THE RADIO PLANET

THE RADIO PLANET

RALPH MILNE FARLEY

WILDSIDE PRESS

Published by Wildside Press LLC.
www.wildsidebooks.com

AUTHOR'S FOREWORD

Could *you* make a radio set? Don't answer rashly. Don't say that you have already built several. For note that we did not ask whether you could assemble a set from parts already manufactured by others, but rather whether you could build the entire set yourself—from the ground up. That means making every part you require, including the vacuum tubes, the acid in the batteries, the wires, the insulation.

If you think that you could do this, let us ask you one further question. Put yourself in the place of the hero of the following story, and imagine yourself stranded amid intelligent savages who have not progressed beyond the wood age. Under such circumstances, with nothing to guide you but your scientific memory, with no tools except those of your own creation, and with no materials save those furnished by nature, could you, though the lives and happiness of your dear ones depended upon it—could *you* make a radio set?

—*R. M. F.*, 1926.

CHAPTER I

SIGNALS FROM MARS

"It's too bad that Myles Cabot can't see this!" I exclaimed, as my eye fell on the following item:

SIGNALS FROM MARS FAIL TO REACH HARVARD

Cambridge, Massachusetts, Wednesday. The Harvard College Radio Station has for several weeks been in receipt of fragmentary signals of extraordinarily long wave-length, Professor Hammond announced yesterday. So far as it has been possible to test the direction of the source of these waves, it appears that the direction has a twenty-four hour cycle, thus indicating that the origin of these waves is some point outside the earth.

The university authorities will express no opinion as to whether or not these messages come from Mars.

Myles, alone of all the radio engineers of my acquaintance, was competent to surmount these difficulties, and thus enable the Cambridge savants to receive with clearness the message from another planet.

Twelve months ago he would have been available, for he was then quietly visiting at my farm, after five earth-years spent on the planet Venus, where, by the aid of radio, he had led the Cupians to victory over their oppressors, a human-brained race of gigantic black ants. He had driven the last ant from the face of continental Poros, and had won and wed the Princess Lilla, who had borne him a son to occupy the throne of Cupia.

While at my farm Cabot had rigged up a huge radio set and a matter-transmitting apparatus, with which he had (presumably) shot himself back to Poros on the night of the big October storm which had wrecked his installation.

I showed the newspaper item to Mrs. Farley, and lamented on Cabot's absence. Her response opened up an entirely new line of thought.

Said she: "Doesn't the very fact that Mr. Cabot isn't here suggest to you that this may be a message, not from Mars, but from him? Or perhaps from the Princess Lilla, inquiring about him in case he has failed in his attempted return?"

That had never occurred to me! How stupid!

"What had I better do about it, if anything?" I asked. "Drop Professor Hammond a line?"

But Mrs. Farley was afraid that I would be taken for a crank.

That evening, when I was over in town, the clerk in the drug store waylaid me to say that there had been a long-distance phone call for me, and would I please call a certain Cambridge number.

So, after waiting an interminable time in the stuffy booth with my hands full of dimes, nickels, and quarters, I finally got my party.

"Mr. Farley?"

"Speaking."

"This is Professor Kellogg, O. D. Kellogg," the voice replied.

It was my friend of the Harvard math faculty, the man who had analyzed the measurements of the streamline projectile in which Myles Cabot had shot to earth the account of the first part of his adventures on Venus. Some further adventures Myles had told me in person during his stay on my farm.

"Professor Hammond thinks that he is getting Mars on the air," the voice continued.

"Yes," I replied. "I judged as much from what I read in this morning's paper. But what do *you* think?"

Kellogg's reply gave my sluggish mind the second jolt which it had received that day.

"Well," he said, "in view of the fact that I am one of the few people among your readers who take your radio stories seriously, I think that Hammond is getting Venus. Can you run up here and help me try and convince him?"

And so it was that I took the early boat next morning for Boston, and had lunch with the two professors.

As a result of our conference, a small committee of engineers returned with me to Edgartown that evening for the purpose of trying to repair the wrecked radio set which Myles Cabot had left on my farm.

They utterly failed to comprehend the matter-transmitting apparatus, and so—after the fallen tower had been reerected and the rubbish cleared away—they had devoted their attention to the restoration of the conversational part of the set.

To make a long story short, we finally restored it, with the aid of some old blue prints of Cabot's which Mrs. Farley, like Swiss Family Robinson's wife, produced from somewhere. I was the first to try the earphones, and was rewarded by a faint "bzt-bzt" like the song of a north woods blackfly.

In conventional radioese, I repeated the sounds to the Harvard group:

"Dah-dit-dah-dit dah-dah-dit-dah. Dah-dit-dah-dit dah-dah-dit-dah. Dah-dit-dah-dit dah-dah-dit-dah. Dah-dit-dit dit. Dah-dit-dah-dit dit-dah dah-dit dit dit dah-dah-dah dah. Dah-dit-dah-dit dit-dah dah-dit-dit-dit dah-dah-dah dah. Dah-dit-dah-dit dit-dah dah-dit-dit-dit-dah dah-dah-dah."

A look of incredulity spread over their faces. Again came the same message, and again I repeated it.

"You're spoofing us!" one of them shouted. "Give *me* the earphones."

And he snatched them from my head. Adjusting them on his own head, he spelled out to us, "C-Q C-Q C-Q D-E C-A-B-O-T C-A-B-O-T C-A-B-O-T—"

Seizing the big leaf-switch, he threw it over. The motor-generator began to hum. Grasping the key, the Harvard engineer ticked off into space: "Cabot Cabot Cabot D-E—"

"Has this station a call letter?" he hurriedly asked me.

"Yes," I answered quickly, "One-X-X-B."

"One-X-X-B," he continued the ticking "K."

Interplanetary communication was an established fact at last! And not with Mars after all these years of scientific speculations. But what meant more to me was that I was again in touch with my classmate Myles Standish Cabot, the radio man.

The next day a party of prominent scientists, accompanied by a telegrapher and two stenographers, arrived at my farm.

During the weeks that followed there was recorded Myles's own account of the amazing adventures on the planet Venus (or Poros, as its own inhabitants call it,) which befell him upon his return there after his brief visit to the earth. I have edited those notes into the following coherent story.

CHAPTER II
TOO MUCH STATIC

Myles Cabot had returned to the earth to study the latest developments of modern terrestrial science for the benefit of the Cupian nation. He was the regent of Cupia during the minority of his baby son, King Kew the Thirteenth. The loyal Prince Toron occupied the throne in his absence. The last of the ant-men and their ally, the renegade Cupian Prince Yuri, had presumably perished in an attempt to escape by flying through the steam-clouds which completely hem in continental Poros. What lay beyond the boiling seas no man knew.

During his stay on my farm, Cabot had built the matter-transmitting apparatus, with which he had shot himself off into space on that October night on which he had received the message from the skies: "S O S, Lilla." A thunderstorm had been brewing all that evening, and just as Myles had placed himself between the coordinate axes of his machine and had gathered up the strings which ran from his control levers to within the apparatus, there had come a blinding flash. Lightning had struck his aerial.

How long his unconsciousness lasted he knew not. He was some time in regaining his senses. But when he had finally and fully recovered, he found himself lying on a sandy beach beside a calm and placid lake beneath a silver sky.

He fell to wondering, vaguely and pleasantly, where he was and how he had got here.

Suddenly, however, his ears were jarred by a familiar sound. At once his senses cleared, and he listened intently to the distant purring of a motor. Yes, there could be no mistake; an airplane was approaching. Now he could see it, a speck in the sky, far down the beach.

Nearer and nearer it came.

Myles sprang to his feet. To his intense surprise, he found that the effort threw him quite a distance into the air. Instantly the idea flashed through his mind: "I must be on Mars! Or some other strange planet." This idea was vaguely reminiscent of something.

But while he was trying to catch this vaguely elusive train of thought, his attention was diverted by the fact that, for some unaccountable reason, his belt buckle and most of the buttons which had held his clothes together were missing, so that his clothing came to pieces as he rose, and that he had to shed it rapidly in order to avoid impeding his movements. He wondered at the cause of this.

But his speculations were cut short by the alighting of the plane a hundred yards down the beach.

What was his horror when out of it clambered, not men but ants! Ants, six-footed, and six feet high. Huge ants, four of them, running toward him over the glistening sands.

Gone was all his languor, as he seized a piece of driftwood and prepared to defend himself.

As he stood thus expectant, Myles realized that his present position and condition, the surrounding scenery, and the advance of the ant-men were exactly, item for item, like the opening events of his first arrival on the planet Poros. He even recognized one of the ant-men as old Doggo, who had befriended him on his previous visit.

Could it be that all his adventures in Cupia had been naught but a dream; a recurring dream, in fact? Were his dear wife Lilla and his little son Kew merely figments of his imagination? Horrible thought!

And then events began to differ from those of the past; for the three other Formians halted, and Doggo advanced alone. By the agitation of the beast's antennae the earth man could see that it was talking to him. But Myles no longer possessed the wonderful electrical headset which he had contrived and built during his previous visit to that planet, so as to talk with Cupians and Formians, both of which races are earless and converse by means of radiations from their antennae.

So he picked up two sticks from the beach, and held them projecting from his forehead; then threw them to the ground with a grimace of disgust and pointed to his ears.

Doggo understood, and scratched with his paw in Cupian shorthand on the silver sands the message: "Myles Cabot, you are our prisoner."

"What, again?" scratched Myles, then made a sign of submission.

He dreaded the paralyzing bite which Formians usually administer to their victims, and which he had twice experienced in the past; but, fortunately, it was not now forthcoming.

The other three ants kept away from him as Doggo led him to the beached airplane, and soon they were scudding along beneath silver skies, northward as it later turned out.

Far below them were silver-green fields and tangled tropical woods, interspersed with rivulets and little ponds.

This was Cupia, his Cupia. He was home once more, back again upon the planet which held all that was dear to him in two worlds.

His heart glowed with the warmth of homecoming. What mattered it that he was now a prisoner, in the hands (or, rather, claws) of his old enemies, the Formians? He had been their prisoner before, and had escaped. Once more he could escape, and rescue the Princess Lilla.

Poor girl! How eager he was to reach her side, and save her from that peril, whatever it was, which had caused her to flash that "S O S" a hundred million miles across the solar system from Poros to the earth.

He wondered what could have happened in Cupia since his departure, only a few sangths ago. How was it that the ant-men had survived their airplane journey across the boiling seas? What had led them to return? Or perhaps these ants were a group who had hidden somewhere and thus had escaped the general extermination of their race. In either event, how had they been able to reconquer Cupia? And where was their former leader, Yuri, the renegade Cupian prince?

These and a hundred other similar questions flooded in upon the earth-man, as the Formian airship carried him, a captive, through the skies.

He gazed again at the scene below, and now noted one difference from the accustomed Porovian landscape, for nowhere ran the smooth concrete roads which bear the swift two-wheeled kerkools of the Cupians to all parts of their continent. What uninhabited portion of Cupia could this be, over which they were now passing?

Turning to Doggo, Myles extended his left palm, and made a motion as though writing on it with the thumb and forefinger of his right hand. But the ant-man waved a negative with one of his forepaws. It was evident that there were no writing materials aboard the ship. Myles would have to wait until they reached their landing place; for doubtless they would soon hover down in some city or town, though just which one he could not guess, as the country below was wholly unfamiliar.

Finally a small settlement loomed ahead. It was of the familiar style of toy-building-block architecture affected by the ant-men, and, from its appearance, was very new. On its outskirts further building operations were actively in progress. Apparently a few survivors of the accursed race of Formians were consolidating their position and attempting to build up a new empire in some out-of-the-way portion of the continent.

As the earth-man was turning these thoughts over in his mind the plane softly settled down upon one of the flat roofs, and its occupants disembarked. Three of the ants advanced menacingly toward Myles, but Doggo held them off. Then all of the party descended down one of the ramps to the lower levels of the building.

Narrow slitlike window openings gave onto courtyards, where fountains played and masses of blue and yellow flowers bloomed, amid gray-branched lichens with red and purple twig-knobs. It was in just such a garden, through just such a window, that he had first looked upon the lovely blue-eyed, golden-haired Lilla, Crown Princess of Cupia.

The earth-man sighed. Where was his beloved wife now? That she needed his help was certain. He must therefore get busy. So once again he made motions of writing on the palm of his left hand with the thumb and forefinger of his right; and this time the sign language produced results, for Doggo halted the procession and led Cabot into a room.

It was a plain bare room, devoid of any furniture except a small table, for ant-men have no use for chairs and couches. The sky outside was already beginning to pinken with the unseen sun.

With a sweep of his paw, Doggo indicated that this was to be Cabot's quarters. Then, with another wave, he pointed to the table, where lay a pad of paper and stylus, not a pencil-like stylus as employed by the Cupians, but rather one equipped with straps for attaching it to the claw of a Formian.

Even so, it was better than nothing. The earth-man seized it eagerly, but before he could begin writing an ant entered bearing a Cupian toga, short-sleeved and bordered with Grecian wave designs in blue. Myles put on this garment, and then quickly filled a sheet with questions:

"How is my princess and my son, the baby king? Whence come all you Formians, whose race I thought had been exterminated? What part of Cupia is this? What is this city? Where is Prince Yuri? And what do you intend to do with me *this* time?"

Then he passed the paper and stylus over to his old friend Doggo. They were alone together at last.

The ant-man's reply consumed sheet after sheet of paper; but, owning to the rapidity of Porovian shorthand, did not take so very much more time than speaking would have required. As he completed each sheet he passed it over to Myles, who read as follows:

"As to your princess and your son, I know not, for this is not Cupia. Do you remember how, when your victorious army and air navy swept to the southern extremity of what had been Formia, a few of our survivors rose in planes from the ruins of our last stronghold and braved the dangers of the steam clouds which overhang the boiling seas? Our leader was Prince Yuri, erstwhile contender for the throne of Cupia, splendid even in defeat.

"It was his brain that conceived our daring plan of escape. If there were other lands beyond the boiling seas, the lands which tradition taught were the origin of the Cupian race, then there we might prosper and raise up a new empire. At the worst we should merely meet death in another form, rather than at your hands. So we essayed.

"Your planes followed us, but turned back as we neared the area of terrific heat. Soon the vapor closed over us, blotting our enemies and our native land from view."

For page after page Doggo, the ant-man, related the harrowing details of that perilous flight across the boiling seas, ending with the words:

"Here we are, and here are you, in Yuriana, capitol of New Formia. But how is it that you, Myles Cabot, have arrived here on this continent in exactly the same manner and condition in which I discovered you in *old* Formia eight years ago?"

When Myles reached the end of reading this narrative, he in turn took the pad and stylus and related how he had gone to the planet Minos (which we call the Earth) to learn the latest discoveries and inventions there, and how his calculations for his return to Poros had been upset by some static conditions just as he had been about to transmit himself back. Oh, if only he had landed by chance upon the same beach as on his first journey through the skies!

Wisely he refrained from mentioning the "S O S" message from Lilla. But his recollection of her predicament spurred him to be anxious about her rescue.

His immediate problem was to learn what the ant-men planned for him; so the concluding words which he wrote upon the pad were: "And, now that you have me in your power, what shall you do with me?"

"Old friend," Doggo wrote in reply, "that depends entirely upon Yuri, our king, whose toga you now have on."

CHAPTER III
YURI OR FORMIS?

The earth-man grimaced, but then smiled. Perhaps, his succeeding to the toga of King Yuri might prove to be an omen.

"So Yuri is king of the ants?" he asked.

"Yes," his captor replied, "for Queen Formis did not survive the trip across the boiling seas."

"Then what of your empire?" Myles inquired. "No queen. No eggs. How can your race continue? For you Formians are like the ants on my own planet Minos."

Doggo's reply astounded him.

"Do you remember back at Wautoosa, I told you that some of us lesser Formians had occasionally laid eggs? So now behold before you Doggo, Admiral of the Formian Air Navy, and mother of a new Queen Formis."

This was truly a surprise! All along Cabot had always regarded the Formians as mannish. And rightly so, for they performed in their own country the duties assigned to men among the Cupians. Furthermore, all Formians, save only the reigning Formis herself, were called by the Porovian pronoun, which corresponds to "he" in English.

When Myles had somewhat recovered from his astonishment, he warmly congratulated his friend by patting him on the side of the head, as is the Porovian custom.

"Doggo," he wrote, "this ought to constitute you a person of some importance among the Formians."

"It *ought* to," the ant-man replied, "but as a matter of fact, it merely intensifies Yuri's mistrust and hatred of me. Now that I am mother of the queen, he fears that I may turn against him and establish Formis in his place as the head of an empire of the Formians, by the Formians, and for the Formians exclusively."

"Why don't you?" Myles wrote. It seemed to him to be a bully good idea, and incidentally a solution of his own difficulties.

But Doggo wrote in horror, "It would be treason!" Then tore up all the correspondence. It is difficult to inculcate the thought of independence in the mind of one reared in an autocracy.

The earth-man, however, persisted.

"How many of the council can you count on, if the interests of Yuri should clash with those of Formis?"

"Only one—myself."

And again Doggo tore up the correspondence.

Myles tactfully changed the subject.

"Where is the arch-fiend now?" he asked.

"We know not," the Formian wrote in reply. "Six days ago he left us in his airship and flew westward. When he failed to return, we sent out scout planes to search for him, and we have been hunting ever since. When we sighted you on the beach this morning we thought that you might be our lost leader, and that is why we landed and approached you."

At about this point the conversation was interrupted by a worker ant who brought food: roast alta and green aphid milk. With what relish did the earth-man plunge into the feast, his first taste of Porovian delicacies in many months.

During the meal conversation lagged, owing to the difficulty of writing and eating at the same time. But now Myles Cabot seized his pad and stylus and wrote:

"Have you ever known me to fail in any undertaking on the planet Poros?"

"No," the ant-man wrote in reply.

"Have you ever known me to be untrue to a principle, a cause, or a friend?"

"No," Doggo replied.

"Then," Myles wrote, "let us make your daughter queen in fact as well as in name."

"It is treason," Doggo wrote in reply, but this time he did not tear up the correspondence.

"Treason?" Myles asked. If he had spoken the word, he would have spoken it with scorn and derision. "Treason? Is it treason to support your own queen? What has become of the national pride of the once great Formians? Look! I pledge myself to the cause of Formis, rightful Queen of Formia. Formis, daughter of Doggo! What say you?"

This time, as he tore up the correspondence, Doggo signified an affirmative. And thus there resulted further correspondence.

"Doggo," Myles wrote, "can you get to the antenna of the queen?"

The ant-man indicated that he could.

"If she has inherited any of your character," Myles continued, "she will assert herself, if given half a chance."

So the Pitmanesque conversation continued. Long since had the pink light of Porovian evening faded from the western sky. The ceiling vapor-lamps were lit. The night showed velvet-black through the slit-like windows. And still the two old friends wrote on, Myles Standish Cabot, the Bostonian, and Doggo, No. 334-2-18, the only really humanlike ant-man whom Myles had ever known among the once dominant race of Poros.

Finally, as the dials indicated midnight, the two conspirators ceased their labors. All was arranged for the *coup d'etat*.

They tore into shreds every scrap of used paper, leaving extant merely the ant-man's concluding words: "Meanwhile you are my prisoner."

Doggo then rang a soundless bell, which was answered by a worker ant, whom he inaudibly directed to bring sufficient draperies to form a bed for the earth-man. These brought, the two friends patted each other a fond good night, and the tired earth-man lay down for the first sleep which he had had in over forty earth hours.

It hardly seemed possible! Night before last he had slept peacefully on a conventional feather-bed in a little New England farmhouse. Then had come the S O S message from the skies; and here he was now, millions of miles away through space retiring on matted silver felting on the concrete floor of a Porovian ant-house. Such are the mutations of fortune!

With these thoughts the returned wanderer lapsed into a deep and dreamless sleep.

When he awakened in the morning there was a guard posted at the door.

Doggo did not show up until nearly noon, when he rattled in, bristling with excitement.

Seizing the pad he wrote: "A stormy session of the Council of Twelve! We are all agreed that you must be indicted for high crimes and misdemeanors. But the great question is as to just what we can charge you with."

"Sorry I can't assist you," the earth-man wrote. "How would it be if I were to slap your daughter's face, or something? Or why not try me for general cussedness?"

"That is just what we finally decided to do," the ant-man wrote in reply. "We shall try you on general principles, and let the proper accusation develop from the evidence.

"At some stage of the proceedings it will inevitably occur to some member of the council to suggest that you be charged with treason to Yuri, whereupon two members of the council, whom I have won over to the cause of my daughter, will raise the objection that Yuri is not our king. This will be the signal for the proclaiming of Queen Formis. If you will waive counsel the trial can take place to-morrow."

"I will waive anything," Myles replied, "counsel, immunity, extradition, anything in order to speed up my return to Cupia, where Lilla awaits in some dire extremity."

"All right," Doggo wrote, and the conference was at an end. The morrow would decide the ascendancy of Myles Cabot or the Prince Yuri over the new continent.

CHAPTER IV
THE COUP D'ETAT

The next morning Myles Cabot was led under guard to the council chamber of the dread thirteen: Formis and her twelve advisers. The accused was placed in a wicker cage, from which he surveyed his surroundings as the proceedings opened.

On a raised platform stood the ant queen, surmounted by a scarlet canopy, which set off the perfect proportions of her jet-black body. On each side of her stood six refined and intelligent ant-men, her councillors. One of the twelve was Doggo.

Messenger ants hurried hither and thither.

First the accusation was read, Myles being furnished with a written copy.

The witnesses were then called. They were veterans who had served in the wars in which Cabot had twice freed Cupia from the domination of its Formian oppressors. They spoke with bitterness of the downfall of their beloved Formia. Their testimony was brief.

Then the accused was asked if he wished to say anything in his own behalf. Myles rose, then shrugged his shoulders, sat down again, and wrote: "I fully realize the futility of making an argument through the antennae of another."

Whereupon the queen and the council went into executive session. Their remarks were not intended for the eyes of the prisoner, but he soon observed that some kind of a dispute was on between Doggo, supported by two councillors named Emu and Fum on one side, and a councillor named Barth on the other.

As this dispute reached its height, a messenger ant rushed in and held up one paw. Cabot's interpreter, not deeming this a part of the executive session, obligingly translated the following into writing:

The messenger: "Yuri lives and reigns over Cupia. It is his command that Cabot die."

Barth: "It is the radio. Know then, O Queen, and ye, members of the council, that when we fled across the boiling seas under the gallant leadership of Prince Yuri, the man with the heart of a Formian, he brought with him one of those powerful radio sets invented by the beast who is our prisoner here to-day.

"Supporters of Yuri still remained among the Cupians, and he has been in constant communication with these ever since shortly after our arrival here. From them he learned of the return of Myles Cabot to the planet Minos.

"Then Yuri disappeared. Those of us who were closest to him suspected that he had gone back across the boiling seas to claim as his own the throne of Cupia. But we hesitated to announce this until we were sure, for we feared that some of our own people would regard his departure as desertion. Yet who can blame him for returning to his father-land and to the throne which is his by rights?"

To which the messenger added: "And he offers to give us back our own old country, if we too will return across the boiling seas again."

"It is a lie!" Doggo shouted.

"Yuri, usurper of the thrones of two continents. Bah!" shouted Emu.

"Yuri, our rightful leader," shouted Barth.

"Give us a queen of our own race," shouted Fum.

"Release the prisoner," shouted the Queen.

And that is all that Myles learned of the conversation, for his interpreter at this juncture stopped writing and obeyed the queen. The earth-man was free!

With one bound he gained the throne, where fighting was already in progress between the two factions. Barth and Doggo were rolling over and over on the floor in a death grapple, while the ant-queen had backed to the rear of the stage, closely guarded by Emu and Fum.

Seizing one of the pikes which supported the scarlet canopy, Myles wrenched it loose and drove it into the thorax of Barth. In another instant the earth-man and Doggo stood beside the queen.

Ant-men now came pouring into the chamber through all the entrances, taking sides as they entered and sized up the situation. If it had still been in vogue among the Formians to be known by numbers rather than names, and to have these identifying numbers painted on the backs of their abdomens followed by the numbers of those whom they had defeated in the duels so common among them, then many a Formian would have "got the number" of many another, that day.

As Myles battled with his pike beside Formis, queen of the ants, he could well imagine the conflicting shouts of "Death to the usurper!" "Formia for the Formians!" "Long Live Queen Formis!" "Long live Prince Yuri!" which must have resounded throughout the chamber; but to him all was silence, for he was without the antennae wherewith to pick up the radiated speech of the contenders.

So as he wielded the pike in silence, he had opportunity to reflect on the incongruity of his position. Here was he, Myles Cabot regent of Cupia, the man who had driven the ants forever from their dominion over his people, and yet now fighting side by side with their leaders defending the life of their queen.

Yet was she not the daughter of Doggo his only friend among the ants? And would not her victory mean the speedy return of Myles to his own continent?

As the earth-man jabbed to right and left among the supporters of his enemy Yuri there came to his human ears the sound of rifle fire. It might prove a godsend or an added menace, according to whose paw held the rifle. But no chances must be taken on the life of the queen. So Myles made frantic signs to Doggo of impending danger.

The queen and her supporters, outnumbered, were fighting with their backs to one of the walls of the room. A short distance along this wall on the side where Cabot stood was a door; so he now began edging his way along the wall to this door. This was not difficult, as the ant-men, having only their mandibles to fight with, greatly respected his pike.

He gained the door and passed by, but not through it. The shots came nearer and nearer. Then Doggo opened the door and slipped through with Formis and the rest of her immediate supporters; the door closed, and Myles Cabot stood guarding the exit with his pike— alone against the hordes of antdom.

He had no difficulty in defending himself from those in front of him, but the ants who began to close in on him from each side were a different matter.

He received several bad scratches on his shoulders and hips, and his toga was ripped and torn; but fortunately he was able to ward off their paralyzing bites. Nevertheless, his enemies pressed so close that it was difficult for him to manipulate his long weapon. In fact, it was only the jamming of the ants upon one another and upon the dead bodies of their slain comrades that kept them from him.

He now was holding his pike by the middle, with both hands, using one end as a club and the other as a dagger. The black circle of the ants was steadily closing in on him. A pair of mandibles from the left snapped angrily within a few inches of his throat. Instantly he drove the point of his lance home between horrid jaws. But at the same instant its butt was seized by a pair of jaws to his right. He could not pull it free.

At last he was weaponless, and not only that, but pinned to the wall by the shaft of his own pike as well.

And then to his surprise the ants before him separated as at a command. The butt of his lance was dropped. As Myles wrenched the point loose from the dead body of the Formian in which it had been stuck, and gazed expectant down the long aisle which had opened before him, he saw confronting him at the other end an ant-man armed with the peculiar type of claw-operated rifle which the Formians had adapted from those which Myles himself had built for Cupian use in the first war of liberation.

Briefly the two surveyed each other. Then slowly the rifle was raised until its aim settled squarely upon the earth-man's chest.

Instantaneously the glance of Myles Cabot swept the black hordes which hemmed him in on each side. There was no escape!

Yet how can man die better,

Than facing fearful odds?

With a wild warwhoop, which was utterly lost on the radio-sense of the assembled Formians, Myles charged down the narrow way, straight into the muzzle of the rifle of his antagonist. The astonished ant-man hastily pulled the trigger. A shot rang out. But still the impetuous rush of Myles continued, and before the rifle could be discharged a second time, Myles had driven his spear deep into the leering insect face.

The Formian staggered back. The rifle clattered to the floor. The earth-man, not waiting to withdraw his own weapon, stooped, seized the fallen firearm, and wheeled to confront his enemies, who fell back in a snarling arc before this new menace.

Myles stood now in one of the entranceways of the council chamber, and thus was secure against flank attack. But not against an assault from the rear. In fact, even as he stood thus irresolute, a rattling noise behind him in the hallways revealed to his human ears the approach of a new enemy. What was he to do? To remain as he was meant *carte blanche* to this newcomer, whereas to turn about would mean that those within the chamber would undoubtedly rush him.

In this predicament Myles grasped his gun firmly, and wheeled backward to the left until he was flattened against the wall of the corridor in which he was standing. From this position he could turn his head slightly to the left and see into the council chamber, or to the right and look down the long hall.

Directly opposite him was one of those narrow, slitlike windows, so typical of Porovian architecture. It was too narrow for the passage of the huge body of an ant-man, but a human being could conceivably squeeze through. Thus it offered a means out, a way of escape.

The lone ant in the corridor was joined by the others. They and their compatriots within the chamber slowly closed in on the cornered earth-man.

There was no time to speculate upon the depth of the drop outside. With a suddenness which caused his aggressors to recoil momentarily, Myles dashed across to the window, forced his way through, and, still grasping his rifle, plunged headlong two stories into a clump of gray lichens in the courtyard below.

Hastily extricating himself, he looked up at the window which he had just quitted. There, framed by the masonry, was the head of an ant-man. A quick shot, and the head stared at him no more.

Before another Formian could take post at the window to observe the direction of Cabot's departure, the latter ran quickly from the courtyard garden into the interior of the building again.

His first thought was to join Doggo, Queen Formis, and their faction; so, taking a firm hold on his rifle, he hurried in the direction in which they had made their escape.

The first ant-man whom he met within the building was Emu, one of the three members of the council who had been a party to the original conspiracy. This ant was fleeing from something in very evident terror, so that it was all Cabot could do to stop him, but the threat of rifle-shooting was finally effective.

Then, extracting a cartridge from the magazine of his firearm, Cabot scratched upon the smooth wall the brief question: "What of Doggo and Formis?"

Emu snatched the cartridge and quickly wrote the reply: "Dead, both dead. The revolution has collapsed. Flee for your life!"

Then the ant-man clattered rapidly off down the corridor, taking the precious cartridge with him. He had not been too flustered to think of that.

Myles heaved a sigh of self-reproach at having brought his friends to this sad end. But then, he reflected, Doggo had been in a situation in which conflict with the authorities and then execution would have been inevitable sooner or later. The revolution had been his one best bet, and it was no one's fault that it had failed.

Now that Doggo and Formis were dead, there was no longer any obligation binding Myles to stay and fight. In fact, he owed it to his loved ones in Cupia to preserve his own life until he could find some way of rejoining them. So he set out to escape from the city.

For some time he threaded the corridors without meeting any ants, although occasionally there drifted down to him the sounds of fighting on the upper levels. But at last, as he rounded a turn, he saw before him a Formian, and it was one whom he recognized, namely the messenger ant who had brought to the trial the radiogram from Prince Yuri. The ant's back was toward him. Cabot cautiously withdrew a step; then raising his rifle, he again advanced and fired full at his enemy.

But the hammer merely clicked. There was no explosion. The magazine was empty.

Cabot's first impulse was to throw the weapon away. Then he reflected that even an unloaded gun might well serve to awe his enemies and hold them at a distance; so he retained it.

By this time the messenger ant had disappeared around a turn farther down the corridor, so Cabot hastened after him; for it had suddenly occurred to the earth-man that this ant was undoubtedly returning to the hidden radio set, whence he had come.

Radio! Means of a communication with his own continent, if he could but reach the instruments!

The messenger had announced at the trial that Yuri was in Cupia and knew of Cabot's presence in this new land. Thus it was certain that complete wireless communication had been established between the two continents. But, equally, undoubtedly, this communication had been established at a wave-length which kept the knowledge of Cabot's return pretty much a secret of Prince Yuri and his own followers. This information would probably induce the renegade prince to speed up whatever nefarious schemes he had afoot in Cupia.

But if Cabot could once get on the air and adjust the Formian sending set to the wave-length of Luno Castle, or run it through all its available wave-lengths, he could broadcast to the Cupian nation the fact that he was alive and well, and would return again—though he knew not how—to lead them. Such news should strengthen the hearts of the loyal Cupians to rally to the cause of his wife, the Princess Lilla, and his son, the baby king.

So he quickened his pace, and soon caught sight again of the messenger ant. From, then on he stealthily stalked his quarry, who led him through many a winding passage-way, before finally they emerged from the city into the open fields.

Beyond the fields lay the rocky foothills of a mountain range. Caution dictated that Cabot remain under the shelter of the city walls until the Formian disappeared among the rocks. Then he ran lightly across the plain to take up the trail once more.

As he, too, gained the rocks, he glanced back to see if his departure had been noted. No, there was no sign of life. Evidently the fighting had drawn all the inhabitants to the interior of the city. So, with a sigh of relief, Myles hurried after the messenger ant.

At the place where Myles had noticed the Formian enter the rocks there was the well-defined beginning of a trail; so up this winding trail he sped, and soon caught sight of his quarry. From that time on more caution was necessary, but nevertheless the pursuer was able to keep the pursued always in sight until, just after a turn in the road had obscured his view, Myles came upon a place where the way forked.

Pausing, he scratched his head in dismay, then carefully examined the ground for evidences of claw marks; but none were apparent. Dropping to his hands and knees, the earth-man scrutinized the dirt with even more care; and at last, imagining that he observed some slight scratches to the right, he took the right-hand branch.

It was necessary for him to proceed with great rapidity, if he would catch up with the messenger ant, so Myles broke into a dog trot. On and on he ran; up, into the rocky mountains.

At last he sat down exhausted on a large boulder, just as the silvery sky turned crimson in the west, and darkness crept up out of the east. It was quite evident that he had taken the wrong road at the fork, and also that he must now spend the night, half clad and alone amid the rocks of the mountains of this strange new continent.

CHAPTER V

LOST AMID THE ROCKS

But although Myles Cabot was lost, he was free for the first time since his return to Poros.

So not disheartened he arose and proceeded along the trail, looking for food and a place to spend the night; and presently came upon a "green cow," as he was wont to call the aphids which are kept both by Cupians and Formians for the honey-dew which they produce.

It made no objection to Cabot's approach, nor to his manipulating the two horns which projected from its back, with the result that the tired man was presently regaling himself with a satisfying drafts of green "milk" from a leafy cup.

The bush, which furnished the leaf to fashion the cup, closely resembled the tartan bushes of Cupia, whose heart-shaped leaves are put to so many uses in that country. Myles Cabot accordingly stripped off a considerable portion of the foliage, and lay down in a bed of warm, thick green for the night.

The morning dawned silver bright. Myles drew another meal from the grazing aphid and then pressed on up the rocky defile. He did not dare return for fear of meeting ant-men; and besides, now that a night's rest had to some extent tempered his chagrin at not catching up with the particular ant-man whom he had been pursuing, he could not be sure he had taken the wrong road after all. So on he went, up the rocky path.

Around noon the path petered out at the top of an eminence which gave Cabot an opportunity to survey the surrounding scenery. To the westward lay the city from which he had fled. What had become, he wondered, of the supporters of his friend Doggo and of Formis, the ant-queen, whose cause he had espoused? According to Emu, Doggo and Formis were both dead, or Cabot would never have deserted them.

Cabot turned his attention next to the northward. To his great joy, on the next peak to the one where he sat, there stood two rough wooden towers, spanned by an aerial.

He decided to cut across country and attempt to approach the installation by stealth. So he started scrambling down into the intervening valley.

Never before had the earth-man traveled through such difficult country. As soon as he had gone a short distance below the summit he encountered a continuous expanse of boulders, ranging in size from a man's head to twenty feet or more in diameter, and piled aimlessly together. Lying crossways in every direction, upon and between the rocks, were the gaunt skeletons of fallen trees in all stages of decay.

The sharp edges of the rocks cut and tore the bare feet of the earth-man, while the splinters of the fallen trees jabbed his body. Time and again he slipped and nearly fell into one of the chasms which yawned between the boulders, and on one of these occasions he must have inadvertently let go the ant-rifle which he had treasured so far so carefully, for presently he noticed that it was gone.

But to all this there was one extenuating feature, although Myles did not realize it at the time, namely that his physical pain and the need for constant vigilance on his part so occupied his mind as to spare him from the mental pain which had been his almost constant companion since his return to Poros. The attention necessary to avoid misjudging a jump, or slipping into a dark deep hole, or being impaled by a tree-branch, crowded out of his mind even his great love and anxiety for Princess Lilla and Baby Kew.

Through the maze of obstacles Cabot toiled all day long.

Oh, to reach the radio station established by his enemy Yuri, and get into touch with his own continent. Thus he could learn what was happening in Cupia, and also give word of his own safe arrival on the planet. Safe, hm! He smiled grimly at the word.

"I *must* reach that station," he thought, "and then, when I have talked with Cupia, I must secure a Formian plane by hook or by crook, and brave the boiling seas. If ants have crossed those seas safely, if Yuri has safely crossed them twice, then why cannot I, the Minorian?"

As he communed thus with himself, a faint pink flush appeared in the sky. Slowly, painfully he continued his way. Gradually the pink light turned to crimson in the west and then darkened to a royal purple. Gradually the black night crept up out of the east. But also gradually the boulders became smaller and smaller as he clambered upward, until just as darkness finally enveloped the planet, the tired man gained the smooth rocks of the summit, and lay down amid some leaves.

He had had nothing to eat or drink since his breakfast of green milk that morning. He had undergone an exhausting journey. His feet were bruised and cut, his body covered with innumerable scratches, and he was weary, thirsty and hungry. But he had almost reached the point which he had been seeking, and this thought comforted him as his eyes closed in healthy and dreamless sleep.

Next morning early he was up, rested, parched and ravenous. As the first faint pink tinged the eastern sky Myles Cabot shook off the leaves and completed the ascent.

It only required a few moments for him to reach the top, a narrow plateau, about a mile in length, near the farther end of which there stood a small cabin with its two towers and aerial.

With a cry of joy—which he knew the earless Formians could not hear—he raced toward it. The huge chain and lock, which secured its door on the outside, indicated that it was unoccupied, and a glance through the narrow slitlike windows confirmed this.

The glance through the window also revealed the presence of a complete radio sending and receiving set of the same general hook-up which he himself had adapted for the use of Cupians and Formians on the other continent.

"Imitation is the most insulting form of flattery," as Poblath, the Cupian philosopher, used to say. Yet Cabot was willing to brook the insult, until suddenly it dawned on him that the set had no earphones nor microphone!

Of course not, since it was designed for use by creatures who possessed neither ears nor vocal speech! Gone then was all hope of news from home, even if he could succeed in breaking in. At the most, he would merely be able, by interposing an interrupter in the primary or secondary of that aerial circuit, to send a dot-dash message across the boiling seas—I use the term "aerial circuit," because "antenna circuit" would be ambiguous, as the latter term might have either its conventional earth significance, or might mean the circuit in which the Formian operator would place *his* living antennae in sending and receiving.

Well, even a chance to send to Cupia a message to the effect that he was free and safe, would be worth something. Myles Cabot tried the slitlike windows, and finding them too narrow, slid quickly down the near-by slope, soon to return laboriously with a twenty-pound rock, which he heaved against the door.

Again and again he heaved the rock, until he had the satisfaction of seeing the door crack and then give. Finally a large enough opening was effected to afford passage for a man, although not for a Formian; and through this breach Myles Cabot squeezed into the station.

A few minutes' scrutiny familiarized him with the details of the hook-up, the generator set, and the trophil-engine. Everything was in running order and the fuel tank was full. So he fashioned a rude sending key, broke one of the circuits and tied in the key. Then he warmed-up and cranked the trophil-engine, clutched-in the generator, threw the main switch, and sat down to flash across the seas the message which was to hold firm his partisans in Cupia until he could join them.

But at that instant an arrow hummed through the hole in the door, and struck quivering in the bench beside him.

Cabot sprang to his feet and slid home the huge beam which barred the door on the inside. This was a precaution which he had neglected to take before. Next he filled the hole in the door with some boards hastily wrenched from the work-bench. Then picking up a Formian rifle and bandolier which hung on the wall, he made his way to one of the slit windows on the same side as the door and peeped cautiously out.

The result was immediate; an arrow sped through the window and passed just above his head. But even as he ducked instinctively, he saw a dark form moving behind a bush at some distance outside; so quickly rising again, he discharged the rifle square at the bush.

There came a cry of pain, followed by silence. And there were no more feathered incursions.

Not knowing whether his enemy had been disposed of, or whether the cessation of the stream of arrows was merely a ruse to entice him from his shelter, Myles did not dare venture forth to investigate.

From the first time the arrow had struck the work-bench until this final squelching of the unknown enemy, Myles had been engrossed in action. Now came the reaction, as he realized how narrowly he had twice escaped from death in the last few minutes. He shuddered at the thought, and turned pale; not, however, at the danger to himself, but rather at the danger to his loved ones in Cupia. He must keep himself alive until he could reach and save them from whatever peril it was that had caused Lilla to send the SOS which had recalled him to Poros.

But being ever the inquisitive scientist, his attention was soon distracted by the arrow which stood sticking to the bench.

Its shaft was of some hard and very springy wood. Its tip was of chipped stone resembling flint, and bound to the shaft by vegetable fibers. Its "feathers" were thin laminae of wood, doubtless because birds, and hence true feathers, are unknown on Poros.

Why on earth—or rather, on Poros—were the ant-men employing such crude weapons? Rifles they had aplenty, and powder was easy to manufacture. Besides what did they know of bows and arrows, which had never been used by them, even in the days before Cabot the Minorian introduced firearms upon the planet?

Thus these arrows presented a perplexing problem. But a practical job remained to be performed before Myles was to have any time for abstract questions. The message to Cupia must be sent off.

The earth-man returned to the radio set. The trophil-engine and the generator were still running. The whole apparatus appeared to be functioning properly. And so Myles ticked off into space the following message:

CQ, CQ, CQ, DE, Cabot, Cabot, Cabot. I have returned to Poros from Minos. I am on the continent of the Formians. I am in complete control there.

That was a lie, but it would serve to hearten his supporters, or throw the fear of the Supreme Builder into the partisans of Yuri, whichever it reached. The message continued:

Do not expect me soon, for first I must consolidate what I have gained here. But when I do come, Yuri beware! My friends, hold out until then. I have spoken.

DE, Cabot.

This message he sent again and again, at every wavelength of which the installation was capable. He repeated and repeated it until he was tired.

And then, for the first time, he remembered his thirst and his hunger. Fortunately there was both food and drink in the shack; so Cabot satisfied his wants, and then went at his message again.

When at last he paused once more for a rest, and shut off the trophil-engine, his human ears caught a familiar rattling sound. Instantly he realized the situation; one or more ant-men were approaching. Sure enough, as he looked out of a window in the direction of the sound, he saw two of these creatures trotting toward him across the plateau.

Both carried rifles slung at their backs; so without waiting for their nearer approach Myles opened fire. One of the Formians dropped, but the other turned and fled; and in spite of the hail of bullets which the earth-man sent after it, reached the crest in apparent safety, and disappeared from view.

Cabot knew what that meant to him. It portended the early return of the fugitive ant with scores of his fellows, to lay siege to the radio station. Then a doubt occurred to him. What if these ants were members of Doggo's faction, and he had killed a friend?

And so at the risk of his life, he unbarred the door and rushed out to inspect the dead body. But it was no ant whom he knew. Time would tell whether the surviving ant would return with friends or foes. Meanwhile Cabot must get busy with his message. So at it again he went, first barring the door again.

From time to time he rested and listened for the approach of Formians. Occasionally he ate and drank. During his longer rests, he carted the rifle, the ammunition and some provisions to a point quite a distance down the mountainside, and cached them there; for he had formulated a plan of escape. But mostly he stuck to his signaling. All Cupia, or such of it as might still possess long-distance radio sets in spite of the renewed dominion of Yuri, must be made to know of the return of Myles Cabot from the earth.

Night fell, and with it came a respite from the danger of Formian attack; for these creatures would never venture forth in the darkness without lights, and lights would betray them. Myles spent part of the night in sending his message, part in watching for approaching lights, and part in dozing.

Finally along toward morning he set about wrecking the set, for he did not wish the Formians to get into communication with Cupia and undo the effect of his own message by pointing out its falsity. Accordingly he smashed the tubes, unwound the inductances and transformers, cut all the wiring into little bits, bent the plates of the condensers, chiseled through the coils of the generator, pounded the trophil-engine to pieces, and drained the trophil tank. It would be many sangths before a new radio set could be built, if indeed these Formians knew enough of the art to ever build another.

His work of destruction completed, he sat down to wait; but the inaction palled on him, and before he knew it he had fallen sound asleep.

He awakened with a start. It was broad daylight. He listened. There was much rattling outside. So he walked to the door, unbarred it, and stepped out.

He was not afraid; for on the evening before he had nailed above the door two crossed sticks, the Porovian equivalent of a flag of truce.

At a short distance stood a band of thirty or forty ant-men, their leader holding a pair of crossed sticks. Accordingly the ragged earth-man advanced. Not one of them did he recognize, but this was no indication of their identity.

Were these members of the Yuri faction, he wondered, or of the faction recently captained by the now deceased Doggo? If the former, they were conquerors intent on adding him to their list of conquests; but if the latter, then they might be fugitives like himself. It behooved him to find out.

So he proceeded to a slight depression in the mountain-top, very near the group of Formians. This depression contained soil, and in it he scratched in Porovian shorthand the words: "Yuri or Doggo?" Then pointed to his message and withdrew for a slight distance.

One of the ant-men advanced alone to the depression, stared at the words, rubbed one part of them, and returned to his comrades, at which Cabot in turn advanced.

The one word remaining written in the dirt was "Yuri!"

So these were victorious enemies, rather than fugitive friends.

Waving a signal that the interview was at an end, Myles Cabot returned with dignity to the shack and pulled down his crossed sticks.

But then, instead of entering, he suddenly dashed around the house and slid down the mountainside amid a shower of pebbles.

Instantly the Formian pack rushed after him, but they were too late; for by the time they had gained the crest he was safely under cover of the bushes, making his way down the slope with his rifle, ammunition, and provision. The ant-men evidently feared an ambush, for they did not follow.

This side of the mountain (the eastern) was wooded, instead of the almost impassable boulders over which he had climbed up the other side two days ago. Accordingly the descent was easy, almost pleasant. Soon he struck a path beside a little brook, and followed it until it led out onto the fertile eastern plains which he had observed when first he had topped this range of hills.

Beneath a large tree beside the brook, at the edge of the plain, Myles Cabot stopped and sat down for lunch; and it was while seated thus, with his back against the tree trunk, that an arrow suddenly whistled through the woods and imbedded itself in the bark just above his head.

Startled, he sprang to his feet, seized his rifle, and looked around.

A second arrow sped through the air, and this one did not miss him.

In due course of time, Myles regained consciousness. He was lying on the ground beneath the same tree. There was an ugly gash in his head. His rifle, ammunition, and food were gone. His face and body were covered with clotted blood, and he felt very faint.

With difficulty he dragged himself to the stream, tore off a piece of his ragged toga, and washed away some of the gore. But it required an almost superhuman effort. He lay on the bank and panted. His head swam. His surroundings began to blur and dance about. And then he swooned again.

After what seemed an interminable time he became dimly conscious that he was lying on something less hard than the ground. Soft arms were around him. Some one was crooning to him sweet words and low.

Was this a dream? Or was he back once more in Cupia with his loved ones?

CHAPTER VI
THE VAIRKINGS

Myles Cabot opened his weary eyes. Around him hung barbaric tapestries. He was lying on a couch covered by the same materials.

Seated on the couch beside him was a creature human in form, but covered with short golden-brown fur. It seemed to be a young woman of some species. But of what species?

Myles threw back his head and studied the creature's face, expecting to see the prognathous features of some anthropoid ape. But no; for eyes, nose, mouth, ears, and all were human, distinctly human, and of high type. They might have been the features of an earth-girl, except for the fact that the short brown fur persisted on the face as on the rest of the body. The general effect reminded Cabot for all the world of a teddy bear. Yes, that is what this creature was, an animated human teddy bear.

Seeing Cabot looking at her, the creature smiled down at him, and murmured some strange words in a soothing musical voice. Also she stroked his cheek with one of her furry paws.

At this moment the hangings parted, and there stepped into their presence a man of the species, wearing a leather tunic and leather helmet, and carrying a wooden spear. Bowing low before the furry lady, he spoke to her in the same soft tongue which she had employed in addressing Myles.

Not a single syllable was familiar to the earth-man, but he caught the words "Roy" and "Vairking" repeated a number of times, and also made out that the furry man had addressed the furry lady as "Arkilu."

Arkilu now arose from the couch and, taking a tablet and a stick of charcoal from a near-by stand, wrote some characters upon a sheet of paper and handed it to the man, who bowed and withdrew.

The pad and charcoal gave Myles an idea. If he was to stay any length of time with these creatures he had better start in at once learning both their written and their spoken language.

And perhaps, when he had mastered it, he could persuade these kindly yet warlike folk to assist him against the Formians. He judged that they were kindly, because of the actions of the furry lady; and they were warlike, because of the habiliments of the furry man.

Putting his idea into action, Myles sat up, gathering a gaudy blanket about his shoulders, and pointed to the writing materials. With a furry smile Arkilu brought them to him.

Having been through this game once before, he knew just where to begin. He pointed to the couch, and handed her the pad and charcoal.

Whereupon the lady spoke some absolutely unintelligible sound, and wrote upon the pad, in unmistakable Cupian shorthand, the familiar Cupian word for couch!

Myles could hardly believe his senses. He stared at the paper, rubbed his eyes, and then stared again. How was it that this creature employed a written character identical with the word used by another race, far across the impassable boiling seas, to designate the same thing? But perhaps this was merely a coincidence.

So he pointed to another object. Again there came a strange sound, coupled with the familiar Cupian symbol.

The experiment was repeated and repeated, always with the same result.

Then Cabot himself took the writing materials and inscribed a number of words which sounded somewhat alike in Porovian antenna speech. To these words Arkilu gave an entirely different set of similar sounds.

"Aha," said Cabot to himself, "this language employs exactly the same words as are used on our continent, but translates the sound-symbols of these words into entirely different sounds!"

Cabot's interpretation of the situation proved correct in the main, which fact made it extremely easy for him to master the new language. Already he could carry on a written conversation with his benefactress; and before long it became possible, by dint of great care, for him to talk aloud in simple sentences.

Of course, all this progress was not made at one sitting, for Arkilu insisted that her patient take frequent rests. From time to time meals were served by female attendants, meals abounding in strange meats, mostly lobsterlike, but some resembling fish and flesh. Each night Arkilu departed, leaving a furry man-creature on guard, with leather armor and wooden spear.

As he mastered the language, Myles learned the following facts from Arkilu. Her people were called the Vairkings, and she was the eldest daughter of Theoph, their ruler. The Vairkings were a primitive race. Apparently they knew nothing of any of the metals, but had made considerable progress in the arts of tanning, weaving and carpentry.

The fact that they had made cloth accounted for the fact that they had paper. Their leather they had obtained from the hides of a large variety of nocturnal reptiles, known indiscriminately as "gnoopers," and ranging in size from that of a cat to that of an elephant, though all possessed the common characteristics of small heads, long necks, stumpy legs, and long heavy tails.

She explained as follows to her guest how he had been rescued: "Our home is in the city of Vairkingi, far away, a little east of north from here. We Vairkings stick pretty close to the cities, for the great open spaces of our land are inhabited by predatory tribes of wild creatures very like ourselves, called Roies. The leader of one of the largest tribes of these, Att the Terrible, sought alliance with my father, and, as the price of this alliance, a union between Att and myself. But I spurned him.

"His hordes then attacked Vairkingi, but we repulsed them and drove them to the southward. At present we are on a punitive expedition into their territory. Our warriors are under the command of Jud the Excuse-Maker; and my father (Theoph the Grim) and I have accompanied the headquarters, so as to witness the downfall of Att the Terrible.

"It was undoubtedly one of the Roies who wounded you, but the approach of our men drove them off before they had time to do you further harm. It was I myself who found you lying beside the brook, and I would fain possess you as my own, you who are unlike any man whom I have ever seen. Whence come you?"

"I am from the planet Minos, O Arkilu the Beautiful," replied Cabot.

But the princess incredulously shook her head, saying, "I know not whereof you speak, nor know I the meaning of the word 'planet.' There are no other worlds than this continent which we inhabit, surrounded by boiling seas on all sides; though rumor says that strange beasts from somewhere have landed and are building a city to the eastward of the mountains."

"Rumor has it right," Myles laconically interjected, "for I had just escaped from those beasts when I was wounded by the arrow of the Roies."

Arkilu opened her eyes in wonder.

"Tell me about them," she breathed.

So the earth-man sat up, swathed in the gaudy tapestries of the Vairkings, and related to the furry princess the story of his adventures on the planet Poros. It was difficult to put it all into words within her comprehension, for neither she nor her people could know anything of radio, of the solar system, of airplanes, or of rifles. Accordingly his account ran about as follows:

"Know, O Princess, that there is another land called 'Minos', or in our own language 'the earth', far above those silver clouds, one million times the distance from here to your capital city, Vairkingi. Also there is, beyond the boiling seas, another land much like this, where dwell hairless men called 'Cupians', and also the black beasts to whom you have referred. These beasts are called 'Formians'.

"Cupians and Formians cannot talk with their mouths as you and I. Nor do they have ears to hear with. Instead, they communicate by a kind of soundless magic, called 'radio'. But they write the same language as do you Vairkings.

"On the earth I was master of this magic, radio. But one day my own magic proved too strong for me, and shot me through the skies to Formia, where the Formians captured me. I found that the Cupians were the slaves of the Formians.

"By means of radio I was able to talk with both races. I escaped from the Formians. By other magic, which could throw small black stones faster than arrows and with more deadly results, I led the Cupians to victory over their oppressors. Their princess, Lilla, became my bride, and our son, Kew, now sits on the throne of Cupia. But Prince Yuri, a renegade Cupian, rebelled against us, for he too loved Lilla!"

Myles continued: "Yuri and his allies possessed magic wagons which could fly through the air—"

"What is 'fly'?" Arkilu interrupted. "If you mean 'swim' it is impossible, for no creature ever lived which could swim in air."

"Ah, but this is magic, you must remember," he assured her. "Have you Vairkings never seen any peculiar black objects sailing through the sky since the rumored arrival of the Formians on your continent?"

Arkilu pursed her lips in thought. "Yes," she admitted, "there have been rumors of that too."

"Well," he continued, "those were the flying wagons of the Formians. When we finally defeated them and drove them across the boiling seas in these wagons, I revisited the planet earth by means of the radio magic of which I have told you. But on my attempted return to Cupia I landed on your continent instead, by mistake, and was again captured by my Formian enemies. Of my escape from them, my wounding by the Roy arrow, and my rescue by you, you already know."

Arkilu smiled ingratiatingly. "You are a pretty spinner of tales. Therefore I shall keep you to amuse me. Methinks that even Theoph the Grim will revel in your fantasies."

And she leaned over and caressed Cabot's cheek with one furry hand. He cringed at the touch, yet strove not to offend her, whose continued friendship might mean so much toward his return to his own country.

He wanted her good will and her influence; but, out of loyalty to Lilla, he dreaded her love.

To change the subject he inquired: "When shall I be well enough to get up?"

"You are well enough now," she replied "Try to stand."

At Myles's insistence, a leather suit was sent for; he soon found himself dressed like a soldier of the Vairkings. Thus arrayed he stood and walked about a little inside the tent, but Arkilu would not permit him to venture outside until he should be stronger.

Before leaving for the night Arkilu announced: "Tomorrow our expedition starts back for Vairkingi. When we reach the city I shall marry you, for I have decided that I love you."

CHAPTER VII
RADIO ONCE MORE

So ARKILU, the furry beauty, planned to marry Myles Cabot, the earth-man, he who already loved and was wed to Lilla of Cupia! A happy prospect indeed! Yet he dared not repulse the Vairkingian maiden, lest thereby he lose his chance of returning to his home and family.

For at last he had formulated a plan of action, namely to arm the hordes of Vairkingia, lead them against the ant-men, seize an ant-plane and with it fly back to Cupia. So, for the present, he appeared to fall in with the matrimonial whim of the princess.

Early the next morning, however, as he was prowling around inside the tent, testing his weak legs, he overheard a conversation on the outside, which changed the situation considerably.

"But, father," remonstrated a voice which Myles recognized as that of Arkilu, "I found him, and therefore he is mine. I want him. He is beautiful!"

"Beautiful? Humph!" a stern male voice sarcastically replied. "He *must* be, without any fur! Oh, to think that my royal daughter would wish to wed a freak of nature, and a common soldier at that!"

"He's *not* a common soldier!" asserted the voice of Arkilu. "He wears clothes merely so as to preserve his health for my sake."

"Well, a sickly cripple then," answered her father's voice, "which is just as bad. At all events, Jud is the leader of this expedition, and therefore this captive belongs to him. You can have him only if Jud so wills. It is the law."

Myles Cabot stealthily crossed the tent and put his eye to an opening between the curtains at the tent opening. There stood the familiar figure of Arkilu, and confronting her was a massive male Vairking. *His* fur, however, was snow white, so that his general appearance resembled that of a polar bear. His face was appropriately harsh and cold. This was Theoph the Grim, ruler of the Vairkings!

The dispute continued. And then there approached another man of the species. The newcomer, black-furred, was short, squat, and gnarled, yet possessed of unquestionable intelligence and a certain dignity which clearly indicated that he was of noble rank. He wore a leather helmet and carried a wooden lance.

Theoph the Grim hailed him with: "Ho, Jud, what brings you here?"

Jud raised his spear diagonally across his chest as a salute, and replied: "A change of plans, excellency. Upon reaching the river, I decided that it would be wiser not to return to Vairkingi by that route."

"Really meaning," Arkilu interposed, with, a laugh, "that you found it impossible to throw a bridge across at that point."

"Why do you always doubt the reasons for my actions?" Jud asked in an aggrieved tone.

"You wrong me," she replied, "I never doubt your reasons. Your *reasons* are always of the best. What I doubt is your *excuses*."

"Enough, enough!" the king shouted. "For I wish to discuss more immediate matters than nice distinctions of language. Jud's reasons or excuses, or whatever, are good enough for me. Jud, I wish to inform you that my daughter has recently captured a strange furless being, whom it is my pleasure to turn over to you. I have not yet seen this oddity—"

"Father, please!" Arkilu begged, but at this juncture, Myles, exasperated by Theoph's remarks, parted the tent curtains and stepped out.

"Look well, oh, king!" he shouted. "Here stands Myles Cabot, the Minorian, beast from another world, freak of nature, sickly cripple, common soldier, and all that. Look well, O king!"

"A bit loud mouthed, I should say," Theoph the Grim sniffed, not one whit abashed.

"Watch him crumple at the presence of a real man," added Jud the Excuse-Maker.

Suiting the action to the word, the latter stepped over to Myles and suddenly slapped him on the face.

As a boy, the earth-man had often seen larger boys point to their cheek or shoulder, with the words: "There is an electric button there. Touch it and something will fly out and hit you." But never as a boy had he dared to press the magic button, for he could well imagine the result.

Such a result now occurred to Jud; for, the instant his fingers touched Cabot's cheek, out flew Cabot's clenched fist smack to the point of Jud's jaw, and tumbled him in the dust.

Jud picked himself up snarling, shook himself, and then rushed bull-like at the earth-man, who stood his ground, ducked the flying arms of his antagonist, and tackled him as in the old football days at college. Jud was thrown for a four-yard loss with much of the breath knocked out of his body.

Theoph the Grim, with a worried frown, and Arkilu the Beautiful, with an entranced smile, stood by and watched the contest.

The Vairking noble lay motionless on his back as Myles scrambled to his knees astride the other's body and placed his hands on the other's shoulders. But suddenly, the underdog threw up his left leg, caught Myles on the right shoulder and pushed him backward. In an instant both men were on their feet again, glaring at each other.

Then they clinched and went down once more, this time with Jud on top. Theoph's look changed to a smile, and Arkilu became worried. But before Jud had time to follow up his advantage, Cabot secured a hammerlock around his neck and shoulders, and then slowly forced him to one side until their positions were reversed, and the shoulders and hips of the furry one were squarely touching the ground.

In a wrestling match, this would have constituted a victory for Myles Cabot, but this was a fight and not a mere wrestling match;

so the earth-man secured a hammerlock again and turned Jud the Excuse-Maker over until he lay prone, whereupon the victor rubbed the nose of the vanquished back and forth in the dirt, until he heard a muffled sound which he took to be the Vairkingian equivalent of the "'nuff" so familiar to every pugnacious American schoolboy.

His honor satisfied, Cabot arose, brushed himself off, and bowed to the two spectators. Jud sheepishly got to his feet as well, all the fight knocked out of him. Theoph stared at the victor with displeasure and at his own countryman with disgust, but Arkilu rushed over to Cabot with a little cry, flung her arms around him, and drew him within the tent.

As they passed through the curtains, Myles heard Jud the Excuse-Maker explaining to the king: "I decided to let him beat me, so that thereby I might give pleasure to her whom I love."

Inside the tent, Arkilu bathed the scratches and bruises of the earth-man, and hovered around him and fussed over him as though he had accomplished something much more wonderful than merely to have come out on top in a schoolboy rough-and-tumble fight.

Myles was very sorry that it all had happened. In the first place, he had lost his temper, which was to his discredit. In the second place, he had made a hero of himself in the eyes of the lady whose love he was most anxious to avoid. And in the third place, he had fought the man who was best calculated to protect him from that undesired love. Altogether, he had made a mess of things, and all he could do about it was meekly submit to the ministrations of the furry princess. What a life!

Finally Arkilu departed, leaving Cabot alone with recriminations for his rashness, longings for his own Princess Lilla, and worries for her safety.

The next day the expedition took up its delayed start homeward, Jud having found a route which required no alibis. The tents were struck, and were piled with the other impedimenta on two-wheeled carts, which the common soldiers pulled with long ropes.

In spite of Arkilu's pleadings, Myles was assigned to one of these gangs, Theoph grimly remarking: "If the hairless one is well enough to vanquish Jud, he is well enough to do his share of the work."

Jud explained to Arkilu that the real reason why he had suggested this was that he sincerely believed that the exercise would be good for Cabot's health.

During one of the halts, when Jud happened to be near Cabot's gang, the earth-man strode over to the commander, who instinctively cringed at his approach.

"I'm not fighting to-day," Myles assured the Vairking with an engaging smile, "but may I have a word with you?"

So the two withdrew a short distance out of earshot of the rest, and Myles continued: "I do not love Arkilu the Beautiful. You do. Let us understand one another, and help one another. You assist me *to* keep away from the princess, and I shall assist you *by* keeping away from the princess. Later I shall make further suggestions as to how we can cooperate to mutual advantage. I have spoken."

Jud stared at him with perplexed admiration.

"Who are you?" he asked, "who stands unabashed in the presence of kings and nobles, who addresses a superior without permission, and yet without offensive familiarity?"

"I am Cabot the Minorian," the other replied, "ruler over Cupia, a nation larger and more powerful than yours. A race of fearsome beasts have landed on the western shores of your continent. They are enemies of mine, and will become enemies of yours as they extend their civilization and run counter to yours."

"Impossible!" Jud exclaimed. "For how could these mythical creatures cross the boiling seas to land on our shores?"

"By magic," answered Myles, "magic which they stole from me. And they held me prisoner until I overthrew their magic and escaped, to be found by your expedition."

"Then you are a magician?"

"Yes."

"Ah, that explains how you defeated me in combat yesterday," Jud asserted with a relieved sigh.

"We will let it go at that," Myles agreed, smiling. "But to continue, let me frankly warn you that unless you destroy these Formians, they will eventually destroy you.

"They now possess magic against which you Vairkings would be powerless; magic methods of soundless speech; magic devices for transmitting that speech as far as from here to Vairkingi; magic wagons which can travel through the air and at such a speed that they could go from here to Vairkingi and back in a twelfth part of a day; and magic bows which shoot death-dealing pellets faster than the speed of sound, and which can outrange your bows and arrows ten to one.

"But if you will give a workroom and materials—and keep Arkilu away from me—I can devise magic which will overcome *their* magic, and which will make Vairkingi the unquestioned master of this whole continent, in spite of the Roies and the Formians. Then I shall seize one of the Formian magic wagons, fly back in it to my own country, and leave you in peaceful dominion over this continent. What do you say?"

"I say," the Vairking replied, "that you are an amusing fellow, and an able spinner of yarns. But you talk with evident earnestness and sincerity. Therefore I shall give you your workshop and your materials; but on one condition, namely, that you entertain us likewise. I have spoken."

And thus it came to pass that Jud the Excuse-Maker attached the earth-man to his personal retinue, and placed a laboratory at his disposal upon the return arrival of the expedition at Vairkingi.

This city was built entirely of wood. It was surrounded by a high stockade, and was divided by stockades into sections, each presided over by a noble, save only the central section which housed the retinue of Theoph himself. Within the sections, each family had its own walled-off enclosure. All streets and alleys passed between high wooded walls. The buildings and fences were carved and gaudily colored.

As the returning expedition approached the great wall, they were met by blasts of trumpet music from the parapets. Then a huge gate opened, and they passed inside. Here they quickly separated, and each detachment hastened to the quarter of the nobleman from whom they had been drawn. Jud and his detachment proceeded down many a high-walled street until they came to a gate bearing the insignia of Jud himself.

Inside there were more streets of the same character through which Jud's retinue dispersed to the gates of their own little inclosures until Jud and Myles Cabot were left alone.

The noble led his new acquisition to a gate.

"This inclosure is vacant," Jud explained. "It will be yours. Enter and take possession. Within, you will find a small house and a shop. Serving maids will be sent from my own household to make you comfortable. Repair to my palace to-night and tell me some more stories. Meanwhile good-by for the present."

And he strode off and disappeared around a bend in the street.

Cabot passed in through the gate.

He found a well, from which he drew water to fill a carefully fashioned wooden pool. Scarce had he finished bathing, when a group of furry girls arrived from the house of his patron bearing brooms and blankets and food.

One of them also bore a note which read as follows:

If you love me you will find a way to reach me.

Arkilu.

"And if not, what?" said Myles to himself.

After he had rested and dined, and the place had been made thoroughly neat, all the girls withdrew save the one who had brought the note. She informed him that her name was "Quivven" and that she had been ordered to remain in the inclosure as his servant.

She was small and lithe. Her hair was a brilliant yellow-gold, and her eyes were blue. If it had not been for her fur, she would have passed for a twin to his own Lilla. This fact brought an intense pang to him and caused such a wave of homesickness that he sat down on a couch and hid his face in his hands.

But the pretty creature made no attempt to comfort him. Instead, she merely remarked half aloud to herself: "I wonder what Arkilu can possibly see in him. Even Att the Terrible is much more handsome."

Finally, Myles arose with more determination and courage than he had felt at any time since his return to Poros.

Guided by Quivven, he set out for Jud's dwelling, firmly resolved to take steps that very night, which should result eventually in his reaching Cupia, and rescuing his family from the renegade Yuri.

Jud's palace was elaborate and barbaric. Jud himself was seated on a divan surrounded by Vairkingian beauties. They all were frankly inquisitive to see this hairless creature from another world, yet they rather turned up their pretty noses at him when they found him dressed like a common soldier.

Cabot regaled the gathering with an account of his first arrival on Poros and of the two wars of liberation which had freed Cupia from the domination of the ants. All the while he was most eager to get down to business with the noble; yet he realized that he had been employed for a definite purpose, namely story-telling, and that his first duty was to please his patron.

Finally, the ladies withdrew, and Myles Cabot, the radio man, began the first discussion of radio that he had undertaken since his return to Poros.

CHAPTER VIII
BUT WHY RADIO?

Three fields of "*magic*" were open to him, rifle-fire, aviation, and radio. The opportunity for building a workable airplane among people who knew no metal arts was obviously slight. To make a radio set should be possible, if he could find certain minerals and other natural products, which ought to be available in almost any country. But easiest of all would be to extract iron from the ore which he had observed on his journey across the mountains, forge rifle barrels and simple breech mechanisms, and make gunpowder and bullets.

Therefore it is plain why he did not attempt to build airships, but it is hard to see why he did not make firearms rather than a radio set. Firearms would have enabled him to equip the Vairkings for battle against the Formians, whereas radio could serve no useful purpose at the moment.

Yet, he took up radio. I think the explanation lies in two facts: first, he wanted above all to get in touch with his home in Cupia, find out the status of affairs there, and give courage to his wife and his supporters, if any of them remained; and secondly, he was primarily a radio engineer, and so his thoughts naturally turned to radio and minimized its difficulties. There would be plenty of time to arm the Vairkings after he found out how affairs stood at home.

So he broached to Jud his project of constructing a radio set, which would necessitate extended journeys in search of materials. But the Vairking noble was singularly uninterested.

"I know that you can spin interesting yarns," he said, "but I do not know whether you can do magic. Why, then, should I deprive myself of the pleasure of listening to your stories, just for the sake of letting you amuse yourself in a probably impossible pursuit? First, you must convince me that you are a magician; then perhaps I may consent to your attempting further magic."

"Very well," the earth-man replied. "Tomorrow evening I shall display to you some of the more simple examples of my art. Meanwhile, I shall spend my time concocting mystic spells in preparation for the occasion."

Then he bowed and withdrew, thanking his lucky stars that he had learned a few tricks of sleight-of-hand while at college.

Myles now recalled several of these, and devoted most of the succeeding day to preparing a few simple bits of apparatus. Then he practiced his tricks before the golden-furred Quivven, to her complete mystification.

That evening, he went again to the quarters of Jud the Excuse-Maker. The same group was there as on the evening before, and in addition, several other Vairking men and their wives.

After an introduction by his host, the earth-man started in. First he did, in rapid succession, some simple variations of sleight-of-hand.

He had wanted to perform the well-known "restoration of the cut handkerchief," but unfortunately the Vairkings possessed neither handkerchiefs nor scissors, and he was forced to improvise a variant. Taking a piece of stick, which he had brought with him for a wand, he stuffed a small part of one of the gaudy hangings through his closed left fist between the thumb and forefinger, so that it projected in a gathered-up point about two inches beyond his hand. Then pulling the curtain over toward one of the stone open-wick lamps which illuminated the chamber, he completely burned off the projecting bit of cloth.

Evidently, this was one of Jud's choicest tapestries, for the noble emitted a howl of grief and rage, and leaped from his divan, scattering the reclining beauties in both directions. If he had interfered in time to prevent the burning, it would have spoiled the trick, but as it was, the confusion caused by his onrush played right into Cabot's hands.

Myles stepped back in apparent terror as Jud seized his precious curtain and hunted for the scorched hole. But there was no hole there; the curtain was intact.

Jud looked up sheepishly into the triumphant face of his protégé, who thereupon stated: "You did not need to worry about your property in the hands of a true magician."

"Oh, I was not afraid," Jud the Excuse-Maker explained. "I merely pretended fear, so as to try and confuse your magic."

"Please do not do it again," the earth-man sternly admonished him.

The Vairking noble seated himself again.

His guests were enthralled.

This was a fitting climax for the evening. The amateur conjurer bowed low and withdrew.

Quivven was waiting for him at his house, and reported that some one had torn a small piece out of one of the tapestries. Several days later she found the piece, but alas, there was a hole burnt in the middle of it.

The next morning Jud the Excuse-Maker called at the quarters of Cabot, the furless. It was a rare honor, so Cabot answered the door in person. Jud expressed his conviction that the earth-man really was a magician, after all, and that therefore he—Jud—was agreeable to an expedition to the mountains in search of rocks whose mystical properties would enable the performing of even greater magic. It was soon arranged that Cabot, with a bodyguard of some twenty Vairking soldiers and a low-ranking officer, should start on the morrow.

Myles was thrilled. Now he was getting somewhere at last! The rest of the day he devoted to preparing a list of the materials for which he must hunt.

To make a radio-telephone sending and receiving set, he would need dielectrics, copper wire, batteries, tubes, and iron. For dielectrics, wood and mica would suffice. Wood was common, and the Vairkings were skilled carpenters and carvers. For fine insulation, mica would be ideal; and this mineral ought to be procurable somewhere in the mountains, whose general nature he had observed to be granitic.

To make copper wire, he would need copper ore—preferably pyrites—quartz, limestone, and fuel. The necessary furnaces he would built of brick; any one can bake clay into bricks.

For cement, Myles finally hit upon using a baked and ground mixture of limestone and clay, both of which ingredients he would have at hand for other purposes.

The Vairkings used charcoal in their open fires, and this would do nicely for his fuel.

For the wire-drawing dies he would use steel. This disposed of the copper questions, and brought him to a consideration of iron, which he would need at various places in his apparatus. This metal could be smelted from the slag of the copper furnaces, using an appropriate flux, such as fluorspar.

Cabot next turned his attention to his power source. For some time he debated the question of whether or not to build a dynamo.

But how about the storage batteries? He wasn't quite sure how to find or make the necessary red and yellow lead salts for the packing plates.

Thus by the time that Cabot reached the contemplation of having either to find or make his lead compounds he decided to turn his attention to primary cells. The jars could be made of pottery, or from the glass which was going to be necessary for his tubes anyhow. Charcoal would furnish the carbon elements. Zinc could easily be distilled from zincspar, if that particular form of ore were found. Sal ammoniac solution could be made from the ammonia of animal refuse, common salt, and sulphuric acid.

Mass production of zinc carbon batteries should thus be an easy matter, and they would serve perfectly satisfactorily, as neither compactness nor portability was a requisite. The radio man accordingly abandoned the idea of dynamos and accumulators in favor of large quantities of wet cells.

The tubes, it appeared to Myles, would present the greatest problem. Platinum for the filaments, grids, and plates had been fairly common in nugget form in Cupia, and so presumably could be found in Vairkingia. Glass, of course, would be easy to make.

Alcohol for laboratory burners could be distilled from decayed fruit.

But the chief stumbling block was how to exhaust the air from his tubes, and how to secure magnesium to use in completing the vacuum. These matters he would have to leave to the future in the hope of a chance idea. For the present there were enough elements to be collected so that he would be kept busy for a great many days. Accordingly he copied off the following two lists:

Materials readily available:

Wood
Wood ashes
Charcoal
Clay
Common salt
White sand
Animal refuse
Decayed fruit
Materials to hunt for:

Mica
Copper ore
Quartz
Limestone
Fluorspar
Galena
Zinc ore
Platinum
Chalk
Magnesium

But that afternoon all his plans were disrupted by a message reading:

To The Furless One:
     You are directed to appear for my amusement at my palace to-morrow. Fail not.

                                              Theoph The Grim.

"That puts an end to my trip," he said to Quivven. "How do you suppose his majesty got wind that I am a conjurer?"

"One of the guests at the show last night must have told him," she replied.

But something in her tone of voice caused Myles to look at her intently, and something in her expression caused him to say, "You know more than you tell. Out with it!"

Whereat Quivven shrugged her pretty golden shoulders, and replied, "Why deceive you? Though you are so stupid that it is very easy. Who brought you the note from Arkilu the night of your arrival here?"

"You did," Cabot answered. "Why didn't I put two and two together before? Then you are connected in some way with Arkilu?"

She laughed contemptuously. "How did you guess it?" she taunted. "Yes, one would rather say I am connected in some way with Arkilu; for I am her sister, set here to spy on you by connivance with the chief woman of Jud's servants, who is an old nurse of ours. I am Quivven the Golden Flame, daughter of Theoph the Grim, and it is from *me* that he learned of your mystic abilities. What do you think of *that*, beast?"

"I think," Myles said noncommittally, "that although you truly are a golden flame, you ought to have been named 'Quivven the Pepper Pot'.''

Whereat she suddenly burst into tears and rushed out of the room.

"Funny girl," Myles commented to himself, as he laid aside the list prepared for his prospecting trip, and set about the concoction of some stage properties for his forthcoming command performance before the King.

It was a sulky Quivven who served his meal that evening, so much so that Cabot playfully accused her of putting poison in his stew. This did not render her any more gracious, however.

"If I did not love my sister very much," she asserted, "I would not stand for you for one moment."

The rest of the meal was eaten in silence during which Cabot had an idea.

So when the food had been cleared away he asked the aureate maiden, "Can you smuggle a note to your sister for me?"

"Yes," she assented gloomily, "and I shall tell her how you are treating me."

At which he could not refrain from remarking, "Do you know, Quivven, I believe that you are falling in love with me."

"You beast!" she cried at him. "Oh, I hate you, I hate you, I hate you!" And she turned her face to the wall.

"Come, come!" said Cabot soothingly. "I don't mean to tease you, and we must both think of your sister. The note. How long will it take you to deliver it and return?"

"Shall I hurry?" she asked guardedly.

"Yes."

"Then it will take me less than one-twelfth of a day."

That would be quite sufficient for his plans. Accordingly he wrote:

> Arkilu The Beautiful:
> Send word how I can see you after the performance. But be-
> ware of Jud.
> Cabot The Magician.

This note he folded up, placed it in the palm of Quivven, and closed her golden fingers over it.

Whereat she sprang back with, "Don't you dare touch me like that!" and rushed out of the house, sobbing angrily.

Really, he must be more careful with this delicate creature; for although her intense hatred furnished him considerable amusement, yet it was possible to go too far. He must at least be polite to the sister of his benefactress.

But there was no time to be given over to worrying about Quivven's sensitive feelings; for the note had been sent merely to give him a slight respite from her prying eyes, in order that he might sneak out for a conference with Jud; of course he had no intention of any secret tryst with Arkilu. Heaven forbid, when he loved his own distant Lilla so intensely!

So he hurried to the quarters of the Vairkingian noble, who received him gladly, being most interested in learning whether there was any rational explanation to be given to the various magic tricks of the evening before. But Myles blocked his inquisitiveness by the flat assertion that all were due to mystic spells and talismans alone, and then got rapidly down to business, for there was no time to be lost.

Myles told Jud of the note from Theoph the Grim requiring his presence at the royal palace, and how he suspected that Princess Arkilu was responsible. Also, he related his discovery that his maid-servant was Quivven the Golden Flame; but he had the decency to refrain from implicating the head of Jud's ménage.

"I shall have her removed at once," the Vairking asserted.

"No, no," Myles hastily interposed, "that would never do; for now that we know she is a spy, it will be easy to outwit her. But a new one we never could be sure of."

Then he told how he had gotten rid of Quivven for the evening by sending her with a note to Arkilu. Jud's brow darkened.

"But," Myles insisted, "that note will serve a three-fold purpose; first, it has enabled me undetected to pay this visit to you; secondly, it will allay Arkilu's suspicions; and thirdly, it will stir you to block my appearance before Theoph to-morrow."

"Oh, I would have done that anyhow," Jud insisted. "My plans are all made. I shall send a runner to Theoph, and warn him to search Arkilu's room for your note. When he finds the note he will certainly cancel the arrangements for your performance. Thus will the note serve a *fourth purpose*.

"Return now to your quarters, and I will send you word of the outcome."

"I wouldn't if I were you," Myles admonished. "For a message from you would reveal to our fair young spy the fact of my secret interview with you this evening. Let Theoph himself send the word."

"So be it. You may count on starting on your expedition to-morrow as planned. Good luck to you."

"Good luck to *you*, Jud the Great, and may you win Arkilu the Beautiful."

So the earth-man hastened back to his quarters, where Quivven, on her return, found him placidly reclining on a divan.

For a few minutes they chatted playfully together, and then she suddenly narrowed her eyelids, looked at him with a peculiar expression, and asked: "Aren't you the least bit anxious to know what answer Arkilu made to your note?"

That was so; he *had* written Arkilu a note; but now that it had served its purpose he had completely forgotten about it. How could he square himself with little Quivven? By flattery?

"Of course I'm anxious to know," he asserted, "but I was so glad to have you come back again that for the moment I neglected to ask you."

Quivven the Golden Flame pouted.

"Now you're teasing me again," she said, "and I won't stand for it."

"But I really want to know," he continued with mock eagerness. "Please do tell me about your sister."

"I gave her the note—"

Just then there came a loud pounding on the gate outside; so loud, in fact, that the sound penetrated within the house. Quivven stopped talking. She and Myles listened intently. The pounding continued.

"Evidently we are to have company this evening," he remarked, glad to change the subject.

Quivven replied, "Such a racket at this time of night can mean naught but ill. Let us approach the gate with care, and question the intruders."

So saying, she took down one of the hanging stone lamps and opened the outside door. It was a typical dark, silent, fragrant Porovian evening, except for the fact that the darkness was broken by the glare of the torches beyond the wall, and that the silence was broken by the pounding on the gate, and that the fragrance was marred by the smoke of Quivven's lamp.

"Who is there?" Quivven called.

To this there came back the peremptory shout: "Open quickly, in the name of Theoph the Grim!"

The golden girl recoiled. Even Cabot himself shuddered as he realized the evident cause of the disturbance; his plot with Jud had produced results beyond what they had planned; and Theoph upon seizing the note, had decided not merely to cancel the sleight-of-hand performance, but also to place his daughter's supposed sweetheart under arrest.

"I am afraid your father has intercepted my letter to your sister," Cabot explained. "I tell you what! *You* leave by the rear door, make your way quickly to Arkilu, and see if the two of you can intercede for me with your stern parent."

So saying, he released her. The slim princess handed him the light, and sped into the interior of the house.

"Cease your noise!" he shouted. "For I, Myles Cabot the Minorian, come to unbar the gate in person!"

He strode down the path. Quickly he slid the huge wooden bolts, swung the gate open, and stepped outside, shielding the lamp with one hand to get a view of the disturbers. But his lamp was instantly dashed from him and his arms bound behind him.

His captors were about a dozen Vairking soldiers in leather tunics and helmets, some carrying wooden spears and some holding torches, while their evident leader was similarly clothed but armed with a sharp wooden rapier.

As soon as the prisoner was securely bound the guard hustled him roughly off down the street.

Thus were his plans rudely dashed to the ground. On the preceding night all had been arranged for his trip to secure the elements for the construction of a radio set with which to communicate with Cupia and his Lilla. That morning he had been forced to postpone his trip, in order to perform before Theoph the Grim. And this evening he was Theoph's prisoner, slated for—what?

CHAPTER IX

A PRISONER

The squad of Vairking soldiers, with Myles Cabot as their prisoner, had traversed nowhere near the distance to the palace, when they turned from the street through a gate.

"Where are they going to take me now?" Myles wondered.

This question was soon answered, for the party entered a building which was evidently a dwelling of the better class. The hall was well lighted, so that Miles blinked at the sudden glare.

The leader of the party placed himself squarely in front of his prisoner, with hands on his hips, and remarked with apparent irrelevance: "Well, we fooled Quivven, didn't we?"

The prisoner stared at him in surprise. It was Jud! Jud, disguised as a common soldier.

Cabot laughed with relief.

"You certainly gave me a bad hundred-and-forty-fourth part of a day," he asserted. "I didn't recognize you in your street clothes. What is the great idea?"

"'The great idea'," the noble replied, "to quote your phrase, is that I did truly represent Theoph the Grim. He authorized me to arrest you in his name. The pretty little spy will report your capture to Arkilu, and her father will stonily refuse to reveal where you are imprisoned.

"Meanwhile I shall give the golden one time to escape, and shall then send a second squad to seize your effects. Your expedition will start immediately. Come, unbind the prisoner."

As soon as his bonds were loosed, Myles warmly grasped the hand of his benefactor.

"You are all right!" he exclaimed. "You have completely succeeded without leaving anything to explain."

"I *always* succeed, and never have to explain anything!" Jud replied a bit coldly.

And so, late that night, the Radio Man, dressed in leather tunic and helmet, and armed with a tempered wood rapier, set out with his bodyguard for the western mountains. In silence, and with the minimum of lights, they threaded the streets of Jud's compound and then the streets of the city until they came to the west gate, where a pass signed by Theoph the Grim gave them free exit. Thence they moved due westward across the plain, with scouts thrown out to guard against contact with any roving Roies.

By daybreak they had reached the cover of the wooded foothills, and there they camped for a full day of much needed rest. Finally, on the second morning following their stealthy departure from Vairkingi, their journey really started.

The commander of the bodyguard was an intelligent youth named Crota. During the meals at the first encampment, Myles described to Crota in considerable detail the particular form of copper pyrites which furnish the bulk of the copper used for electrical purposes on the continent of Cupia.

After listening intently to this description for about the fifth time, Crota smiled and said, "We Vairkings place no stock in pretty stones, except as playthings for our children, but I do recall the little golden cubes with which the children of one of the hill villages are accustomed to play tum-tum. This village, Sur by name, is only a day's journey to the southward. Let us turn our steps thither and learn from the children where they get their toys."

"'Out of the mouths of babes and sucklings,'" the earth-man quoted to himself.

And so they set out to the southward, following a trail which wound in and out between the fertile silver-green hills, which were for the most part scantily wooded.

Toward the close of the day, Crota's scouts established contact with the outposts of the village which they were seeking; and after an exchange of communications by runner, the expedition was given free passage to proceed. Shortly thereafter they came in sight of the village itself.

From among the surrounding verdant rolling terrain there arose one rocky eminence with precipitous sides, and with a flat summit on which stood the village of Sur surrounded by a strong wooden palisade.

Up the face of the cliff there ran a narrow zigzag path, cut in the living rock, and overhung by many a bastion from which huge stones could be tumbled or molten pitch poured on any invaders so rash as to attempt the ascent.

Along this path the expedition crawled in single file with many pauses to draw their breath; and before they reached the summit Cabot realized full well how it was that Sur, the southernmost outpost of Vairkingian civilization, had so long and so successfully withstood the onslaughts of the wild and savage Roies.

The inhabitants, furry Vairkings, turned out in large numbers to greet the visitors and especially to inspect the furless body and the much overfurred chin of the earth-man. Guides led the expedition to a large public hall where, after a speech of welcome by the headman of the village, they were fed and quartered for the night.

Between the meal and bedtime the visiting soldiers strolled out to see the sights by the pale pink light of the unseen setting sun. Cabot and Crota together walked to the west wall to observe the sunset.

As the two of them leaned on the parapet, a rattling noise on the rocky walk beside them disturbed their reverie. Looking down, they saw three furry children rolling some small objects along the ground. With a slight exclamation of surprise and pleasure, the Vairking soldier swooped down upon the youngsters, scooped up one of the toys, and handed it to the earth-man.

"Tum-tum," Crota laconically announced, and sure enough it was one of the small game-cubes, which he had described to his companion.

But before the latter had had the slightest opportunity to examine it, the bespoiled infant let out a howl of childish rage, and commenced to assail Myles with fists and teeth and feet.

"Stop that!" Crota shouted, grabbing him by one arm and pulling him away. "We don't want to keep your tum-tum; we merely want to look at it. This gentleman has never seen a tum-tum."

"Gentleman?" the boy replied from a safe distance. "Common soldier! Bah!"

But Myles Cabot was too engrossed to notice the insult. The small cube in his hand was undoubtedly a metallic crystal, but whether chalcopyrite or not he could not tell in the fading light. In fact, it might be the sunset which gave the stone its coppery tinge.

Taking a small flint knife from a leather sheath that hung from his belt, Myles offered it to the child in exchange for the toy, in spite of Crota's gasping protest at the extravagance.

The boy eagerly accepted the offer, remarking: "Thank you, sir. You should take off those clothes."

It was a very neat and subtle compliment. Gentlemen Vairkings never wore clothes. Cabot was impressed.

"Your name, my son?" he asked, patting the furry little creature on the head.

"Tomo the Brief," was the reply.

"I shall remember it."

Then he hurried back to the public hall, eager to examine his purchase by the light of the oil flares.

Sure enough, it turned out to be really pyrites, and by its deep color probably a pyrites rich in copper. To the Radio Man it meant the first tangible step toward the accomplishment of the greatest radio feat ever undertaken on two worlds; namely the construction of a complete sending and receiving set out of nothing but basic materials in their natural state without the aid of a single previously fabricated man-made tool, utensil, or chemical. To this day Myles wears this cube as a pendant charm in commemoration of that momentous occasion.

As he lay on the floor of the public building that night the earth-man reviewed the events of the day until he came to the episode of the purchase of the cubical pyrite crystal from little Tomo.

"Your name, my son?" Cabot had asked him.

"'My son'," thought Cabot. "I have a son of my own across the boiling seas on the continent of Cupia, and a wife, the most beautiful and sweetest lady in Poros. They are in dire danger, or were many months ago when I received the S O S which led me to return through the skies to this planet. Oh, how I wish that I could learn what that danger was, and what has happened to them since then!"

Thus he mused; and yet when he came to figure up the time since his capture he was able to account for less than three weeks of earth time. Perhaps there was still a chance of rescue, if he would but hurry.

The danger which had inspired his Lilla's call for help was undoubtedly due to the return of Prince Yuri across the boiling seas. For all that Myles knew, Princess Lilla and the loyal Cupians were still holding out against their renegade prince.

The message which Cabot had ticked out into the ether from the radio station of the ants had been sent only a few days after the S O S. If received by Lilla or any of her friends, it had undoubtedly served to encourage them to stiffen their resistance to the usurper; and if received by Yuri, it had undoubtedly thrown into him the fear of the Great Builder.

Musing and hoping thus, the earth-man fell into a troubled sleep, through which there swirled a tangled phantasmagoria of ant-men, Cupians, whistling bees, and Vairkings, with occasional glimpses of a little blue-eyed blond head, sometimes surmounted by golden curls and two dainty antennae, but sometimes completely covered with golden fur.

Shortly after sunrise he awoke, and aroused Crota. No time must be lost! The Princess Lilla must be saved!

But there was nothing they could do until their hosts brought the food for the morning meal. From the bearers they now ascertained that the tum-tum cubes were gathered in a cleft in the rocks only a short distance from the village; and that, although the perfect cubes were rare and quite highly prized, the imperfect specimens were present in great quantities. In fact, hundreds of cartloads had been mined and picked over in search of perfect cubes, and thus all this ore would be available in return for the mere trouble of shoveling it into carts.

As soon as arrangements could be made with the headman of Sur, Cabot and his party, accompanied by guides, crept down the narrow zigzag path to the plain below the village, and proceeded up a ravine to the quarry, where they verified all that had been told them.

It was a beautiful sight; a rocky wall out of a cleft in which there seemed to pour a waterfall of gold.

But on close inspection, every cube was seen to be nicked or bent or out of proportion, or jammed part way through or into some other cube.

The soldiers, both those from Vairkingi and those from Sur, scrambled up the golden cascade and started hacking the crystals out of the solid formation, in search for perfect cubes, while their two leaders watched them with amusement from below.

All at once there came a shriek, and one of the Vairkings toppled the whole length of the pile, almost at Cabot's feet, where he lay perfectly still, the wooden shaft of an arrow projecting from one eyeball.

"Roies!" Crota shouted.

Instantly every member of the party took cover with military precision behind some rock or tree.

They had not long to wait, for a shower of missiles from up the valley soon apprised them of the location of the enemy. So the Vairkings thereafter remained alert. Those who had bows drew them and discharged a flint-tipped arrow at every stir of grass or bush in the locality whence the missiles of the enemy had come.

"We know not their number," Crota whispered to Cabot. "And since we have accomplished our mission let us return to Sur as speedily as possible."

"Agreed," the earth-man replied.

The withdrawal was accomplished as follows. Crota first dispatched runners to the village to inform the inhabitants of the situation. Then, leaving a small rear guard of archers and slingers to cover their retreat, he formed the remainder of the expedition in open order, and set out for Sur as rapidly as the cover would permit.

The enemy kept pretty well hidden, but it was evident from the increase of arrows and pebbles that their numbers were steadily augmenting. Noting this, Crota sent another runner ahead with this information.

It now became necessary to replenish and relieve the rear guard, of which several were dead, several more wounded and the rest tired and out of ammunition. This done, Crota ordered the main body of his force to leave cover and take up the double quick.

The result was unexpected. A hundred or more Roies charged yelling down the ravine through the Vairking rear guard, and straight at Cabot's men, who at once ran to cover again and took deadly toll of the oncoming enemy.

But the Roies so greatly outnumbered the Vairkings that the tide could not be stemmed, and soon the two groups were mingled together in a seething mass. The first rush was met, spear on spear. Then the sharp wooden swords were drawn, and Cabot found himself lunging and parrying against three naked furry warriors.

The neck was the vulnerable spot of the Vairkings, and it was this point which the Roies strove to reach, as Cabot soon noted. That simplified matters, for guarding one's neck against such crude swordsmen as these furry aborigines was easy for a skilled fencer such as he. Accordingly, one by one, he ran three antagonists through the body.

Just as he was withdrawing his blade from his last victim, he noted that Crota was being hard pressed by a burly Roy swordsman; so he hastened to his friend's assistance. And he was just in time, for even as Cabot approached, the naked Roy knocked the leather-clad Vairking's weapon from his hand with a particularly dexterous sideswipe, and thus had Crota at his mercy.

But before the naked one could follow up his advantage, the earth-man hurled his own sword like a spear, and down went the Roy, impaled through the back, carrying Crota with him as he fell.

Cabot paused to draw breath, and was just viewing with satisfaction the lucky results of his chance throw, when a peremptory command of "Yield!" behind him caused him to wheel about and confront a new enemy. The author of the shout was a massive furry warrior with a placid, almost bovine, face, which nevertheless betokened considerable intellect.

"And to whom would I yield, if I did yield?" Myles asked, facing unarmed the poised sword of his new enemy.

"Grod the Silent, King of the Roies," was the dignified reply.

"I thought that Att the Terrible was king of your people," the earth-man returned, sparring for time.

"That is what Att thinks too," the other answered with a slight smile.

But the smile was short-lived, for Myles Cabot, having momentarily distracted his opponent's attention by this conversation, stepped suddenly under the guard of the furry Grod, and planted his fist square on Grod's fat chin. Down crashed the king, his sword clattering from his nerveless hand. In an instant Myles snatched up the blade and bestrode his prostrate foe.

Just as he was about to plunge its point into Grod's vitals, there occurred to him the proverb of Poblath: "While enemies dispute, the realm is at peace."

With Grod the Silent and Att the Terrible both contending for the leadership of the Roies, Vairkingia might enjoy a respite from the depredations of this wild and lawless race. He would leave the fallen Roy for dead, rather than put him actually in that condition. Accordingly, he sprang to the aid of his companions.

Crota was already back in the fray, his own sword in his hands once more, and the sword of his late burly opponent slung at his side. Quite evidently he did not intend to be disarmed again.

Three Vairking common soldiers and Crota and Myles now confronted seven Roies. This constituted a fairly even match, for the superior intelligence and the leather armor of the men of Vairkingi and Sur, offset the greater numbers of their aboriginal antagonists. What the outcome would have been can never be known, for at that moment, the reinforcements from the village came charging up the ravine; and at the same instant, the tops of the cliffs were lined with Roies, who sent a shower of arrows upon those below.

The contending twelve immediately separated. Cabot and his followers passed within the protection of his rescuers and the return to Sur was renewed. The commander of the rescue party threw out a strong rear guard, and the Vairking archers on both flanks peppered the cliff tops with sling shots and arrows, but the marauding Roies harassed every step of the retreat.

There was some respite when Cabot's party reached the plain where stood the rocky peak with the village of Sur on its summit, for arrows could not carry from the cover of the surrounding woods to the foot of the rocks. But, as the tired party began the ascent of the narrow path on the face of the cliff, they noted that the Roies were forming solid banks of wooden shields and were advancing across the plain.

Arrows now began to fly from below at the ascending Vairking party, several of whom toppled and fell down the face of the cliff. And then the warrior just above Myles on the narrow path clutched his breast with a gasp and dropped square upon the earth-man, who braced himself and caught the body, thus preventing it from being dashed to pieces at the foot of the rocks.

Whether or not the furry soldier was dead could not be ascertained until Myles should have reached the summit, so up he toiled with his burden until he gained the protection of the palisade, where he laid the Vairking gently on the ground and tore open his leather tunic to see if any life were present.

The wounded man still breathed, though hoarsely, and his heart still beat; but there was a gaping hole in one side of his chest.

No arrow protruding from this hole. Myles tenderly turned the man over to see if the wound extended clear through. It did—almost. And from the man's side there projected the tip of a bullet, the steel-sheathed tip of a leaden rifle bullet!

CHAPTER X
THE SIEGE OF SUR

Myles quickly extracted the bullet from the back of the wounded Vairking. Then tender furry female hands bore the victim away, as the earth-man stood in thoughtful contemplation of his find.

There could be no doubt of it. This was a steel-jacketed bullet, identical with those used in the rifles of the ant-men. How came such a weapon in the hands of the savage and untrained Roies?

It was inconceivable that these uncultured brutes had overwhelmed New Formia and captured the weapons of the ant-men. No, the only possible explanation was that the Formians had formed an alliance with the Roies, and were either fighting beside them or at least had furnished them with a few firearms, the use of which they had taught them.

But this last idea was improbable, due to the well-known shortage of rifles and ammunition at Yuriana, capital of the new ant empire. No, if the ant-men were in alliance with these furry savages, there must be ant-men present with the besiegers, and the shot in question must have been fired by the claw of a Formian.

This opened up new terrors for the village of Sur and its inhabitants. Myles glanced apprehensively at the southern sky, half expecting to see and hear the approach of a Formian plane, but the radiant silver expanse was unmarred by any black speck. Sur was safe for the moment.

His musings thus completed, Myles hurried to the public hall to communicate this discovery to Crota and the village authorities. He found the headman already there in conference with Crota.

Said Myles, exhibiting the bullet: "Here is one of the magic stones thrown by one of my own magic sling-shots, which is capable of shooting from the ground to the top of your cliffs and even penetrating your palisade. It is big magic! With its aid, the Roies can overcome us. Without it, I am powerless. Therefore, we must secure possession of it. What do you suggest?"

Crota replied: "It is now sunset. Let us select a squad of picked scouts and try to stalk the camp of the enemy."

"No, no!" the headman of Sur exclaimed in horror. "Never have our men dared to attack the Roies by dark."

"Do the Roies know this?" Myles asked with interest.

"Most certainly," was the reply.

"Then," he said, "all the more reason for attempting it They will be unprepared."

The magistrate shrugged his furry shoulders with: "If you can persuade any men of Sur to attempt anything so foolhardy, I shall interpose no objection."

Within a twelfth of a day, Crota had enrolled twenty scouts, and with Myles Cabot, they had all begun the stealthy descent of the narrow winding path down the face of the cliff. Before starting, they had observed the direction of the Roy camp-fires on one of the surrounding hills; so now they crept quietly toward that hill, and then slowly up to its crest.

In spite of the dense blackness of the Porovian night, they were able to find their way, first by starting in the correct direction and then by keeping the lights of their own village always behind them.

As Cabot had expected from the remarks of the headman, there were no sentinels on post, for the enemy were quite evidently relying on the well-known Vairking fear of the unknown terrors of the dark. Indeed, it spoke volumes for the individual courage of the twenty-one members of this venture, and for their confidence in their earth-man leader, that they had dared to come.

Finally, the party emerged from the underbrush at the top of the hill, a few score of feet from the tents and camp-fires of the Roies. There, motioning the others to remain where they were until he gave a signal, Myles crawled forward, always keeping in the shadow of some tent, until he was able to peek through a small bush beside one of the tents, directly at the group around one of the camp-fires.

Just as Cabot arrived at this observation post, a Roy warrior was declaiming: "I told you it would work, for had I not seen it demonstrated fully to me? You yourselves saw it kill. Now will you not believe me?"

Another spoke: "I cannot understand its principle. How can a weapon kill afar, and yet not resemble either a sling or a bow?"

And another: "Show us how it works, friend. Then perhaps we may be persuaded."

And a third: "I do not believe that he has it."

Whereat, the original speaker, nettled, spoke again: "It is in my tent there, you doubters," indicating the one beside which Cabot crouched.

Quick as a flash, Cabot wriggled beneath the back of the tent into its interior. The campfire light, penetrating through the slit opening in front, revealed nothing but rumpled blankets on the floor, and ordinary weapons slung to the tent pole; so the intruder commenced rummaging among the bedding. The conversation outside continued.

"Prove, or be silent!" said a voice.

"You saw the Vairking fall, did you not?" the original speaker replied.

"True, but I did not see you sling any pebble."

Meanwhile, Cabot continued his frantic search. At last, it was rewarded. In one corner of the tent, his groping fingers closed upon a Formian rifle and a bandolier of cartridges. A thrill ran through him at the touch.

"To prove it to you," the voice outside was saying, angrily, "I will get it for you; and if you do not believe me, I shall slingshot you with it. *That* ought to be proof enough even for a stupid one like you.

I have said it!"

"The signal for my exit," Myles said to himself, as he hastened to crawl out through the back of the tent, but then he reflected: "No, I want more than this gun and ammunition; I want information."

So he remained.

As the Roy entered the tent and felt for the rifle, the crouching earth-man flung himself upon him; and before the startled furry one could utter even a gasp, strong fingers closed upon his windpipe, throttling off all sound. The struggle was over in a few moments.

When Myles Cabot finally crept out of the enemy tent, it was with a limp form under one arm, and a bandolier and a rifle slung across his shoulders.

The conversation at the camp fire continued.

One of the warriors was saying: "Our friend takes long to find his wonderful sling-shot. Methinks he was lying and does not dare to face us."

Said another voice: "Let us pull him from his tent and confront him with his perfidy."

At this, Myles sprang to his feet and ran to the cover which concealed his followers.

"Rush in among them as we planned," he urged, "while you two come with me."

Then on he sped down the hillside towards the lights of Sur with his captive and trophies and two previously-picked members of the band, while Crota and the remaining eighteen charged yelling into the midst of the Roy camp, upsetting tents, scattering camp fires, and laying about them with their swords. Straight through the camp they charged, shouting: "Make way for Att the Terrible!" Then they circled the hill under cover of the darkness and rejoined Myles.

The startled Roies were taken completely by surprise. From the cries of Crota and his followers, they assumed that the intruders were Roies, partisans of Att the Terrible, attacking them for being partisans of Grod the Silent. As they came rushing out of their standing tents, or crawled from beneath such tents as had been wrecked, they met others of their own camp, similarly rushing or crawling, and mistaking them for enemies, started to fight.

The confusion was complete, and never for a moment did the naked furry savages suspect that the whole trouble had been caused by a mere handful of Vairkings.

Truly, as Poblath the Philosopher has said, "While enemies dispute, the realm is at peace."

While the Roy followers of Grod the Silent fought among themselves until they gradually discovered that there was no one there except themselves, Myles Cabot and his Vairkings safely regained the Village of Sur with the rifle, the ammunition, and the still unconscious Roy warrior.

In the public hall, under the tender ministrations of Vairking maidens—who would far rather have plunged a flint knife into him—the captive finally regained his senses and looked around him in bewilderment.

"Where am I?" he asked, rubbing his eyes.

"In Sur," some one replied.

"Then are we victorious? For never before has a Roy set foot in Sur."

"No, your forces are not victorious," Crota answered. "You are a prisoner. And it is only by the grace of Cabot the Minorian that you are permitted to come here even as a prisoner. For the men of Sur take no prisoners, and give no quarter."

In reply, Myles himself stepped forward.

"I myself, am Cabot the Minorian," he said.

To which Crota added impressively: "The greatest magician of two worlds!"

The prisoner shook his head.

"I know of only one world," he asserted, "and this man before me is dressed as a mere common soldier, as are all of you."

"Know then, O scum of Poros," the earth-man admonished, "that there are other worlds beyond the silver skies, and that in the world from which I come, all soldiers are gentlemen."

But the Roy warrior was not to be subdued by language. "How did I come here?" he asked.

"You did not come here," Myles answered. "You were brought. I brought you."

"But how?"

"By magic."

"What magic?"

"My magic cart which swims through the air as a reptile swims through the waters of a lake."

"True," the Roy mused, "there be such aerial wagons, for I have seen them near the city of the beasts of the south."

"Mark well!" Myles interjected to the assembled Vairkings, then to the prisoner again: "I captured you because you possessed the magic sling-shot, and presumed to use it on one of my own men. This effrontery could not be permitted to go unpunished; hence your capture. The offending weapon is now mine, and you are my prisoner."

"What do you propose to do with me?" the captive asked. "I propose to ask you some questions," Myles evaded. "First where did you get the magic sling-shot?"

"The great magician knows everything," the Roy replied, with a sneer. "Why, then, should I presume to tell him anything?"

But the earth-man remained unruffled. "You are correct," he countered. "I ask, not because I do not already know, but because I wish to test whether it is possible for one of your degraded race to tell the truth."

"Why test that?" came back the brazen Roy, "for doubtless you, who know everything, know that, too."

Myles could not help admiring the insulting calm with which this furry man of inferior race confronted his relentless captors.

"Who are you, rash one?" he asked.

The prisoner drew himself up proudly, with folded arms, and answered: "I am Otto the Bold, son of Grod the Silent."

"Ah," Myles said, "the son of a king. And I am the father of a king. Well, then, as one man to another, tell me where you got this gun."

"Gun?" Otto queried. "Is that the name of this weapon of bad omen? Know then that I got it from you yourself when I wounded you beneath the tree beside the brook at the foot of the mountains, before the Vairkings of Jud the Excuse-Maker drove me off. I have spoken!"

"And spoken truly," Cabot replied, concealing his surprise with difficulty. Of course. Why had he not guessed it before? But there were still some more points to clear up, so he continued: "Why did you shoot those two arrows at me in the house at the top of the mountains?"

"Because we wished to explore the house. But you killed my companion, whereupon I resolved to kill you in revenge, and to capture the noisy 'gun'—and is that the right word? So I trailed you. The rest you know."

"Remember, I know *everything*," Myles said, grinning. "But did you ever see any one but me shoot the gun?"

"You know I never did," was the reply. "No one on Poros, save Cabot the Magician and Otto the Bold, has ever done this big magic. I saw the results, but not the means, when you killed my companion; so I experimented for myself after I had stolen your gun, and soon I learned how, after which I carefully conserved the magic stones until last night when I shot one of the Vairkings of Sur, so as to give visible proof of my magic powers to my doubting comrades."

The earth-man heaved a sigh of relief. There existed as yet no alliance between the Formians and the Roies. Pray Heaven that such a calamity would never suggest itself to the minds of either race; for if so, then woe to Vairkingia!

"Son of a king," he said, "return to your people and your father. Give him my greetings, and tell them that you are the friend of a great magician, who lent you his 'gun', who transported you through the air within the walls of Sur, where no Roy has ever stood or will ever stand, and who last night caused phantom warriors to attack your camp under the guise of followers of Att the Terrible. Go now. My men will give you safe conduct to the plain below."

"And what is the price of this freedom?" Otto disdainfully inquired.

"The friendship of a king's father for a king's son," Myles Cabot replied with dignity.

The two drew themselves up proudly and regarded each other eye-to-eye for a moment.

"It is well," Otto the Bold declared. "Good-by." And he departed under the escort of a Vairking guard.

"The master knows best," Crota remarked, sadly shaking his head, "but I should have run the wretch through the body."

The next morning Cabot thanked the headman of Sur for his hospitality, and took up the return trail for Vairkingi, the vacancies in his ranks being filled by the loan of soldiers from Sur. The party had gone but a short distance when they found the way barred by a formidable body of Roies. But before these came within bow-shot a bullet from Cabot's rifle brought two of them to the ground, whereupon the rest turned and fled precipitately.

Later in the day a bend in the road brought them suddenly upon a furry warrior. Myles fired, and the man instantly fell to the ground.

But when they reached the body there was not even a scratch to be found on it; the bullet had missed.

"Dead of fright," Myles thought; but no, for the heart was still beating, although faintly, and the lungs were still functioning.

"Sit up there!" Myles ordered.

"Can't," The Roy replied. "I'm dead."

"Then I'll make you alive again," his captor declared, placing his hands on the head of the Roy. "*Abra cadabra camunya.*"

Thereat the soldier sat up with a sigh of relief, and opened his eyes.

"Stand up!" Myles ordered.

For reply the Roy jumped to his feet and started running for cover.

"Halt!" the earth-man commanded. "Halt, or I'll kill you again!"

The man stopped.

"Return!"

The man returned, like a sleep walker.

"What do you mean by running away? Now listen intently. Are you one of the men of Grod?"

"Yes."

"Then go to Otto, the son of Grod, and tell him that it is the order of Cabot the Magician that Vairking expeditions into these mountains, in search of golden cubes and other minerals, be unmolested. Tell Otto that he can recognize my expedition by the blue flags which they will carry hereafter. Now go. I have spoken."

The Roy warrior ran up the trail and this time was not halted.

"Another mistake," Crota remarked, half to himself.

The rest of the return to Vairkingi was without event. On the way the radio man made notes of the best deposits of quartz, limestone, and fluorspar. Also he carried with him a few large sheets of mica. But he found no traces of galena, zinc ore, or platinum. These would require at least one further expedition.

Crota spared no extravagant language in relating to Jud the exploits of Cabot the Minorian in raising the siege of the village of Sur; and Jud repeated the story with embellishments to Theoph the Grim. Also the long deferred sleight-of-hand performance was held at the palace, to the great mystification of the white-furred king.

Arkilu did not show up to mar the occasion. In fact, little Quivven reported that her sister was very indignant at the earth-man for trifling with her affections, and had turned to Jud in her pique. Needless to say, Jud had taken every possible advantage of Cabot's absence to reinstate himself with the chestnut-furred princess. But neither Myles nor Quivven appeared to exhibit any very great sorrow at this turn of affairs.

So long as Arkilu's hostility did not become active, the support of Jud and Theoph ought to prove quite sufficient.

The standing of Cabot the Minorian as a magician was now well established, and accordingly Jud the Excuse-Maker and even Theoph the Grim were willing to accord him all possible assistance in the gathering of the materials with which he was to perform his further magic, namely radio.

Theoph made a levy upon all the nobles, and turned over to the earth-man upward of five hundred soldiers with their proper carts and equipment. Jud (himself,) Quivven (still unknown to her father), and Crota (the soldier who had demonstrated on the expedition an intelligence far above his social class), were enrolled as laboratory assistants. Several inclosures adjoining Cabot's yard were vacated and converted into factories, in one of which were mounted a pair of huge millstones such as the Vairkings use in grinding certain of their food.

Myles divided his men roughly into three groups. One group, under Crota, he established at the clay deposits to the northeast of the city, to make bricks and charcoal.

The second group, under Jud, were engaged in the mining operations, digging copper ore, quartz rock, fluorspar, limestone, and sand, at various points in the mountains, and carting some of the limestone to the brickyard, and the rest with the other products to Vairkingi. The carters carried back with them to the mountains all the necessary supplies for the expeditions.

The third group, under Quivven, were engaged in setting up the grist mill, and in other building and preparatory operations.

At the claypits the first operation was to scrape off the surface clay and spread it out thin in the open air, so it would age fast.

The limestone, upon its arrival at the brickyard, was burned in raw brick ovens, and then carted to Vairkingi, to be ground at the mill. It was then shipped back to the brick plant, where it was mixed with the aged clay—first screened—molded into bricks, baked, burned, and carted to Vairkingi, to be ground into cement.

Some of the ground limestone was retained at Vairkingi for use in later glass-making, and some of the unground for smelting purposes.

Other aged clay was screened, moistened, molded, and baked to form ordinary brick. Fire-brick was similarly made by the addition of white sand finely ground at Vairkingi, but this kind of brick had to be baked much more slowly.

Thus only a week or two after this whole huge industrial undertaking had begun, the radio man was in possession of fire-brick and fire-clay with which to start the building of the smelting furnaces.

Meanwhile Myles Cabot, with a small bodyguard, kept traveling from one job to another, giving general superintendence to the work. And when everything was well under way he set out on another exploring expedition in search of galena, zinc ore, and platinum.

Quivven had furnished the inspiration for this trip by suggesting that the sparkling sands of a large river, which ran from west to east, about a day's journey north of Vairkingi, might contain the silver grains which he sought. So thither he set out one morning, with camping equipment and a detachment of soldiers.

All day they marched northward across the level plains. Toward evening they reached a small estuary of the main stream, and there they camped.

As the silver sky pinkened in the west Myles Cabot ran quickly down this brook to inspect the sands of the river, which lay but a short distance away.

The pink turned to crimson, and then purple. The darkness crept up out of the east, and plunged the whole face of the planet into velvet and impenetrable black. But Myles Cabot did not return to the camping place.

CHAPTER XI
ATT THE TERRIBLE

When Myles Cabot left his encampment beside the little brook, he hastened down stream to where the brook joined the big river, along the edge of which there stretched a sandy beach. Falling on his knees, he picked up handful after handful of the silver sands.

There was still plenty of daylight left for him to examine the multitude of shiny metallic particles.

There could be no doubt of it, these sands held some metal which could be separated out in much the same manner as that in which the California gold miners of 1849 used to wash for gold, but only time would tell whether or not this metal was the much-to-be-desired platinum which the radio man needed for the grids, filaments, plates, and wires of his vacuum tubes.

On the morrow he would wash for this metal, using the wooden pans which he had brought for that purpose. The precious dust he would carry back to Vairkingi, melt it into small lumps if possible, and then try to analyze its composition in his laboratory.

As he sat on the sandy beach and thus laid his plans, his thoughts gradually wandered away from scientific lines, and he began again to worry about Lilla.

It was many days since she had sent the S O S which had recalled him from earth to Poros. Whatever she had feared must have happened by now. It was possible that he would never be able to effect a return to Cupia. Why not then accept the inevitable, settle down permanently among the Vairkings, and solace himself as best he could?

Even an ordinarily stalwart soul would have done his best and have been satisfied with that. But Myles Standish Cabot possessed that indomitable will which had given rise to the Porovian proverb: "You cannot kill a Minorian."

To such a man, defeat was impossible. He *would* rescue the Princess Lilla in the end; that was all there was to it.

So he laid his plans with precision, as he sat on the sandy shore of the Porovian river in the crimsoning twilight.

Before the velvet darkness completely enveloped the planet, the earth-man arose from the sands, and began his return up the valley of the little estuary. But, as he was hurrying along, and was passing through a small grove of trees, a dark form noiselessly dropped on him from above.

The creature lit squarely upon his back, wrapping its furry legs around his abdomen and its furry arms around his neck. Although taken completely by surprise, Cabot wrenched the creature's feet apart and then threw it over his head as a bucking broncho would throw a rider, a jiujitsu trick which he had learned from one of the Jap gymnasts at college.

The Roy, for that is what Cabot's assailant proved to be, scrambled quickly to his feet, although a bit stunned, and crouched, ready to spring at him again. The earth-man planted his feet firmly apart, clenched his fists, and awaited the onslaught; then, when the creature charged, he met him on the point of the jaw with a well-aimed blow. Down crashed the furry one!

Cabot was rubbing his bruised knuckles and viewing his fallen antagonist with some satisfaction, when suddenly he was seized around the knees from behind, and was hurled prone by one of the neatest football tackles he had ever experienced.

Squirming quickly to a sitting position, he dealt the Roy who held his legs a stinging blow beside the ear. The grip on his knees loosened, and he was just about to scramble erect, when a third assailant caught him around the throat and pulled him over backward. Then scores of these furry savages swarmed upon him from every side. Yet still he fought, until his elbows were pinioned behind his back, his eyes were blindfolded, and a gag was placed between his teeth.

Thereupon, he ceased struggling, not because there was no fight left in him, but rather because he wisely decided to save his strength for some time when he might really need it. So he offered no further resistance when he was picked up and thrown across a pair of brawny shoulders, and carried off, he knew not whither.

Finally, after what seemed many hours, he was unceremoniously dumped onto the ground, and then jerked roughly to his feet.

His bandage was snatched off, and he found himself standing in the center of a circle of flares, confronting a large, squat, and particularly repulsive gray-furred Roy, who sat with some pretense of dignity upon a round boulder in front of him. Beside him stood another Roy, evidently the one who had brought him thither.

This one now spoke. "See the pretty Vairking which I have brought you."

"If that's a Vairking," the fat one remarked, "then I'm my own father."

"If he *isn't* a Vairking," the other countered, "then why does he wear Vairking leather armor? Answer me that."

"Vairking or not," the fat one declared, "he will do very nicely to string up by the heels and shoot arrows at. For quite evidently, he is no Roy. What say you to that, my fine target?"

The guard removed the gag.

"I say," Myles evenly replied, "that you had better not take any such liberties with me."

"And why not, furless?" the seated Roy sneered.

"First, let me ask *you* a question," Myles said. "Who is King of the Roies, Grod the Silent or Att the Terrible?"

"Grod the Silent, most assuredly. Why do you ask?"

"And do you know Prince Otto, his son?"

"Otto the Bold? Most assuredly."

"Know then," the captive asserted, "that I am no Vairking, but rather a Minorian, which is a sort of creature I venture you have never met before. Furthermore, I am a particular personal friend of Otto the Bold. He will not thank you to string up Cabot the Minorian by the heels, and shoot arrows into him. I demand that I be taken before Prince Otto."

Thereat the fat Roy smiled a crafty smile. "I shall take you before Att the Terrible," he said.

It thus became evident that this fat chieftain had falsely asserted his belief in the kingship of Grod for the purpose of securing from Myles an admission as to which side the earth-man favored.

The rest of the night Myles spent on a pile of smelly bedding in a tent. He was still bound, and was kept under constant surveillance by a frequently changing guard. By morning, his arms below the elbows had become completely numb, in spite of his having loosened his bonds somewhat by straining against them.

When the velvet night had given place to silver day, the guard brought some coarse porridge in a rough stone bowl, which he held to the prisoner's lips until it was all consumed. Myles thanked him politely, and then asked if he would mind chafing the numbed arms.

For reply, the soldier kicked him savagely.

"Get up!" he ordered. "The time is here to start the march. You'll wish the rest of you were numb, too, when Att the Terrible starts shooting arrows into your inverted carcass."

Presently, Myles was driven into the open, the tents were struck and loaded onto carts—probably stolen from the Vairkings—and the furry warriors took up the march, with their prisoner in their midst. The fat chief alone rode in a cart; all the others walked.

By straining at the thongs which bound his arms, Myles further loosened them sufficiently to relieve the pressure on his blood vessels, and then by wiggling his fingers, he managed finally to restore the circulation.

After that he began to take some interest in his surroundings.

His captors were a coarse-looking lot of brutes, with long gangling arms, thickset necks, low foreheads, and prognathous jaws. In general, they more closely resembled the anthropoid apes of the earth than they resembled the really human, although furred Vairkings.

Their weapons—wooden spears and swords, and flint knives—were like those of the Vairkings, only cruder. They marched without any particular order or discipline, and jested coarsely with each other as they ambled along.

After taking in all this, Myles next turned his attention to the country through which they were passing. The trail led upward into mountains. This at once aroused his interest. Here and there he noted what he felt sure must be zinc-blende. Yes, and cropping out of the rocks on the left was an unmistakable rosette of galena crystal!

The radio man was sincerely glad that he had been captured. And so he even joked jovially with the soldiers around him, until they became quite friendly.

At one point, their route lay across a foaming mountain stream, by means of a log bridge. As they were crossing over, one of the furry soldiers had the misfortune to stumble, and in another instant completely lost his footing and plunged headlong into the stream below. He happened to be one who had recently become particularly chummy with the captive.

"Poor fellow," one of the guard casually remarked. "It's too bad he can't swim."

"*I* can," Myles shouted. "Quick, some one cut my cords!"

And, before any one could interfere, a young and impetuous Roy had drawn his knife and severed the earth-man's bonds, thus permitting him to dive after the poor creature who was rapidly being washed down stream by the swift current.

It had all happened in an instant. A few swift strokes brought Myles up to the other. But it became no easy matter to reach the shore. However, the troop of Roies showed much more interest in regaining their captive, than they had shown in rescuing their comrade; and thus, by the aid of their spears, finally dragged the two ashore.

Then Cabot was bound again, and the march resumed. The carts had detoured, and so the fat chief had not seen the episode.

"Better not tell him, any one," one of the guard admonished, "or it will go hard with the youngster. Our leader would not relish any chance of not being able to present this furless Vairking to Att the Terrible."

"And will Att shoot arrows into me?" Myles asked.

"Most assuredly."

Myles thought to himself: "I guess they are right, especially if Att knows how I was befriended by Arkilu, whom he covets!" Then he asked: "And when am I to see the Terrible One?"

"To-morrow morning," was the reply.

However, Myles Cabot fell asleep at the encampment that night wondering when he would get that radio set finished for a talk with Lilla and wondering whether that really was galena crystal which he had passed on the road.

But galena crystal wasn't going to help him any with Att the Terrible.

CHAPTER XII
COMPANIONS IN MISERY

In the morning Myles Cabot was to be brought before Att the Terrible, king of the Roies—for execution in the diabolical manner common to these furry aborigines, namely by being strung up by the heels and then used as a target for the archery of the king.

In spite of this, he slept soundly and dreamed of radio sets and blast furnaces and galena mines, until he was awakened by a soft furry paw shaking his shoulder.

A voice spoke close to his ear: "A life for a life."

"So you have that proverb on this continent as well as in Cupia?" was his reply. "Who are you, and what do you want?"

"I am the soldier whom you saved from the raging mountain torrent, and what I want is to repay that favor. It is really true that you are a friend of Otto the Bold?"

"Yes."

"Then come. The forces of Grod the Silent, Prince Otto's father, are encamped but a short distance from here. I am on guard over you for the moment. Come, while there is yet time."

Cabot arose in haste. The other promptly severed the cords which bound his elbows. Oh, how good it felt to have his arms free once more! He held them aloft, and flexed and reflexed the lame and bloodless muscles. Excruciating pain shot through the nerves of his forearm, but it was pleasant pain, easy to bear, for it portended peace and rest to his tired members.

He wiggled all his fingers rapidly, and the pain gave way to a prickly tingling, which in turn gradually faded off as the blood coursed freely through his veins and arteries once more. He drew a deep sigh of relief.

"Come!" the guard commanded.

Together the two left the tent, and threaded their way among the other tents out of the camp, and down a rocky hillside path, the Roy in advance, with Myles following, holding the other's hand for guidance.

Myles lost all sense of direction in the jet black starless night, but the other, born and reared on Poros, and hence used to the daily recurrences of twelve hours of absolute darkness, walked sure-footedly ahead, and seemed to know where he was going.

Finally, after about two hours of this groping treadmill progress lights appeared ahead, and presently there came the sentry's challenge: "Halt! Who is there?"

"Two messengers with word for Grod the Silent," Cabot's conductor replied.

In an aside, Cabot interestedly inquired: "How does it happen that this camp is guarded, whereas the camp which besieged the village of Sur was not?"

"There is no need to post sentinels when fighting against the Vairkings, for Vairkings never go out in the dark, but we Roies are different."

"Why, then, did we meet no sentinels when leaving your camp?"

"Because we were going *out*. We passed one but he did not challenge us. Coming *back* would be different."

At this point the hostile guard interposed: "Stop that whispering among yourselves. Ho there, a light!"

Whereat a small detachment arrived on the double quick, with torches. The leader shaded his eyes with one palm, and inspected Myles and his companion carefully.

"This is a Vairking," he said in surprise, noting the leather trappings of the earth-man. "You are spies. Seize them!"

In an instant they were seized and bound, and thrown into separate tents under guard.

When morning came, Myles was fed and then led before Grod the Silent. The earth-man smiled ingratiatingly as he entered, but there was no sign of recognition on the stern face of the King of the Roies.

"Who are you?" the latter asked, "and what are you doing here?"

"I am Cabot the Minorian," was the reply, "a recently escaped prisoner of Att the Terrible."

"Do not mention that accursed name in my presence!" thundered the king; then: "I do not seem to recall your name, but your face looks familiar. Where have I seen you before?"

"In the ravine near Sur."

Grod's brow clouded.

"I remember. You felled me with your fist," said he, darkly; then brightening a bit: "But you spared me. Why?"

"Because your death would please the Roy whose name you do not permit me to mention."

"You improve," Grod declared, smiling. "Know, then, that we Roies hold to the maxim, 'A life for a life.' Accordingly, I shall set you free, and shall content myself with shooting arrows into merely the soldier who brought you here."

"You give me a life for a life unconditionally?" asked Myles.

"Yes."

"Then give me the life of the poor soldier who saved me from the unmentionable one. Shoot your arrows into my body instead."

"Very magnanimous of you," Grod said. "And really, it makes but little difference to me just whom I practice archery upon. Ho guard! Bring the other prisoner in."

One of the soldiery accordingly withdrew, and presently returned with—Quivven! Quivven, of all persons!

Cabot gasped, and so did the golden-furred Vairking maiden; then both uttered simultaneously the single word, "You!"

The savage chief smiled. Said he, "A slight mistake, guard; I meant you to bring the Roy soldier who was captured with this fur-less one early this morning. But evidently it has turned out to be a fortunate mistake, for it has brought to my attention the fact that this common Vairking man and this noble Vairking lady are acquainted."

While the Roy was speaking an idea occurred to Cabot: He was entitled by the code of honor of this savage race to save a life. Chivalry demanded that he save the life of this maiden rather than that of himself, or even the soldier who had rescued him from Att the Terrible. Yet what would Lilla think?

Did he not owe it to Lilla to save his own life in order that he might some day return across the boiling seas to save *her* from the unknown peril which menaced her? For him to sacrifice himself and her, or even merely himself, for the sake of some strange woman, would fill Lilla with consuming jealousy.

Luckily Lilla was not here to see him make his choice. He was an officer and a gentleman, to whom but one course lay open. And if he decided in the way that would displease Lilla, then that very decision would forever prevent Lilla from knowing.

So, his mind made up, he spoke: "O king, you still owe me a life. Inasmuch as your guard has made the mistake of substituting this young lady for the Roy warrior, whose life I had elected to save, I now accept the substitution, and elect that you shall spare her life in place of mine."

Quivven the Golden Flame stared at him with tears of gratitude and appreciation in her azure eyes. Grod the Silent smiled knowingly in a manner which infuriated Myles, but fortunately Quivven did not notice this, so Myles let it pass.

Then the Roy king spoke: "We shall see about that later. Meanwhile, guard, bring in the *right* prisoner."

The guard sheepishly withdrew, and soon returned with the soldier who had befriended Myles.

"Why did you rescue this furless Vairking, who was a prisoner of your forces?" Grod asked the newcomer.

"Because he rescued me from a mountain torrent, O king," was the reply. "A life for a life."

"Quite true," Grod admitted, nodding his head contemplatively. "But was it altogether necessary to that end that you leave your own forces?"

"No, O king," the soldier replied, "but I fain would battle on your side. I have had quite enough of the fat one who commands our outfit."

"Good!" cried Grod, clapping his hands. "We shall need every man we can muster. Thus have you bought your own life and freedom. Unbind him, guards, and give him weapons, so that he may fight for us. As for you, you yellow minx, the quicker you get out of here the better it will suit me. We are at war, and women have no place in warfare. Therefore I gladly give you your life, which this furless one had purchased.

"Do not think," he continued, "that I do not know who you are, or that I do not realize that I could hold you for high ransom. But for the present it suits my purposes to release you; for my mind is a one-cart road, and at present I am engaged in an important and highly personal war.

"Besides, if I were to keep you, my enemy might get hold of you and collect the ransom himself, which would never do. Twelve days from now, if I should be in need of carts, a messenger from me will call at the palace of Theoph the Grim; and if you are at all grateful, you will make me a present of about twenty sturdy wagons.

"As for you," turning to Myles, "your life is mine, since you failed to redeem it. Some day I may call upon you for it, but for the present I wish to use it. You are detailed, as my personal representative, to escort this lady safely to Vairkingi. Now both of you get out of here, for I have more important things to do. I must put my army on the march."

One of the guards stepped up to Myles and cut his bonds. Quivven had not been bound.

"May I have arms, O king, so that I can fulfill your mission with credit to you?" Myles asked, with a twinkle in his gray eyes.

"You keep on improving," Grod replied. "Yes, you may. Here, take my own sword. You are a brave man and an able warrior, as my chin well remembers. May the Builder grant that some day we shall fight side by side."

This gave Cabot an idea. "Why can that not be now?" he suggested. "Why not form an alliance with Vairkingi against the unmentionable one?"

But Grod the Silent shook his head. "No," he said positively, "it cannot be. In the first place, the unmentionable one is himself seeking to make such an alliance against me; and in the second place, this is my own private fight. I have spoken."

Then Cabot had a further idea. "About the wagons," he said, "would you mind sending for them to my brickyard north of Vairkingi? That would be more convenient."

"Very well," Grod replied.

Roy warriors then supplied the two prisoners with portable rations, and escorted them for quite a distance from the camp, until they struck a mountain trail. This, the escort informed them, led to Vairkingi. There the Roies left Myles and Quivven alone.

The first thing that she asked was, "With all these mountains full of warring Roies, do you believe that we shall be safe?"

"I think so," Myles replied. "The very fact that they are at war will keep them much too busy to bother about us. Come on."

As they hurried down the trail, each related his or her adventures to the other. Cabot's have already been set down. As for Quivven, she had gone with a few soldiers to hunt for Myles after his prospecting party had returned and reported his disappearance by the river; but her party had been killed, and she had been taken prisoner.

"Did Grod treat you with respect?" Myles asked, with clenched fists.

"Absolutely," she replied, tossing her pretty head. "I never knew a man so impersonal. I am accustomed to have men recognize my presence and pay some attention to my existence. But this brute— why, I might just as well have been a piece of furniture or one of his servants. I don't believe he knows now what color my eyes are, or whether I'm pretty or not. And you're just as bad as he is," she added somewhat irrelevantly.

"Your eyes are blue, and you are very pretty," Cabot replied. "In fact, you closely resemble my own wife, the beautiful Princess Lilla, who waits for me far across the boiling seas."

"Which reminds me to ask," Quivven said abruptly. "How successful was your expedition, apart from your being captured and getting yourself into all kinds of trouble?"

So he told her about the glistening metallic particles in the sands of the river. Also how he had found what were probably zinc-blende and galena. Then they discussed in detail his plans for his various factories. From time to time they munched some of the food which had been given them.

The day quickly sped, and evening drew near, yet still they were upon the mountain road with no sight of Vairkingi or of any landmark familiar to either of them. Quivven was for stopping and resting, but Myles urged her on.

"No matter how tired you are," he said, "it is not safe to stop in this strange country."

So still she struggled on. The sky darkened without the usual pinkening of the west. All too well they knew what that portended— one of the heaven-splitting tropical storms so common on Poros. And they were right. The storm broke, the thunder roared in one continuous volume of sound, the lightning and the rain alike poured down in continuous sheets. The trail became a mountain torrent, so that they had to cease their journey and crawl upon a huge boulder, in order to avoid being engulfed by the water.

The rain stopped as abruptly as it had begun. Again the silver sky appeared overhead. The extempore brook rapidly disappeared, but left in its wake a wet, muddy, and slippery trail, down which the two took up their journey once more.

Several times Quivven stumbled and fell, until at last her companion had to help her in order to keep her going at all. But, in spite of this assistance, she finally broke down and cried.

"I shall not go one step farther," she asserted.

Myles seated himself beside her and talked to her as one would soothe a child. And that was what she was, a tired little child.

"You can't stay here," he urged, "the ground is damp, the night is coming on, and your fur is sopping wet."

"I don't care anything about anything," she sobbed. "All that I know is that I positively cannot go on."

So he decided that it would be necessary to change his tactics. "I am ashamed of you," he replied, "You, the daughter of a king, and can't stand a little exercise! Why, I believe you are just plain lazy."

For reply she jumped to her feet in a sudden rage. "Oh, you beast!" she cried. "You insulting beast! You common soldier, you! I'll show you that I can stand as much hardship as the pampered womenfolk of your Cupia, though the men of my country, even our common soldiers, would be gentlemanly enough not to force a lady to endure any more than is absolutely necessary. Oh, I hate you, I hate you, I hate you!"

"You are not being forced to endure more than is necessary," her escort harshly replied. "In the first place it *is* necessary to go on; and, in the second place, I am not forcing you. *You* can go on or not, just as you see fit, but as for me, I don't intend to spend the night here in this wet valley. Good-by!"

For reply Quivven raced ahead of him with, "Oh, how I hate you!" and disappeared around a turn in the trail.

CHAPTER XIII
FURTHER PROGRESS

His change of tactics had worked, although it made him feel like a brute. But only by arousing Quivven's anger could he stir her to continue the journey; and to remain would have menaced her safety and her health.

She had a good head start of him. The silver sky was turning crimson in the west. Night was coming on. So he hurried after her down the wet and slippery trail.

At last it became so dark that he had to slow down and walk; and finally merely grope his way, shoving his feet ahead, one after the other, in order to be sure to keep to the trail and not to stumble.

Time and again his foot would touch something soft, which he would picture as some strange and weird Porovian animal, a gnooper for instance. Quickly he would withdraw the foot. Then waiting in suspense for the creature either to go away or to spring upon him, at last he would cautiously push his foot forward, touch the object again, kick it slightly, and find that it was only a clump of Porovian grass or a rotted piece of lichen log.

Poor Quivven! How terrified *she* must be at such encounters!

After a while he got a bit used to these occurrences, and accordingly each succeeding one of them delayed him less than the preceding.

"You know," he said to himself, "this will keep on until finally one of these obstacles will actually turn out to be a gnooper, and it will eat me alive before I can get out of the way."

Just then his groping foot touched another of these soft objects.

"Get out of my way," Cabot shouted, and gave it a kick. But this time it was not attached to the soil. It yielded and wriggled a bit. Then it gave a peculiar groaning sound.

Myles leaped backward and waited. But nothing happened; so he tried to circle the creature. Again the groan. His scientific curiosity got the better of his caution. He approached once more and investigated more closely, reaching down with his hand. The animal was covered with wet and muddy fur.

It was Quivven!

Tenderly he raised the crumpled form in his arms, and groped on down the treacherous trail.

Myles wondered how long he could bear up with this dead weight in his arms. But just as he was beginning to stagger, the road gave a turn and flattened out, and there before him were lights, the flares and bonfires of a city! They had reached the plain.

"Quivven!" he cried joyfully. "This is home! There ahead lies

Vairkingi!"

But she made no reply. Her body was cold and still.

Quickly he laid her on the ground and placed one ear to her chest. Thank the Great Builder! Her heart still beat. So he chafed her hands and feet, and worked her arms violently back and forth until she began to groan protestingly.

"Quivven!" he cried. "Wake up! We are home!"

"Are you here, Myles?" she murmured faintly,

"Yes."

"And you won't make me walk any more?"

"No."

"Then I'll wake up for you," she murmured cheerfully, and promptly fell fast asleep.

Again lifting her tenderly in his arms, he resumed the journey.

On reaching the city he circled the wall until he came to one of the gates, where he stood the girl on the ground and shook her gently into consciousness.

"Where am I?" she asked.

"At the gates of Vairkingi," Myles answered.

She ran her hands rapidly over her mud-caked fur.

"Oh, but I can't go in like this," she wailed, "I'm covered with mud from head to foot! Think how I must look! No, I refuse to go in."

"If you stay here," he urged mildly, "then when morning comes every one will see you, the Princess Quivven, bedraggled with mud, hanging around outside the city gates. Better far to go in now, and take a chance of being seen by only one sentinel."

"Oh, you beast, you beast!" she sobbed, beating him futilely with her tiny paws.

For reply he seized her in his arms, swung her across one hip, and shouted: "Open wide the gates of Vairkingi for Cabot the Minorian, magician to Jud the Excuse-Maker, and to his Excellency Theoph the Grim!"

The gates swung open, and the sentinel stared at them with surprise and some amusement. Myles whipped out his sword, and the smile froze on the soldier's face.

"Thus do I teach men not to laugh at Myles Cabot," the earthman growled. "Remember that you have seen nothing."

And he handed the soldier the choice blade of Grod the Silent.

The soldier smiled again.

"I have seen nothing but a Roy, whom I robbed of his sword and drove off into the darkness. It is a fine sword, and I will remember that I have seen nothing. May the Great Builder bless Myles Cabot the Minorian."

Cabot glanced at his burden, Quivven, the beautiful. No wonder she did not want to be seen. It always humiliates a lady not to look her best in public. But by the same token, no one could possibly recognize her. He might perfectly well have saved the sword.

So he passed on through the city streets. Finally he had to put the girl down, and ask her to help him find the way, which she did grudgingly. At the gate of Jud's compound, Myles again swung her across his hip, before he demanded entrance. No swords this time, for diplomacy would take the place of payment.

"Myles Cabot demanding entrance," he cried.

The local guard inspected them carefully by the light of his torch.

"It is Cabot all right," he replied, "and you look as though you had seen some hard fighting. But who is this with you?"

"A girl of the Roies," answered Myles. "That is what the fighting was about."

"Not for mine!" the soldier asserted, grimacing. "Though there is no accounting for tastes. They are filthy little beasts, and spitfires as well, so I'm told. My advice to you, sir, is to throw it down a well."

Quivven wriggled protestingly.

"Perhaps I will," Myles laughed.

At their own gate at last, he placed her once more on her feet, whereat she shook herself free, raced into the house, slammed the door of her room.

Cabot himself went right to bed, without waiting to wash or anything, and dropped instantly to sleep the moment he touched his pile of bedding; yet, so intent was he on wasting no time in getting Cupia on the air that he was up early the next morning.

He found his laboratory force sadly demoralized, owing to the absence of Quivven and himself, but he quickly brought order out of chaos, and set the men to work on their first real construction job, to which all the other work had been mere preliminary steps.

Quivven kept to her rooms, but one of the other maids roguishly informed him: "The Golden One says she hates you."

Now that his fire-bricks were ready, Myles Cabot laid out on paper the plans for his smelting plant, all the units of which were to be lined with fire-brick.

First he designed a furnace for roasting his ore. This furnace was to be in two sections, one above the other, the lower holding the charcoal fire, and the upper holding the ore. Later he planned to use the sulphur fumes of this roaster to make sulphuric acid, which in turn he would use to make sal ammoniac for his batteries. But at present he had not yet figured out this process in detail.

The smelting furnace, for smelting the roasted ore into copper-matter, was to consist of a chimney about two feet in diameter, sloping sharply outward for about two feet, and thence sloping gradually inward again for a height of about ten feet. Near the bottom were to be a number of small holes leading from an air passage.

This air passage and the vent for the hot flames from the top of the smelter were to run in parallel pipes made of hollow brick tile, to two chambers containing a checkerwork design of fire-brick. The two pipes were to be interchangeable; so that, when the exhaust had heated one of the checkerwork grids to a red heat, the pipes could be switched, and the incoming air would be warmed by passing through the heated grid. From gnooper hide and wood he could easily construct bellows to pump in the air for the blast.

Molten copper-matte and slag would be separately run off through two separate openings at different levels near the bottom of the blast furnace.

To further refine the matte, he designed a Bessemer converter, that is to say, a barrel-shaped box of layers of fire clay, the inner layer being very rich in quartz sand. This barrel, when filled with molten matte, would be laid on its side; and a hot blast introduced through holes near this side would convert the matte into pure copper in about two hours.

The first converter which he made was rather small, as he expected that it would not last very well without metal reinforcements, and of course he would have no metal for reenforcing purposes until after he had run off at least one heat.

For the extraction of iron, he made crucibles of fireclay, which he set in deep holes in the ground.

On the second morning after the unpleasant homecoming, Quivven appeared. All her rage had burned out, and she was meek and subdued.

With downcast eyes she reported to Myles: "I am ready to go to work now."

With a welcoming smile he patted her golden-furred shoulder, whereat her old anger started to flare again, but this one remaining ember merely flickered and died out, and she submitted with a shrug of resignation.

So the Radio Man explained to her his plans for the furnaces; then, leaving her in charge of the work, he set out once more to the river of the silver sands, this time accompanied by a heavy guard of Vairking soldiers, and flying a blue flag, as agreed on with Prince Otto of the Roies.

As he was departing, Quivven flung her arms around him and begged him not to go to certain destruction, but he gently disengaged himself, smiling indulgently at this show of childish affection.

"My dear little girl," he admonished, "most of our troubles last time came from your following me. This time I warn you that I shall be very displeased if you fail to stick closely to home and complete my two magic furnaces for me. Promise me that you will."

So, with tears of dread in her blue eyes, she promised; and the expedition set forth. They were gone about five days. The trip proved uneventful from any except a scientific viewpoint. They returned, bearing several pounds of silvery grains, placermined from the river sands; also some large lumps of galena crystal, and nearly a ton of zinc-blende. They found that, under the skillful direction of little Quivven, the furnaces were nearly completed.

Quivven the Golden Flame was overjoyed at Cabot's safe return, while even he had to confess considerable relief. He complimented her warmly on the progress of the furnaces, and noted her pleasure at his expressions of approval.

A few details which had perplexed her were quickly straightened out, and the work was rushed to completion.

He next tested the silver grains which he had brought from the river. His method was a very simple one, invented by himself. It consisted in filling a clay cup with water and weighing it, then weighing a quantity of the metal, and then putting this metal in the water and weighing the whole. A simple mathematical calculation from these three weights gave him the specific gravity of the metal. This process was repeated a number of times to avoid error, and gave as an average the figure 21.5, which he remembered to be the specific gravity of pure platinum.

As a further test he hammered some of the supposed platinum into a thin sheet, and attempted, without success, to melt it. Then he laid a sliver of one of his lead bullets on it, and tried again, with the result that the lead melted and burned a hole through the metal sheet. This test convinced him that he truly had found platinum.

Cabot next turned his attention to glass making. For ordinary glass he would need quartz, soda, potash, and limestone.

The reason for his employing both soda and potash instead of merely one or the other, was that together they would have a lower fusing point, and thus be easier for him to handle with his crude equipment. For glass for his tubes he would use litharge in place of the limestone.

The quartz and the limestone were already available. Soda would be a byproduct of his sal ammoniac when he got around to making it, but this would not be until he had made sulphuric acid from his copper ore, which was a most complicated process as he remembered it.

Potash could be got simply by dripping water through wood-ashes, evaporating the water, roasting the sediment, dissolving again in water, letting the impurities settle, and then evaporating the clear liquid, and roasting again. He started this process at once.

But he had no idea how to make litharge. Furthermore, he could not blow his glass until he had metal tubes, so he abandoned further steps for the present.

While he was pondering over these problems a messenger arrived, demanding his immediate presence at the quarters of Jud the Excuse-Maker.

Jud was in a state of great excitement when the earth-man arrived.

Said Jud: "Do you remember what you told me about the beasts of the south, who swim through the air, talk soundless speech, and use magic slingshots like yours which you captured from the Roies near Sur?"

"Yes," Cabot replied. "I hope that by this time I have given sufficient demonstration of my truthfulness so that you now believe the story."

"Oh, I believed it at the time," Jud hastily explained, "But now I have proof of it, for we have captured one of these beasts. That is, we *think* it is one of them. I want you to see and identify it, before we present it to Theoph the Grim."

"Thereby displaying commendable foresight," Myles commented. "Where is this Formian?"

"In a cage in the zoo," the Vairking noble replied. "Come; I will take you there."

So together the two threaded the streets of Vairkingi to the zoo. This was part of the city which the earth-man had never before visited. Its denizens fascinated him.

There were huge water snakes with humanlike hands. There were spherical beasts with a row of legs around the equator, a row of eyes around the tropic of cancer, and a circular mouth rimmed with teeth at the north pole. There were—

But at this point Jud urged him on into another room, where he promptly forgot all the other creatures in the sight which met his eyes.

In a large wooden cage in the center of the room was an enraged ant-man gnawing at the bars, while a score or so of Vairking warriors stood around and prodded him with spears.

"Stop!" Jud shouted at the soldiery, whereat they all fell back obediently.

This called the attention of the imprisoned beast to the newcomers, so he looked up and stared at them. Cabot stared back.

Then he rushed forward to the cage!

CHAPTER XIV
OLD FRIENDS

"Doggo!" he cried. "Doggo! They told me you were dead!"

But of course all this was lost on the radio speech sense of the prisoner. Vairking soldiers interposed their spears between Myles Cabot and what they believed was sure destruction at the jaws of the black beast. Cabot recoiled.

"Jud," he called out, "order off your henchmen! I am not crazy, nor do I court death. This creature is the only one of the Formians whom I can control. He will prove a valuable ally for us, if I can persuade him to forgive the indignities which your men have already heaped upon him."

"I do not believe you," Jud replied, "for how can men communicate with beasts, especially with strange beasts such as this, the like of which man ne'er set eyes on before?"

"Remember that I am a magician," Myles returned somewhat testily. Then seeing that Jud was still obdurate, he addressed the guards. "You know me for a magician?"

"Yes," they sullenly admitted.

"And you know the magic on which I am now engaged, and to which all of my recent expeditions relate?"

"Yes," one replied. "You seek to call down the lightnings of heaven, and harness them to transport your words across the boiling seas."

"Rightly spoken!" the Radio Man asserted. "Therefore, if you do not stand aside, I shall call those lightnings down for another purpose, namely, to blast you. Stand aside!"

One of the guards spoke to another, "Why should we risk our lives to save his? Let the magician save himself!"

So they stood aside. Myles stepped up to the cage, and he and Doggo each patted the other's cheek through the bars.

Jud the Excuse-Maker sheepishly explained, "I knew that you were speaking the truth, but I wished to learn what method you would use to handle the soldiers. You did nobly."

"Bunk!" the earth-man ejaculated, well knowing that the Vairking would not understand him.

"What means that word?" Jud inquired, much interested.

"That," Myles replied, grinning, "is a complimentary term often applied on my own planet, the earth, to the remarks of our great leaders."

Jud, highly complimented, let it go at that. Myles now ordered paper and a charcoal pencil, and began a conversation with his ant friend.

"They told me you were dead," he wrote. "Or I never would have left the city of Yuriana or deserted your cause."

"My cause died with my daughter, the queen," Doggo replied. "I alone survive. I escaped by plane, and have been flitting around the country ever since, until my alcohol gave out. Then these furry Cupians captured me. They got me with a net so that I could not fight back.

"Also, I was distant from my airship at the time, or it would have gone hard with them for the ship is well stocked with bombs, and rifle cartridges, and one rifle. Now tell me of yourself. How do you stand with these furry Cupians?"

"They are not Cupians." Myles wrote. "They are Vairkings, a race much like myself, who send messages with their mouths and with their ears, instead of using their antennae for both, as the Cupians and you Formians do. Do you remember the old legend of Cupia, that creatures like me dwell beyond the boiling seas? Well, it appears to have been true, though how any one could have known or even suspected it, is a mystery to me."

"You have not yet told me how you stand," the ant-man reminded him.

"They recognize me as a great magician," Myles answered, "and I have promised to build them a radio set, and to lead them to victory over the Formians."

"Just as you did for the Cupians," Doggo mused. "But you will have a harder task here, for these furry creatures appear to know no metals, nor any of the arts save woodcarving."

They patted each other's cheeks again. Then, before any one could interfere, Myles Cabot unbolted the door of the cage, and out walked Doggo, a free ant once more.

The soldiery, and Jud with them, promptly scattered to the four walls of the room.

"Come over here, Jud," Myles invited, "and meet my friend—that is, unless you are afraid."

"Oh, no, I do not fear him," Jud the Excuse-Maker replied, "but I do not consider it consistent with the dignity of my position to be seen fraternizing with a wild beast."

It was typical. Myles laughed. Then he led the huge ant home with him to his quarters.

Quivven was amazed, but not at all frightened, at the great black creature; and when an introduction had been effected on paper, she and Doggo developed quite a strong liking for each other.

As soon as the Formian had been fed and assigned to a room in the ménage—some improvement over the menagerie, by the way—his host and hostess took him on a tour of inspection of their laboratory.

With the true scientific spirit so characteristic of the cultured but warlike race which once dominated Cupia, Doggo plunged at once into the spirit of the almost super-Porovian task which Myles had undertaken; and it soon became evident that the new comer would prove to be an invaluable accession. His scientific training would dovetail exactly with that of the earth-man, and would supplement it at every point.

Almost at the very start he suggested a solution of the problems which had been puzzling Myles.

Cabot's recollection of the process of sulphuric acid manufacture had been that it required a complicated roasting furnace, two filtering towers, and a tunnel about two hundred feet long made of lead, and into which nitric acid fumes had to be injected. His recollection of nitric acid manufacture was that it required sulphuric acid among other ingredients. So how was he to make either acid without first having the other? And furthermore, where was he to procure enough lead to build a two-hundred-foot tunnel?

Doggo solved these problems very nicely—by avoiding them.

"What do you need sulphuric add for?" he wrote.

"Merely to use in making hydrochloric acid," wrote the earth-man in reply.

"And that?"

"To use in making sal ammoniac for my batteries."

"Do you need nitric acid for anything except the manufacture of sulphuric?"

"No."

"Then," Doggo suggested, "let us make our sal ammoniac directly from its elements. We shall build a series of about twenty vertical cast-iron retorts, as soon as you have smelted your iron. These we shall fill with damp salt, pressed into blocks and dried. We shall heat these retorts with charcoal fires, and through them we shall pass then, air, and the sulphur fumes of your ore-roasting.

"After about fifteen days we shall daily cut out the first retort, dump out the soda which has formed in it, refill it, and place it at the farther end of the series. The liquid, which condenses at the end of the series, will be diluted hydrochloric acid. By passing the fumes of roast animal-refuse through it we shall convert it into sal ammoniac solution."

Accordingly, the quicker they started their foundry operations, the better.

By this time chalcopyrite, quartz, and charcoal were present at Vairkingi in large quantities. The ore was first roasted, and then was piled into the smelter with the quartz and charcoal; the air-bellows were started, fire was inserted through the slaghole, and soon a raging pillar of flame served notice on all Vairkingi that the devil-furnace of the great magician was in full blast. By this time it was night, but no one thought of stopping.

Of course, there were complications. The furry soldiers deserted the pumps at the first roar of green-tinged flame, but Doggo instantly stepped into the breach and operated all of the bellows with his various legs. Finally the warriors, on seeing that Myles and Quivven had survived the ordeal of fire, sheepishly returned to their posts, and were soon loudly boasting of their own bravery and of how their fellows would envy them on the morrow when they should relate their experiences.

Along toward morning Cabot drew his first heat of molten matter into a brick ladle and poured it into the converter. It was an impressive sight. The shadowy wooden-walled inclosure, lit by the waving greenish flare of a pillar of fire, which metamorphosed the white skin of the earth-man into that of a jaundiced Oriental, tinged Quivven with green-gold, and glinted off the shiny carapace of Doggo as off the facets of a bloodstone. In the darkness of the background, toiled the workers at their pumps.

Then there came a change. The fires died down, the pumping ceased, oil lamps were lit, and the ghostly glare gave place to a faint but healthy light, although over all hung the ominous silence of expectancy.

The ladle was brought up, a hand-hole-cover removed, and out flowed a crimson liquid, tinting all the eager surrounding faces with a sinister ruddiness.

Again the red glare, as the ladle was poured into the barrel-shaped converter. Then the pumps were started again, and the blast from the converter replaced that of the furnace with its ghostly light. Two hours later the converter was tipped, and pure molten copper was poured out into the ladle. Once more the sinister ruddiness.

Quickly the molds were filled, the red light was gone, the spell was broken, conversation was resumed. The first metallurgy of Vairkingi was an accomplished fact.

Day came, and with it loud pounding on the gate. Cabot answered it, carelessly and abstractedly sliding back the bolt before inquiring who was outside. The gate swung open with a bang, almost knocking Myles into a flower bed, and in rushed a Vairking youth with drawn sword and panting heavily.

"You beast!" he cried, lunging at the earth-man as he spoke.

But in his haste and anger he lunged too hard and too far; so that Cabot, although unarmed, was able to step under his guard and grasp him by the wrist before he recovered. Quick as lightning the boy's sword arm was bent up behind his back, and he was "in chancery", to use the wrestling term.

Slowly, grimly, Cabot forced the imprisoned hand upward between the shoulder-blades of his opponent, until with a groan the latter relinquished the sword, and it fell clattering to the ground.

Smiling, Cabot stooped down and picked it up, and forced the young intruder against the wall.

"Now," said the earth-man, "explain yourself."

The boy faced Myles like a cornered panther.

"It's Quivven," he snarled. "You have stolen my Quivven."

"Nonsense!" Myles exclaimed. "What do you mean?"

"I am Tipi the Steadfast," the youth replied. "Long have I loved the Golden Flame, and she me, until you came to this city. When you arrived I was away on a military expedition, winning distinctions to lay at the tiny feet of my fair one. Last night I returned to find her working at your laboratory. One or the other, you or I, must die."

"You are absurd!"

"In *my* country," Tipi returned, looking the earth-man straight in the eye, "no common soldier is permitted to dictate manners to a gentleman. I repeat that Quivven—"

But at this point, Myles cuffed the young Vairking over one ear, knocking him flat upon the walk; and, as he scrambled sputtering to his feet, dealt him another blow which sent him reeling into the street. Then Myles barred the gate, and turned toward the house.

In the doorway stood Quivven, shaking with laughter. Myles was immediately embarrassed. He hadn't known that his encounter had been observed. He hated to show off, and was afraid that his actions had appeared very melodramatic.

"Isn't Tipi silly?" she asked.

"But he may make trouble with your father," Myles said, with a worried frown.

"Oh, I'm not afraid of father."

"But he will put an end to my experiments."

So Quivven went home to chat with her father before young Tipi could get there to stir up possible trouble. She returned later in the day to resume her work. While she was gone, Cabot conferred with Doggo.

"Why are you building this radio set?" the ant-man wrote. "I did not ask you before in the presence of the lady, for I felt that perhaps you did not wish her to know your plans."

"Doggo, you show remarkable intuition," Myles wrote in reply. "It is true that I do not wish any of the Vairkings to know. My idea is to communicate with Cupia, learn how Lilla is getting along, and encourage my supporters there to hold out until in some way I can secure a Formian airship and return across the boiling seas."

"Then cease your work," Doggo wrote, "for my plane, in perfect condition, lies carefully hidden in a wood not a full day's journey from this city. All that we need is alcohol for the trophil-engines."

CHAPTER XV
PLANS FOR ESCAPE

"We can make the alcohol in a few days in my laboratory," Cabot wrote, "but it will not do for us to escape too precipitately, lest our plans be discovered and blocked. The Vairkings like sleight-of-hand, and wish to keep me with them as their court magician. Let us bide our time until they become sufficiently accustomed to you, so that they will not question your accompanying me on an expedition. Then, away to the plane, and off to Cupia!"

The ant-man assented. It seemed logical. And yet I wonder if this logic would not have done credit to Jud the Excuse-Maker. I wonder if Cabot was not subconsciously influenced by a scientific desire to complete his radio set in this land of people who used only wood and flint. I wonder.

At all events, the work proceeded.

He had planned to use the slag from the copper furnace as the "ore" for his iron, but the more he thought about it, the more he realized that its high sulphur content would probably ruin any steel which he produced. Fortunately, however, he ran across a deposit of magnetic iron ore near Vairkingi.

This he ground and placed in his crucibles with charcoal, and they built charcoal fires in the pits around them. The slag he slammed off with copper—later iron—ladles. The melting had to be repeated many times in order to purify the iron sufficiently, and further in order to secure just the right carbon content for cast-iron, steel, or wrought-iron, according to which he needed for any particular purpose. This securing the proper carbon content was largely a matter of cut-and-try.

With iron and steel available, he now made pots, retorts, hammers, anvils, drills, wire-drawing dies, and a decent Bessemer converter.

Copper tubes for glass-blowing, and copper wire were drawn. A simple wooden lathe was made for winding thread around the wires. This thread, by the way, was the only Vairkingian product which the earth-man found ready to his hand.

As soon as the iron retorts were available, the joint manufacture of sal ammoniac and soda was started, as already outlined by Doggo.

In iron pots, Cabot melted together finely ground white sand, with lime, soda, and potash, and blew the resulting glass into bottles, retorts, test tubes, and other laboratory apparatus; also jars for his electric batteries. He used both soda and potash, as this would render the glass more fusible than if made with either alone.

Lead was melted from galena crystal in small quantities for solder. Thus was suggested to Doggo, the manufacture, on the side, of bullets, gunpowder, and cartridges, for the rifle which Myles had in his quarters, and for the one which lay in the concealed airplane.

Tales of the copper-smelting had spread among the populace, who evinced such great interest that double guards had to be placed and maintained about the laboratory inclosure. And every returning military expedition brought with it samples of unusual minerals.

Meanwhile, Cabot instituted a regular campaign of getting Vairkingi accustomed to Doggo. Every day, Doggo would parade the high-walled streets, with Quivven the Golden Flame perched upon his back. The ten-foot ant inspired great interest and considerable fear.

She enjoyed her rides thoroughly, not only for the novelty of the thing, but also because her seat on his six-foot-high back brought her head above the level of the fence palings, and thus enabled her to survey the private yards of everyone.

Tipi had not been seen or heard from.

Arkilu the Beautiful thoroughly made up with the earth-man, and even admitted that her love for him had been a mistake. Plans for her wedding with Jud proceeded rapidly. When this coming marriage was publicly announced, Att the Terrible sent in a Roy runner with the message that he didn't in the least care.

Quivven now lived in the palace, so as to be near her father, but came to work regularly each day. Theoph the Grim interposed no objection to this, and, in fact, frequently accompanied his daughter to the laboratory. He loved to mess around the bottles and retorts, and lost much of the grimness when engaged in this childish meddle-someness.

So every one was happy except Tipi the Steadfast and Att the Terrible.

Jud continued the operation of the brickyard, even though Cabot had no more need of bricks, for Jud planned to build himself a brick palace which would outshine even the palace of King Theoph.

Melting the platinum for the wires presented a problem, until Myles thought of electrolizing some ordinary water into its constituent hydrogen and oxygen, and then burning these two materials together in a double blow-pipe, much like that used in oxyacetylene welding.

But to do this he had to make batteries. To this end he already had sal ammoniac and jars. He needed carbon and zinc. For carbon he pressed charcoal into compact blocks. To extract zinc from the blend ore he made long cylindrical retorts of clay, with a long clay pipe for a vent. The ore, after being thoroughly roasted in the copper-roasting furnace to remove all sulphur, was ground, mixed with half its weight of powered charcoal, and then charged into the retorts, where it was baked. The result was to distill the pure zinc, which condensed on the walls of the tubes.

Cabot now at last had all the elements for his batteries, and so was able, by employing about seventy cells in multiple, to get the two volts, three hundred fifty amperes, necessary to electrolize the oxygen and hydrogen for melting his platinum.

The platinum proved to be quite free of iridium, and so was easily drawn into wires.

Needless to state, the distilling of alcohol in large quantities, ostensibly for the laboratory burners, but actually for Doggo's airplane, was commenced as soon as they had blown their first glass retorts.

Myles was going strong!

One day, in the midst of all this technical progress, as Myles was passing through one of the streets of Vairkingi on some errand or other, and admiring the quaint and brightly colored wood carvings on the high walls which lined the way, his attention was arrested by the design over one of the gateways.

It was a crimson swastika within a crimson triangle, the insignia of the priests of the lost religion of Cupia, the priests who had befriended him in their hidden refuge of the Caves of Kar, when he was a fugitive during the dark days of his second war against the ant-men.

Could it be that the lost religion was also implanted upon *this* continent? Myles had never discussed religion with Arkilu, or Jud, or Quivven, or Crota, or any of his Vairking friends. Somehow the subject had never come up. Full of curiosity, Cabot knocked in the door.

Immediately a small round aperture opened and a voice from within inquired "Whence come you?"

For reply, the earth-man gave one of the passwords of the Cupian religion. To his surprise, the gate swung open, and he was admitted into the presence of a long-robed priest, clad exactly like his friends of the Caves of Kar.

"What do you wish?" asked the guardian of the gate.

Having made his way so far, Myles decided to continue, on the analogy of the religion of his own continent. Accordingly, he boldly replied, "I wish to speak with the Holy Leader."

"Very well," said the guard; and closing the gate and barring it, he led Myles through many winding passages, to a door on which he knocked three times.

The knock was repeated from within, the door opened, and Myles entered to gaze upon a strangely familiar scene. The room was richly carved and colored. On three sides hung the stone lamps of the Vairkings. Around the walls sat a score or more of long-robed priests, some on the level and some on slightly raised platforms. On the highest platform of all, directly opposite the point where Cabot had entered, sat the only hooded figure in the chamber, quite evidently the leader of the faith.

Him the earth-man approached, and bowed low.

Whereat, there came the unexpected words: "Welcome to Vairkingi, Myles Cabot."

Then the priest descended, took the visitor by the hand, and led him to a seat at his own left. A few minutes later, the assembly had been temporarily suspended, and Myles and his host were chatting together like old friends.

Myles told the venerable prelate the complete history of all his adventures on both continents of the planet Poros, not omitting to dwell with considerable detail upon the vicissitudes of the lost religion of Cupia. This interested the priest greatly, and he asked numerous questions in that connection.

"Strange! Strange!" he ruminated. "It is undoubtedly the same religion as ours. So there must at some time have been some connection between the two continents."

"Yes, there must have been," the earth-man assented, "for the written language of both Cupia and Vairkingi is the same. Yet the totally different flora and fauna of the two continents negatives this history."

"Where did the Cupians originate, if you know?" the priest inquired.

"We do not know," Myles replied, "but there are two conflicting legends. One is that the forerunners of the race came from across the boiling seas. The other is that they sprang, fully formed, from the soil. There is also a legend that creatures like me dwell beyond the boiling seas; and *this* legend, at least, appears to be borne out by the existence of your Vairkings."

"Strange! Still more strange!" the prelate declared. "For we have but *one* story of *our* origin. The race of Vairkings descended from another world above the skies. Who knows but that we, like you, came from that place which you call the planet—Minos, I think, you said?"

After some further conversation, the conclave was called to order again, and Myles took this as the signal for his departure. He was given a warm invitation to return.

Truly, a new avenue of speculation had been opened up to him by his chance meeting with the Holy Leader. Myles firmly resolved to return again at the earliest opportunity. But, from this time on, events moved with such rapidity that never again did he enter the sacred precincts.

First, he was stumped by his radio tubes. How was he to make a vacuum-pump which would exhaust the air?

The solution, when it finally occurred to him, was absurdly simple; he utilized atmospheric pressure.

He made a glass tube thirty feet long, and sealed his grid, his plates and his lead-wires into one end, closing that end off hermetically. Then he fashioned a piston of waterproof cloth fiber so as to fit into the closed end, almost touching these elements and yet free to move away from them without tearing them. Then he filled the tube with water, and inverted it. But the water did not drop away to a height of about twenty-eight feet, as it would have done on Earth.

Of course not, for this was Venus—Venus of an atmospheric pressure practically equal to that of earth, holding the water up; and yet with a gravity much less than that of Earth, tending to pull, the water down!

But, by lengthning the pipe sufficiently, Cabot finally got the proper balance, the fiber piston was pulled down, and a partial vacuum, practically free of water-vapor had been created. He then sealed off the upper portion of the glass tube with his blow-torch, and had his radio triad.

For these radio tubes, the glass was made according to a special formula. Of this same glass, Cabot fashioned lenses for the goggles which he and Doggo planned to wear on their trip home across the boiling seas.

One of the constituents of this special glass is lead monoxide, commonly known as litharge. This gave the Radio Man some concern, until Doggo suggested melting lead in a rotating cylindrical iron drum with spiral ribs. By pumping cold air in one end of this drum, fine particles of litharge were driven out through the other, where they accumulated in a stationary container.

About this time the king and Jud began clamoring for results, so Cabot made a few electric lights with platinum filaments. And entirely apart from pacifying his two patrons it was well that he did this, for the speedy burning out of these lights showed him that he had a new problem to face, namely: the elimination of all traces of oxygen in his tubes. He got rid of considerable by placing tubes in a strong magnetic field while exhausting, but this was not quite enough.

It looked as though his experiments would have to end at this point; for with an immense quantity of alcohol completed, and with pyrex glass for their goggles, everything was all set for the conspirators to locate Doggo's hidden plane and fly across the boiling seas to Cupia.

The Vairkings were by now sufficiently used to the huge ant-man and to his participation in Cabot's scientific experiments, so that no objection would be raised to his accompanying the radio man on one of the latter's expeditions in search of certain minerals which he believed could be found in the country.

Two carts, laden with tents, food and bedding, were taken along, and beneath these supplies he placed the alcohol and goggles. There was no need to conceal them, for none of the Vairkings, except Quivven, ever had any very distinct knowledge of what he was about, and to her he explained that the alcohol was for the purpose of loosening certain materials from the solid rocks, and that the goggles were to protect his and Doggo's eyes from the fumes.

A squad of soldiers pulled the carts. Doggo had demurred at this, suggesting that the soldiers be left behind, and offering to pull them himself, but Myles pointed out how easily he could scatter the Vairkings when the time came, by threatening them with his "magic sling-shot" (i. e., rifle).

Early in the morning they set forth, just as the unseen rising sun began to tint the eastern sky with purple. When the time came to say farewell to Quivven Myles found to his surprise that his voice was positively choked with emotion.

"Good-by, Golden Flame," he said. "Please wish me a safe journey."

"Of course I do," she said, "But why so sad? You sound as though you never expected to see me again."

"One never can tell," he replied.

"Your food has disagreed with you," she bantered. "I feel confident that you will return. For have you not often quoted to me: 'They cannot kill a Minorian?' Run along now, and come back safely."

Thus he left her, a smile on her face and a tear in his eye. He hated to deceive Quivven, who had been a good little pal, in spite of her occasional flare-ups of temper. He looked back and waved to her where she stood like a golden statue upon the city wall; it would be his last glimpse of a true friend. Then he set his face resolutely to the eastward.

Not only did he feel a pang at leaving Quivven, but he felt even more of a pang at leaving his radio-set half finished. The scientist always predominated in his makeup; and besides, like the good workman that he was, he hated an unfinished job.

But he realized that his radio project had been only a means to an end—the end being to get in touch with his friends and family in Cupia—and that this end was about to be accomplished more directly.

Just think, to-morrow night he would be home, ready to do battle for his loved ones against the usurper Yuri! The thought thrilled him, and all regrets passed away.

Lilla! He was to see his beautiful dainty Lilla once more; and his baby son, Kew, rightful ruler of Cupia! He resolved that, once back with them again, he would never more leave them. Lilla had been right; his return to Earth had been a foolhardy venture; results had proved it. As Poblath, the Cupian philosopher, used to say, "The test of a plan is how it works out."

Cabot was eager, even impatient, to see the ant-plane which was to carry him home. He was bubbling over with questions to ask his ant-man companion; the condition of the plane, its exact location, how well it had been concealed, and so forth. But his only means of communication with Doggo was in writing, and it would never do to delay the expedition for the purpose of indulging in a written conversation. So he merely fretted and fumed, and urged the Vairking pullers of the carts to greater speed.

But along toward evening a calm settled over him, a joyous calm. He was going home, going home! The words sang in his ears. He was going to Cupia, to baby Kew, and Princess Lilla. A nervous warmth flooded through his being, and tingled at his fingertips. He felt the strength to overcome any obstacles which might confront him. He was going home!

Just before sunset the party encamped on the outskirts of a small grove of trees, which Doggo indicated as the hiding-place of his plane and other supplies. It had already been agreed that they should not inspect the machine before morning for they did not wish to give even the slow brains of Vairking soldiers a chance to figure out their ulterior purpose, and perhaps to dispatch a runner to Vairkingi with a warning to Theoph and Jud.

So Myles was forced to possess his soul in patience, and await the dawn. To keep his mind off his troubles he sat with the furry warriors about their camp fire, and told them tales of Cupia and the planet Earth.

Never before, in their experience, had this strange furless leader of theirs been so graciously condescending or so sociable. It was an evening which they would long remember.

Finally they all turned in for the night. The earth-man slept fitfully, and dreamed of encounters in which, with his back to the wall, he fought with a wooden sword alone against Prince Yuri, and ant-men, and Vairkings, and Cupians, and whistling bees, in defense of Lilla and her son.

Yet such is the strange alchemy of dreams that sometimes Lilla's face seemed to be covered with golden fur.

With the first red flush of morning Cabot and Doggo bestirred themselves, and informed their campmates that they intended to do a bit of prospecting before breakfast. Then they set out into the interior of the wood, the ant-man leading the way. At last they came to a small clearing and beyond it a thicket, which Doggo indicated with one paw as being the spot which they sought. There was to be the plane!

Parting the foliage, they looked inside. But the thicket was empty!

On the farther side the bushes had been recently chopped down, and thence there lay a wide swath of cut trees clear out of the woods. It was only too evident that the precious plane had been stolen!

CHAPTER XVI
AFTERTHOUGHTS

There could be no doubt of it. Doggo's plane was gone, and with it had vanished all hopes of a speedy return to Cupia. Sadly the two returned to camp, and gave directions to start back to Vairkingi.

But Myles Cabot was not a man to despair or he would have yielded to fate many times in the past during his radio adventures on the silver planet. Already, as the porters were loading the carts, his agile mind was busy seeking some way whereby to snatch victory from defeat.

So when the expedition was ready to start he led it around the woods until he picked up the trail of the stolen airship. Quite evidently the theft had not been made by ant-men, for they would have *flown* the machine away, upon clearing the woods. No, it had obviously been taken by either Roies or Vairkings, who had wheeled or dragged it away. If he and Doggo could follow its path, they might yet be able to locate and recover the stolen property.

The trail led north until it struck, at right angles, a broad and much-rutted road which ran from Vairkingi to the northeast territory of the Vairkings. And at this point the trail completely vanished.

Myles held a written conference with Doggo, at which it was decided to return at once to the city and make inquiries there as to the stolen plane. If no one there knew of it, Doggo was to be dispatched on a new expedition into the northeast territory, and in the meantime Cabot was to rush the completion of his radio set. So they turned to the left and took up the march to Vairkingi.

It was a tired and disgusted human who returned that evening to the quarters which he had never expected to set eyes on again. Myles Cabot gave himself up to a few moments of unrestrained grief.

As he sat thus a soft, sympathetic voice said: "Didn't you succeed in finding that which you sought? I am so sorry! At least you came back safely to me."

But the blandishments of little Quivven, his pal, failed to comfort him.

That evening when Jud returned from the brickyard, Myles sought an audience with him and demanded news of the plane. Said Myles: "This beast friend of mine came near here in a magic wagon which travels through the air. Possession of this magic wagon would mean much to Vairkingi in your wars, and especially if the beasts ever take it into their heads to attack you, as they undoubtedly will do sooner or later.

"Yesterday Doggo and I embarked on a secret expedition to bring this magic wagon as a surprise to you and Theoph. But we find that it has been stolen. We have traced it to the northeast road, and there the trail ends. It must be either in this city or in the northeast territory. Will you help me to find it?"

But Jud smiled a crafty smile, and said: "It is not in Vairkingi—of that I am certain. Nor will I send into the northeast territory to find it for you; for I well know that you would use it to return to your own land beyond the boiling seas. We wish you to stay with us and do wonders for us. We believe that we can make your lot among us a happy one.

"But remember that, although you are treated with great honors, you are nevertheless still my slave. Any attempt on your part to locate the magic wagon will be met with severe punishment, and an end will be put to your experiments. I have spoken."

Myles Cabot met the other's eye squarely. "You have spoken, Jud," he said.

Myles was now convinced that Jud knew more about the missing plane than he was willing to admit; so the only thing to do was to lie low, bide his time, keep an ear out for news of the plane, and continue the manufacture of the radio set. Thus the earth-man ruminated as he walked slowly back to his quarters.

And then the linking of radio and airplanes in his mind gave him an idea. He had felt all along that he was doing the correct thing in building a radio set rather than in manufacturing firearms with which to attack the Formians, or in trying to fabricate an airplane for a flight across the boiling seas.

His intuition had been correct; his subconscious mind must have guided him to make the radio *in order to phone Cupia for a plane to come over to Vairkingi and get him.* Why hadn't he realized this before? It gave him new heart.

With a laugh he reflected that this afterthought was pretty much like those so characteristic of the man whom he had just left. Jud the Excuse-Maker, always bungling, and always with a perfectly good excuse or alibi, thought up afterward to explain why he did something which, when he did it, was absolutely pointless. Myles had always looked down on the Vairking noble because of this failing.

But now what he found himself going through exactly the same mental processes, he began to wonder if perhaps Jud were not guided by a fairly high-grade intuition. Perhaps Jud's afterthoughts and excuses were but the breaking through of a realization of some real forethoughts on the part of Jud's subconscious mind. Myles wondered. He was still wondering when he fell asleep that night.

The next morning he plunged into his work with renewed vigor. He now had copper wire, copper plates, wood, mica, solder, platinum, glass, and batteries—everything that he needed for his radio set except a better vacuum for his tubes; but without that he was as far from success as when he started.

Of course he knew what he needed—magnesium. But it was one thing to step into a drug store on the earth, or into a chemical laboratory in Cupia, and take magnesium off the shelves, and quite another matter to pick this elusive element out of thin air in Vairkingi.

Nevertheless, in spite of this lack, Myles kept on working. He wound his inductances, transformers, earphones, and rheostats. He assembled his variable condensers and microphones. He fashioned his sockets and lamp bases. He strung his antennae. He wired up his baseboard and panel.

Small sets were installed in Quivven's rooms at the palace, at Jud's house, and at the brickyard. Each of these was equipped with a transformer-coupling for Doggo's antennae, as well as with mouthpieces for the others, so that now at last oral conversation was possible with his Formian friend. Later he would prepare a portable headset such as he had worn in Cupia.

Laboratory experiments demonstrated the success of his sets in everything except durability of tubes. Yet in spite of this drawback he was able to communicate across his laboratory, and even with Jud's house, and under favorable conditions with Quivven at the palace by using a cold-tube hookup. But this was not powerful enough to send as far as the brickyard, let alone Cupia.

At this juncture there appeared one morning at his gate a Vairking soldier in leather tunic and helmet, requesting entrance with important secret news. Myles grudgingly left his work-bench and gave audience. The fellow had a strangely familiar appearance and smiled in a quizzical manner; yet Myles could not place him.

"Who are you?" Myles asked.

"Do you not know me?" the other asked in reply.

"No."

The soldier doffed his leather cap. "Do you know me now?"

"No."

"A life for a life?"

"Now I know you!" Cabot exclaimed. "You are Otto the Bold, son of Grod the Silent, who is King of the Roies. To paraphrase one of the proverbs of my own country, 'A face that is familiar in Sur is oft a stranger in Vairkingi.' I did not recognize you away from the surroundings in which we met. What good fortune brings you here?"

"Not *good* fortune, but *bad*," the Roy replied. "It is true that Grod, my father, is our king, but it is also true that Att the Terrible likewise claims the kingship. Att loves Arkilu, and is even at this moment on the march against Vairkingi with the largest army of Roies ever gathered."

Myles smiled. "We are grateful for the information," he said. "With this forewarning we are secure against attack."

"If you will pardon me," Otto continued, "I think that you are *not* secure. For one of your own Vairkings, Tipi by name, marches with Att. Att has promised Tipi the glorious golden Quivven in return for Tipi's support. And Tipi has many partisans within this city."

Myles continued to smile. "We can deal with traitors," he asserted smugly. "There are many lamp-posts in our city."

But Otto kept on: "Sur has fallen."

"What!" the earth-man shouted, at last shocked out of his complacency. "The rock-bound impregnable fortress of Sur fallen? Impossible!"

"Not impossible to those who travel through the skies and drop black stones which fly to pieces with a loud noise," Otto calmly replied. "The beasts of the south have made alliance with Att the Terrible, and Tipi the Steadfast, and are marching with them. Good Builder! They are upon us even now. Quick, the beasts enter this very room. Come, draw, defend yourself!"

Wheeling quickly, Cabot confronted Doggo standing in the doorway. Much relieved, he explained to Otto who this newcomer was; then, seizing a pad and a lead stylus of his own manufacture, he hurriedly sketched the situation to his Formian friend.

In reply Doggo wrote: "At last I have magnesium ore. Some soldiers brought it in, attracted by its pretty red color. There is no time to be lost. To the laboratory. You must complete our set and summon aid from Cupia. Meanwhile I will get Jud on the air, and call him here for a conference. We have no time to wait upon him, or even Theoph, in this emergency."

Myles read the message aloud to Otto.

"It is well," the latter commented. "Now, if you will excuse me, I must be running along. My disguise as a Vairking soldier will get me safely out of your city, and I must join my father, who is planning to counter-attack, if a fit opportunity presents itself. Till we meet again."

"Till we meet again, in this life or beyond the waves," the earth-man replied. "And may the Builder bless you for your help this day." Then he rushed to the laboratory.

Doggo was already tuning the set. "Jud is not at home," he wrote. "Shall I waste a tube on the brickyard?"

"No," Myles signified with a shake of his head; then seizing the pad and stylus again, he wrote: "I will try and get Jud. You meanwhile attempt to extract magnesium from this piece of carnallite."

The ant-man knew exactly how to proceed. Grinding the ore, he mixed it with salt and melted the mass in an iron pot, which he connected electrically with the carbon terminal of a line of electric batteries. In the boiling pot he placed a copper plate connected with the zinc elements of his cells.

By the time the earth-man returned from calling Jud on the radio, a coating of pure magnesium had begun to form on the copper anode.

An hour or so later he scraped off his first yield of the precious metal, the final necessity of his projected radio set.

At this stage Jud appeared. "Pardon the delay," he started to explain. "You see, I—"

But Myles cut him short with: "Never mind explanations now. It is enough that you are here. Sur has fallen. The beasts of the south and Att the Terrible are on the warpath. They seek to rob you of your Arkilu. With their aerial wagons they will drop magic rocks upon this city and destroy it. Give Doggo back his plane, and he will try to combat them."

But Jud shook his head. "You would merely escape," he replied, "and then we would be worse off than now."

"Then you admit that you know the whereabouts of Doggo's plane?" Myles eagerly asked.

"Not at all, not at all," the Vairking suavely replied. "I was merely stating that, even if I knew where this 'plane,' as you call it, is—"

"For Builder's sake, man!" Cabot cut in. "This is no time to quibble over words! Give us the plane, if you would save Theoph, yourself, and Arkilu."

"It's hardly necessary," Jud asserted, unruffled. "Don't get so excited! If Att wants Arkilu, he certainly won't drop things on the palace. And we can defend the palace against all the Roies in Vairkingi."

"But not against magic slingshots," replied the earth-man.

"Perhaps not," the noble said with a crafty smile; "but we shall see. Now I go to prepare the defense. You are at liberty to come with us, if you will, or putter around your tubes if you had rather. Goodby."

"Shift for yourselves then!" Myles shouted after him, and frantically resumed his work. His attempt to get the plane by stratagem had failed. Perhaps Jud did not know anything about the plane after all. It would be typical of him.

Myles had plenty of sets of grids, plates, and filaments all prepared. Also plenty of long tubes of pyrex glass. All that remained necessary was to coat the platinum elements with magnesium, fuse them into the tube, exhaust the air by the water method as before, seal the tube, and his radio set would be complete.

"Where is Quivven?" he wrote to Doggo. "She ought to be here helping with this."

"On her way from the palace," the ant-man replied. "I radio-phoned her there."

Presently she entered, and jauntily inquired what all the excitement was about. Myles explained as briefly as possible.

Her only answer was to shrug her golden shoulders and remark, "Tipi is a little fool. He can have me if he can get me."

Then she took her seat at the workbench.

After a while she inquired, "Why the rush with the radio set, when Vairkingi is in peril?"

Myles replied, "Our only hope now is to get Cupia on the air, and persuade my followers there to send across the boiling seas enough aerial wagons to defeat the beasts of the south, or 'Formians,' as we call them."

"And will you talk with your Lilla?" she asked innocently.

"Yes, if the Builder wills," he eagerly and reverently replied.

To his surprise, Quivven jumped to her feet with flashing eyes, and, seizing a small iron anvil from the workbench, she held it over the precious pile of platinum elements.

"And if I drop this anvil, you will *not* talk to her. Is not that so?"

Myles, horrified, sat rooted to his seat, unable to move.

CHAPTER XVII
THE BATTLE FOR VAIRKINGI

But the flaming Quivven did not drop the anvil on the precious tube elements. Instead she flung it from her to the floor and sank limply into her seat, her golden head on her arms on the workbench.

"I couldn't do it," she moaned between sobs, "for I too know what it is to love. Talk to her, Myles, and I will help you."

He gasped with relief. "You wouldn't spoil all our days and days of labor, I am sure," he said. "What was the matter? I don't understand you."

"*You* wouldn't," was her reply, as she shook herself together and resumed work.

After a while one of the soldiers attached to the laboratory brought in word that the Roies and Formians were attacking the walls, and that "planes" were sailing around in the sky overhead. Cabot gave word to mass his men to defend the laboratory at all costs and went on working.

One by one the tubes were completed and tested.

From time to time Quivven would step into the yard, glance at the sky, and then report back to Myles. The Formian planes were scouting low, but were not dropping bombs. Jud had apparently been right in one thing—that the beasts would not risk injuring the expected prizes of war, namely Arkilu and Quivven.

From time to time runners brought word of the fighting at the outer wall of the city. It would have been an easy matter for the ant-men to bomb the gates, and thus let in their Roy allies, but evidently they were playing safe even there. At last, however, word came that traitors—presumably friends of Tipi—had opened one of the gates, and that the enemy was now within the city.

Still Myles worked steadily on.

Suddenly Quivven returned from one of her scouting trips in the yard with the cry, "One of the air wagons has seen me, and is coming down!"

At that the Radio Man permitted himself to leave his bench for a few moments and go to the door. True, the plane was hovering down, eagerly awaited by a score or so of Cabot's Vairking soldiers armed with swords, spears and bows. As the Formians came within bowshot they were met with a shower of arrows, most of which, however, glanced harmlessly off the metallic bottom of the fuselage.

The ant-men at once retaliated with a shower of bullets. Two Vairkings dropped to the ground, and the others frantically rushed to cover within the buildings, forcing back Myles and his two companions, as the fugitives crowded through the door.

"Where is *your* magic slingshot?" one of them taunted him as they swept by.

The earth-man shook himself and passed the back of one hand across his tired brow, then hurried to his living room. Seizing his rifle, he cautiously approached one of the slit windows which overlooked the yard, and peeked out. The plane was on the ground. Four ants were disembarking.

Here at last was a chance to secure transportation!

Myles opened fire.

The Formians were taken completely by surprise. Oh, how it did

Cabot's heart good to see those ancient enemies drop and squirm as he pumped lead into them! They made no attempt to return his fire, but scuttled toward their beached plane.

Only one of them reached it; but one was enough to deprive the earth-man of his booty. Up shot the craft, followed by a parting bullet from Myles. Then he proceeded to the yard once more. His furry soldiers, brave now that all danger was over, were already there before him, putting an end to the three wounded ant-men, with swords and spears.

A strong and pungent odor filled the air. Myles sniffed. It was alcohol in large quantities. The plane could not last long, for he had punctured its fuel tank.

Each of the dead enemies had been fully armed, so that, although Myles failed in his plan to secure the airship, the encounter had at least netted him three rifles and three bandoleers of cartridges. These he bestowed on Doggo, Quivven, and the captain of his guards, saying, "You three, with four or five others, had better go at once to Jud's compound before the fighting reaches here; for, now that the Formians have located Quivven, they are sure to attack again, sooner or later."

But the golden-furred princess remonstrated with him: "Let us stay together, fight together, and, if need be, die together."

"For the Builder's sake, run along," he replied testily. "We are wasting valuable time. I will join you if the fighting gets too thick hereabouts."

"But how can you?"

"By the back way which you taught me."

"But you need the help of Doggo and myself."

"No longer, for the set is complete. All that remains to be done is to tune in and either get Cupia on the air or not. Now, as you are my true friends, please run along!"

So, with a shrug and a pout; she left him. And with her went Doggo, and the captain, and five of the guard. Much relieved, the Radio Man returned to his workbench. Although the move truly was wise for the safety of Quivven, the real motive which actuated Myles was a desire to have her absent, when and if he should talk to his Lilla.

He leaned his rifle against the bench, hung the bandoleer handily near by, and set to work. A few more connections and his hookup was complete. He surveyed the assembled set with a great deal of satisfaction; for, although it really was a means to an end, yet it was a considerable end in itself after all, as any radio fan can appreciate.

Once more Myles Standish Cabot, electrical engineer, had demonstrated his premiership on two worlds. He had made a complete radio set out of basic natural elements, without the assistance of a single previously fabricated tool, or material! It was an unbelievable feat. Yet it had been completed successfully.

With trembling hands, he adjusted the controls, and listened. Gradually he tuned in a station. It seemed a nearby station.

A voice was saying: "We could not report before, O master, for we have only just repaired the set which this Cabot wrecked. The Minorian lied when he told you that he had affairs well in hand, for even at that moment he was a fugitive.

"He is now with the furry Cupians who live to the north of New Formia. Today our forces are attacking their city. It is only a matter of a few parths before he will be in our hands. I have spoken, and shall now stand by to receive."

This was the supreme test. Could Myles Cabot hear the reply? Adjusting his set to the extreme limit of its sensitivity, he waited, his hands on the wave-length dials.

Faintly but distinctly came the answer in the well-known voice of Yuri the usurper: "You have done well. Now I will hand the antenna-phones to the Princess Lilla, and I wish you to repeat to her what you have just told me, so that she may hear it with her own antennae and believe."

A pause and then Cabot heard the ant-man stationed at the shack on the mountains near Yuriana recount the tale of Doggo's abortive revolution and flight, of Cabot's wrecking the radio set and disappearing, of the Formian alliance with Att the Terrible, of the fall of Sur, and of the attack on Vairkingi, ending with the words which he had already caught.

As he listened to this narration, the earth-man was rapidly making up his mind what to do, and, as soon as the ant-man signed off, Cabot cut in with: "Lilla, dearest, do not show any sign of surprise, but listen intently, as though the Formian were still speaking. This is your own Myles. I am sending from a station which I have only just completed after many sangths of intensive work.

"It is true that the Formians are now attacking our city but they cannot win. Sur fell because we were taken by surprise, but we were warned in time to defend Vairkingi. Already I, myself, have driven off one plane and killed three Formians.

"As yet I have been unable to secure an airship, or I should have flown back to you. Please get in touch with Toron, or some other of my friends, and persuade them to fly across the boiling seas and bring me back.

"Yuri has made it twice, and 'what man has done, that can man do.' Now I am about to finish. When I sign off, please request Yuri for permission to talk to the Formian at Yuriana, to ask him some questions. Then tell me as much as you can of yourself, our baby, and the situation in Cupia, before Yuri shuts you off. I have spoken, dearest."

And Myles stood by to receive.

With what a thrill did he hear his own Lilla's voice answer: "Oh, Formian, I have Prince Yuri's permission to speak to you. You may answer what I ask you, and reply to what I tell you, but he himself will receive, lest I hear something which I ought not. This leads me to believe that affairs are not so bad with Cabot as you report."

"She is doing fine," Myles remarked to himself, admiringly. "So far, Yuri will not suspect that she is talking to me."

Lilla's voice continued: "You and the other Formians may be interested to know that Prince Yuri is in complete control here. Baby Kew and I are well, and are being respectfully treated by Prince Yuri as his guests in the palace at Kuana. He has promised me that if I will marry him, Kew can have the succession after his death. And this I might have accepted for the baby's sake, but now that I know that you still live, this cannot be."

"She has made a slip," Cabot moaned.

Evidently she realized it herself, for her voice hurried on: "You see, the whistling bees—"

Then Yuri's voice cut in abruptly with: "Congratulations, Cabot. I don't see how you did it. Your ex-wife would have gotten across a lot more information to you if she hadn't inadvertently let me know to whom she was talking by her careless use of the word 'you'. I don't know what you said to her, but I shall be on my guard. No more radio for the Princess Lilla, until my henchmen in New Formia report your death, which I hope will be soon. Good-by, you cursed spot of sunshine. Yuri, king of Cupia, signing off for the night."

So that was that. Myles switched off the set, and sat submerged in thought. Lilla and his baby were safe. He doubted not that she would sooner or later find means to send him a plane. He had given Yuri cause to doubt the glorious story told by the Formian radio operator. The new set had fulfilled its mission.

But how had Yuri succeeded in climbing into power again in Cupia, nine-tenths of the inhabitants of which were loyal to Princess Lilla and the baby king?

Then Myles remembered her closing words: "The whistling bees—" It was as little Jacqueline Farley had prophesied on her father's New England farm, during Cabot's brief revisit to the earth. Cabot had stated: "There can be no peace on any continent which is inhabited by more than one race of intelligent beings"; whereat little Jacqueline had pointed out that the whistling bees were intelligent beings.

Doubtless, Yuri had stirred up trouble between the bees and their Cupian allies, and had ridden to the throne on the crest of this trouble. Portheris, king of the bees, had undoubtedly been deposed; for he was too loyal to Myles to stand for this.

The earth-man's reverie was rudely interrupted at this point by one of his soldiers who rushed into the laboratory shouting: "Sir, there is fighting in your very yard!"

Cabot slipped the bandoleer over his shoulders, adjusted the straps, picked up his rifle, and hurried to the door. In the yard, his guards were struggling in hand-to-hand combat with a superior force of Roies.

He could tell them apart, not only by the contrast between the fine features of his own men and apelike faces of the intruders, but more easily by the contrast between the leather tunics of the Vairkings and the nakedness of the Roies. So, standing calmly in the doorway, Myles began picking off the enemy, one by one, with his rifle. It was too easy; almost like trap-shooting.

But it didn't last long, for the Roies soon learned what was up, and, breaking away from their opponents, crowded out through the gate, followed by a shower of missiles and maledictions.

Cabot's Vairkings were for following, but their master peremptorily called them back, and directed them to barricade the laboratory. It was well that he did so, for presently the heads of the enemy began to appear above the top of the fence. Evidently they had built a platform in the street.

Soon arrows and pebbles began to fly at the windows of the

house. The Vairkings replied with a volley, but Cabot cautioned them to conserve their ammunition, and watch him pick off with his rifle, one by one, the heads which showed themselves above the paling.

This soon ceased to be interesting. So, giving the rifle and bandoleer to one of the more intelligent of his men, and instructing them to hold the laboratory at all costs, the earth-man set out, sword in hand, by the back way to rejoin Doggo and Quivven.

The alleys which he threaded were deserted. He reached the rear of Jud's compound without event, and passed in to one of the inclosures through a small and well concealed gate in the face of the wall. Quivven had pointed this route out to him before, but never had he traversed it farther than this point. He looked cautiously around him. Then he rubbed his eyes, and looked again! He could hardly believe his senses!

There stood a Formian airplane in apparently perfect condition. Approaching it gingerly with drawn sword, he circled it carefully to make sure that it contained no enemies. But it was deserted. A hasty inspection disclosed that everything was in working order, except that the fuel tank was empty.

Probably then, this was the plane at which he had fired. But no, for this plane did not even *smell* of alcohol. The tank had evidently been dry for some time, and there was no sign of any bullet hole in it. Gradually the fact dawned on him that this was Doggo's plane, which Jud had concealed from them for so long. He must reach Doggo and tell him.

At the farther side of the inclosure from the side at which he had entered, there was a door. Myles raced toward it, and flung it open. Beyond it there was a second inclosure similar to the first. Myles raced across this one as well, and flung open another door, whereupon out poured a crowd of Roies, upsetting him and throwing him sprawling upon the ground.

But they were as surprised as he was at the encounter, and this fact enabled him to regain his sword and scramble to his feet before they were upon him again, with parry and thrust.

Good swordsman as he was, they had soon forced him, his back against the wall, to defend his life with his trusty wooden blade. Time and again one of their points would reach his tunic, but he kept his neck well guarded, and so was able to stand them off.

When he had drawn his breath and got his bearings, and his defense had become slightly a matter of routine, he recognized the leader of the enemy as none other than the traitor Tipi. His first thought was to run Tipi through for his treachery. But then he reflected that quite likely Quivven really loved Tipi after all. It would be a shame to kill this boy merely because his unrequited love had caused him to lose his head.

From then on, Myles had no time to reflect on anything, for he was engaged in the difficult task of trying to defend himself without hurting Tipi.

The young Vairking had recognized the earth-man, and was hurling vituperations at him, but Myles saved his breath for his swordplay. Even so, he gradually tired. His sword hand no longer instantly responded to every command of his agile brain, and even his brain itself became less agile. It was only a matter of time when he would be certain to make a misplay, and go down before his opponents. Yet, still he struggled on.

And then suddenly a new complication entered the game, for he was seized from behind the arms and was lifted struggling and kicking off the ground.

CHAPTER XVIII
THE FALL OF VAIRKINGI

As Miles was lifted from the ground by the unknown force behind which had seized him beneath the armpits, his Roy opponents fell back away from him in surprise. But immediately their expressions changed to intense pleasure. Quite evidently they regarded this mysterious new power as an ally.

Myles could not squirm around to see what was holding him; so still grasping his sword in his right hand, he felt with his left hand under his right armpit, and found there—the claw of a Formian! In another moment he would be within reach of its horrid jaws, and then would came the paralyzing bite which he knew so well from past experience. Nevertheless he could die fighting.

Shifting his sword quickly, so that he held it point upward, he struck backward with it across his shoulder, and had the satisfaction of hearing and feeling it glint on the carapace of his captor. A few more strokes, and by lucky chance his blade might find a joint in the black shell of the ant-man.

But just as he was about to strike again a familiar voice behind him called out, "Stop, Myles, for Builder's sake, stop! It is Doggo who holds you, and is rescuing you from your enemies."

It was the voice of Quivven. Tipi and the Roies instantly understood and made a rush at their late victim; but they were too late, for Doggo had lifted the earth-man safely over the wall. There stood Quivven and the members of their guard.

"Quick, Doggo, the rifles!" Myles shouted. "Your missing plane is in the next inclosure. We must reach it before the enemy does."

Of course, this was all lost on the radio-sense of the Formian, but the other members of the party acted at once. On their side of the wall there was a platform near the top. Springing lightly onto this, the furry maid and the captain of the guard covered the Roies with their rifles.

"You!" exclaimed Tipi in surprise.

"What did you expect?" Quivven taunted. "You attacked this city in search of me. Here I am. You can have me, if you can catch me. But you had better not try it just now, for I and my friends have these magic sling-shots, which can kill at almost any distance. Go quickly before I try it on you. For old times' sake, go!"

But Tipi and his Roies stood steadfast. The captain and Quivven fired; two Roies dropped, and the others fled precipitately out through the gates by which they entered. Tipi the Steadfast was left alone confronting Cabot and his companions. But he never budged.

Over the fence vaulted the five Vairking guardsmen in their leather armor, and attacked their renegade countryman, who, being a noble, wore only a leather helmet. The unequal contest could have but one result. Yet Quivven looked on complacently at the impending downfall of her former sweetheart.

Cabot, however, had more heart. Running along the platform within the wall, he vaulted over at a point distant from the contest, sneaked steadily up on Tipi, and suddenly throttled him from behind, at the same time shouting to his own henchmen to desist. The five Vairkings obediently dropped their swords, and then trussed up the young noble with his own leather belt and sword-sling by placing him in a sitting posture, tying his ankles together, slipping a piece of stick beneath his knees, placing his elbows under the ends of this stick, and tying his wrists together in front of his shins. Also they gagged him. And thus they left the traitor, rolled ignominiously into a corner, his eyes blazing with a piteous hate.

Meanwhile Doggo, exploring the exits, had seen his plane! He returned to the group, bristling with excitement, and made signs to them to follow him. Out of respect for his joy, none of the party let on that Cabot had been the first to find the airship and had already informed them of it. So they followed Doggo and gave every indication of being much impressed.

With loving touch the huge black ant-man caressed each strut and brace, and guy, and joint, and lever, as he made a thorough inspection of his long-lost craft. All appeared to be in perfect condition. Even the bombs, the rifle, and the ammunition were intact.

From somewhere in the interior of the fusilage Doggo produced a pad of paper and a Formian stylus, and wrote: "Alcohol. We must have alcohol. Then away from these accursed shores forever."

Seizing the writing materials Myles replied, "You have four rifles. Let me take one of them. Protect this plane with the other three, while I return alone by the back way and bring the alcohol here under convoy of the entire laboratory guard."

Then, giving no time for dissent, he seized the rifle and bandoleer from the plane, and was gone. Out through the next inclosure he went, slid open the secret door in the wall, and peered cautiously out. One lone ant-man with rifle and bandoleer was parading the alley.

Myles fired, but missed. The Formian promptly took cover behind a pile of rubbish, and fired back. Myles hastily withdrew, then cautiously put his head through the opening again in order to take a shot at his enemy. But the enemy fired first, the bullet grazing the leather helmet of the earth-man and stunning him considerably. So he sat on the ground within the inclosure, and rubbed his sore head for a few minutes. What a narrow escape!

Then he had an idea. He propped his hat on a stick, so that it would sway gently in the breeze, its rim just projecting through the opening in the wall giving every indication of life. Then he ran quickly along inside the wall until he came to a corner, which he judged must be about opposite the rubbish heap which sheltered the Formian. Climbing quietly up the studding at this point, he peered carefully over. There lay his black enemy, only a few feet away, steadily watching the bobbing edge of the helmet.

Two shots from Cabot's rifle, and the vigil was over; and soon the earth-man, his helmet regained, and with an extra rifle and cartridge belt flung across his shoulders, was proceeding unmolested down the alley.

He reached the laboratory without further adventure, and found everything as he had left it. The guard, however, reported that they had had to repulse three assaults by Roies, the last of which had been led by a Formian armed with a rifle.

"If it had not been for this magic sling-shot which you left with us," said the guardsman, "we should have been beaten. But the surprise of the savage ones at finding us thus armed was so great that even their leader could not rally them, though the beast did kill several of our men before he finally fled with his Roy henchmen."

The Radio Man then informed them of his intention to cart the alcohol to Jud's inclosure, where new wonders would be performed. Accordingly, all except a few sentinels withdrew into the laboratory to load up.

First Myles sorted out the bottles which were small enough to carry conveniently, and then filled these bottles with alcohol from the large carboys in which it was stored. This left a dozen or so carboys still unemptied. It would be a pity to leave these behind, but it would be impossible to get a cart out by the back way.

So the Radio Man gave hasty directions to take an empty cart through his front gate under guard, and attempt to get it around by the various winding streets into the alley without its being captured by the enemy. Meanwhile all the alcohol was moved to the alley gate, and heavily guarded there.

While this was being done Myles Cabot took a few minutes time for a farewell glance around his laboratory, which he was about to quit for the last time. He had enjoyed working here, for there is no human pleasure greater than the joy of accomplishment, and here he had accomplished the almost superhuman task of building up a complete sending and receiving radio set out of its basic elements. Even though he was at last about to journey home to his Lilla and his baby son in Cupia, he hated to leave this precious set.

An irresistible impulse drew him to it, as a loadstone draws a magnet. He placed his fingers on the controls. He tuned to the same wave length in which he had talked and received earlier in the day.

A voice was speaking in the language of Formia and Cupia: "Vairkingi is about to fall, O master, and with it the Minorian must certainly get into our hands, for our scout fliers are circling the outer walls to the city to prevent his escape."

So that was why the ant planes hadn't bothered them recently.

"But O master," the voice of the ant-man continued. "I have bad news to report along with the good; for while practically our entire populace was engaged with the hordes of our ally, Att the Terrible, in besieging Vairkingi, other hordes of furry savages under Grod the Silent have attacked and captured our own city of Yuriana, and with it have seized our reserve planes and supplies of ammunition. I have—"

But before the Formian could complete his signing off, Myles slammed over the leaf switch, and cut in with: "Cabot speaking. Cabot speaking. Know then, O Yuri, that Vairkingi will not fall. My arms are victorious here as at your ant city of Yuriana. Presently you will cease to receive any further messages from either here or your own mountain station, and then you will know that the last of your Formians has perished off the face of this continent.

"Soon you may expect me and my furry allies to fly across the boiling seas to redeem Cupia, but of our coming we shall give you no further warning. Tremble and await us. Meanwhile believe none of the stories which your henchmen will falsely send you to keep up your courage. Answer me now, and tell me that you have received my message. I have spoken."

Then he set the switches to receive.

Back came the answer, but it was from the mountain station to the south, and it came from Prince Yuri in Cupia: "It is a lie. The Minorian lies."

Of course it was a lie, but it was war; and Yuri would not know which version to credit. If anything should happen to the sending set near the city of the ants, Yuri certainly would believe the worst from that time on. Cabot smiled to himself. The Formian continued denying, and explaining, and apologizing. Finally he signed off, and then Prince Yuri got on the air. "Listen, O Formian," he said, "and you, O Cabot. I received both of your messages. Naturally, I believe my own man. Call me again when you have something further to report. I have spoken."

"He may believe his own henchman *now*," Cabot muttered to himself, "but later he will begin to doubt."

Then, shutting off his set, he penned a hurried note in duplicate to Otto the Bold.

Congratulations on the capture of the city of the black beasts. Destroy their hut in the mountains, where you first shot arrows at me, and first saw me use the magic slingshot. Destroy it at all costs, for with it ends the power of the beasts.

Cabot the Minorian.

One copy he gave to each of two of the most trusted of his laboratory guards, and adjured them at all costs to break through the lines separately and get the message to the prince of the friendly faction of the Roies.

"If either of my Vairkings succeeds in reaching Prince Otto," Myles said to himself, "it will mean the end of Yuri's reports from this continent."

Then with a sigh the Radio Man picked up an iron mallet and demolished his own radio set, the work of so many hours of care. When he had finished, there was not a fragment left intact.

"This, too, must pass," he quoted sadly.

At this point one of his Vairkings rushed in upon him with a shout: "A party of Roies is attacking the alley gate."

Shaking himself together, the Radio Man bade farewell to his beloved laboratory, picked up his two rifles and his ammunition, and hastened to take command of his forces. He found that his cart had safely got around to the gate, but that a hand-to-hand conflict for its possession was now in progress between the guard and a large force of Roies. So inter-mingled were the contestants that the leader of the Vairkings had not dared to use the rifle.

Cabot, however, had the confidence of greater experience. A few well placed shots fired by him from the gate, and the enemy broke away and retreated down the alley. Myles handed out one of his own two rifles, thus raising the number of his riflemen to two. These, with several bowmen, took cover down the alley to hold off any counter-attack by the enemy.

The carboys of alcohol were then quickly loaded into the cart, along with all the reserve ammunition which Doggo had manufactured, and the expedition set forth. Cabot with his rifle in the lead, the other two riflemen and the archers forming a rear guard, closely followed by the hostile band of Roies. But, in spite of this pursuit, all went well until the party turned into the alley of the secret door to Jud's enclosure.

Here they found the way blocked by a formidable body of the

furry savages, led by half a dozen ant-men armed with rifles. Luckily there was plenty of rubbish in the alley behind which to take cover from those ahead. Those behind were not much of a problem, not having any firearms other than bows and arrows.

But it was aggravating to be stopped within sight of one's goal. Furthermore, three of the rifle-armed ants promptly departed, doubtless for the purpose either of bringing up reenforcements, or of joining the Roies who were on the other side of Cabot's party.

There was no time to be lost. The rifles were now three to three. Accordingly the earth-man called his archers from the rear and ordered a charge. Of course, his porters could not fight while carrying a bottle of alcohol under each arm, so all the bottles were piled around the cart and left with a small guard.

The attack proved temporarily successful. Step by step the three ants and their Roy allies were driven back. But, just as Cabot and his Vairkings were about to gain the secret opening in the wall, word was brought that the Roies in the rear were attacking the cart; so Cabot had to order a speedy retreat to save his precious alcohol, thus giving up in an instant the ground which it had taken so long to gain.

The Roies were readily repulsed from the cart and retreated down the alley in disorder, but the party with whom Cabot and his Vairkings had just been fighting formed at once for a counter-attack.

At this juncture a row of heads suddenly and unexpectedly appeared over the top of the wall, Quivven the Golden Flame, Doggo the ant-man, and six Vairking guardsmen. Quivven and two guardsmen held rifles with which they promptly covered the approaches to the alley, while Doggo started hurling airplane bombs into the group of Roies led by his three countrymen.

When the smoke cleared the alley was cleared as well. Here and there were arms and legs and other anatomical sections of Roies and Formians. All the survivors had fled. Myles picked up two ant rifles and the twisted remains of a third, and hurriedly passed what was left of his precious liquid fuel in through the little gate in the wall.

Nearly half the bottles and carboys had been broken during the fighting. The Vairking dead numbered about a dozen, with several more wounded. These were brought within the inclosure and ministered to by Quivven.

By this time the pink twilight had begun to settle over the planet Poros. Departure that day was now out of the question. Accordingly guards were posted, and the rest of the party prepared to spend the night close to the plane, on tapestries filched from the palace of Jud the Excuse-Maker.

The Radio Man himself was nearly exhausted, having worked steadily for thirty-six hours on the completion of his set and the subsequent fighting. Yet before he turned in he inquired about the state of the battle.

It appeared that little was known, save that the city was overrun by ant-men and the furry savages of Att the Terrible, and that isolated groups of Vairkings were defending as best they could their respective inclosures against the invaders. Cabot reported the capture of the ant city by Grod the Silent, which news served to hearten his own little band considerably.

The mention of the radio set, whereby he had obtained this information, suggested to him to ask: "Have you tried to get the palace of Theoph the Grim with the small set in Jud's quarters?"

"Yes," Quivven replied, "repeatedly, but no one answers. You see, the palace set is in my own rooms, and it has probably not occurred to anyone to go there."

Then they lay down for a fitful night of shouts and shots and flares. But no one attacked the inclosure which they occupied.

Along toward morning the earth-man fell into a soundless sleep, only to be awakened by one of his Vairking soldiers shaking him roughly by the shoulders.

"Awake!" the leather-clad warrior shouted. "Awake! Vairkingi is in flames. The fire is rapidly eating its way toward us."

It was true. All around them was the uncanny red of the conflagration. Overhead there sped flocks of sparks against a background of billowy clouds of smoke, and a further background of jet-black sky. Immediate steps were necessary to protect their airship from the flying embers.

Accordingly the bottles and carboys of alcohol were emptied into the fuel tank of the craft, and then filled with water. Brooms of brush were brought and used to beat out such sparks as endangered the plane. Doggo tested the motors, and found them in good order.

The tapestries were loaded on board. Then there remained nothing they could do except keep watch, guard the plane, and await the dawn; although, of course, if the holocaust should approach too near it would become necessary for them to fly, night or no night.

Meanwhile it occurred to Myles to try once more to get the palace on the air; so, with rifle and ammunition slung over his shoulders, and carrying a torch, he proceeded to Jud's quarters.

On the way he espied a dark form crouching in a corner of the fence of one of the inclosures.

CHAPTER XIX
THE BATTLE IN THE AIR

Cabot unslung his rifle, held his torch high above him, and approached the crouching figure.

The crouching figure groaned. It was Tipi, still trussed up, forgotten by all. Myles cut his bonds and helped him to his feet, but he collapsed again with a groan. So, leaving him lying there, the earth-man hastened back to the plane, and then returned with one of his Vairkings, whom he instructed to take charge of the young noble until he was able to walk, and then turn him loose through the secret gate into the alley. There was no point in leaving even an enemy to be burned to death, trussed up in a corner.

Tipi attended to, Myles proceeded to Jud's quarters, where he tuned in the palace. The result was immediate.

"Jud speaking," said a voice. "Answer, Cabot. For Builder's sake, answer!"

"Cabot speaking," he replied. "I am at your quarters, O Jud. With me are Quivven, Doggo, and about two dozen of the laboratory guards. We have eight magic slingshots now, and also the magic aerial wagon, which you have so long concealed from me. As soon as day breaks we shall rise in the air and do battle with the beasts. If you had let me have this wagon before, I could have prevented the fall of Vairkingi. Now it may be too late. How are things with you?"

Back came the answer. "Theoph the Grim, Arkilu the Beautiful, and I are safe in the palace, with most of the army of the Vairkings. So far we have repulsed every assault of the beasts and their Roy allies, but their magic slingshots do frightful havoc. Come and rescue us, O magician."

To which Cabot replied: "With daylight I shall come."

As he came out of the house he looked up at the sky. The background, against which swirled the smoke clouds, now showed faintly purple. By the time he rejoined his party by the plane, day had come.

And it was well, for the buildings in the next inclosure had started to burn.

Cabot gave his parting instructions to the captain of the guard: "Take six of these eight rifles. Convoy the Princess Quivven to her father's palace."

"But am I not going with you?" she interrupted in surprise.

"I am afraid not, my dear," Myles sadly replied. "You have been a good little pal, and I hate to leave you, but you would be entirely out of place among the Cupians. Besides there is every chance of our perishing in crossing the boiling seas."

"Then you are going home?" she wailed. "You are planning to desert us in our extremity?"

"No," he answered, "I shall first fight the ant-men, and do all that I can to save Vairkingi. When I am done, you will be safer here than you would be with me."

But she sank to the ground by his side and buried her head on her arms, sobbing: "Myles, Myles, I love you. Can't you see that I loved you all this time? Oh, you are so blind. You *must* take me with you. Your Quivven. Your own little Golden Flame."

The earth-man sternly put her in the care of one of the guards, saying grimly: "This makes it more impossible for you to go with me, Quivven, for I have a wife and child in that other land across the seas. I am sorry, sorrier than I can say, that you have come to love me. Can't you see, Quivven, that this effectually seals the question? If it had not been for this, I might have yielded to your entreaties, but now it is impossible."

Then to the captain of the guards: "With these six rifles, march to the palace and join the forces of Theoph and Jud. I will endeavor to destroy as many of the beasts as possible before I finally leave you and depart for my own country. Start at once, leaving only two or three of your number to help us."

So the guard marched away, dragging a reproachful and tear-stained Quivven with them. Three leather-clad Vairkings remained, and these shortly were joined by a fourth. Cabot half consciously noticed this new arrival, but paid little attention in the bustle of his preparations.

The tapestries which were to serve in place of fire-worm fur to swathe himself and Doggo in their flight across the boiling seas were rearranged so as to take up less room. The goggles, which he had brought from the laboratory, were packed with them. The bombs and rifle ammunition were placed in handy positions. A small quantity of provisions were added. Everything was lashed down.

Then Myles drew Doggo to one side for a conference and wrote: "I plan first to attack those Formians and Roies who are besieging Theoph's palace; then to dispose of as many as possible of the scout planes. How many of these are there?"

"We had seven airships in our city in the south," wrote Doggo in reply. "This is one of them here. One is probably temporarily disabled by the shots which you fired in the laboratory yard. That should leave five."

"Can we fight five?"

"Most assuredly," Doggo wrote, agitating his antennae eagerly.

"Then let's go!" wrote Cabot.

With a quick take-off diagonally down the inclosure, the huge bombing plane rose slowly into the air amid shouts from the Vairking soldiers below. It was now broad daylight. Myles glanced over the rail, and noted that there were now only three leather-clad warriors. He vaguely wondered what had become of the fourth, but it was too late to inquire.

Up through the swirling sparks and smoke they rose, up, up, until they could get a bird's-eye view of the whole city of Vairkingi. There, on a slight eminence in the center, stood the palace and inclosures of the white-furred king, its walls manned by leather-clad Vairking warriors, surrounded by savage besiegers. The flames had not yet reached that part of the city, and with a change in the wind, appeared to be sweeping past it.

As Myles and Doggo circled the palace they noted that practically all the ant-men within sight were massing in a side street, evidently preparing for an assault. How convenient! Myles took the levers and swooped low, while Doggo deluged his fellow countrymen with bombs. When their sudden attack was over, fully half of the Formian menace to the city had been wiped out.

Now for the scout planes. These, five in number, could be seen circling the outskirts of the city. The two friends were able to approach one of these without being suspected of being an cncmy. Before its flyers realized the peril it had gone down in flames from one well-placed bomb.

The other four scout planes at once realized that their own countryman, Doggo, had returned to do them battle, and accordingly converged upon him. Again the two friends exchanged places. And then there took place one of the finest examples of aerial warfare which the earth-man had ever witnessed.

This was not like the battles with the whistling bees before the advent of Cabot-made rifles on the planet Poros, when the fighting tail of the plane was pitted against the sting of the bee. For now it was rifle against rifle, bomb against bomb.

One by one the enemy planes crashed to the ground, as Doggo spiraled, looped, tailspun, and side-slipped. At last there was only one Formian opponent left.

Doggo maneuvered to a position just above it, and Cabot reached for a bomb to give it the *coup de grâce*.

But the bombs were all gone! And the ant-men in the plane below were raising their rifles, watching for a good opening.

What was to be done? With Doggo's deafness to sound waves, it would be impossible to explain the situation to him in time for him to veer away. He naturally assumed that, as he maneuvered the ship into this position of advantage, Cabot would at once put an end to the fight.

In this extremity the earth-man suddenly thought of the obsolete fighting tail. Its levers were there. Was it still in operation? He would see.

Grasping its levers, he manipulated them swiftly, and drove the tip of the tail through the fuel tank of the enemy. Two bullets zipped by him. Then the machine below careened and soared to earth—or rather, Poros—followed by a stream of shots from the earth-man's rifle. The battle was over.

Cabot relieved Doggo at the controls, and circled the palace once more. His own squad of laboratory guards were just entering one of the palace gates. The captain waved to him. But he noted that Quivven was not among them. Poor girl! What could have become of the poor little golden creature?

But there was no time to ask. With so many of the ants killed, all their aircraft disabled and the Vairkings firmly entrenched in the palace and supplied with at least six ant-rifles, Quivven's people were in as good a position as possible.

For Cabot to stop now might mean not only renewed complications with the golden maid, but also possibly the confiscation of his plane by Jud. It would not pay to take any chances; he must hasten home to Lilla, leaving the ants, the Roies, and the Vairkings to contend for the possession of the burning city.

As he turned the nose of the airship upward and began the ascent preparatory to flying across the western mountains to the sea, he observed a large marching body of troops far to the south. These might change his responsibility with respect to his late hosts; it would only take a few minutes to investigate; so southward he turned the plane.

The marching troops were Roies, as he judged by their absence of leather armor. Swooping low he picked out the face of their leader. It was Otto the Bold, son of Grod the Silent, the leader of the friendly faction of the furry wild-men of the hills. Having captured and sacked the city of the ants, they were now evidently on their way to relieve Vairkingi.

The last feeling of obligation passed from the earth-man, as, waving to his savage friend, he turned the nose of his plane upward once more. Then it occurred to him that, having flown so far south, he might just as well take a final look at the ant-city. Besides, this would place him in exactly the location where the ant-men had landed when they flew east across the boiling seas from Cupia to found New Formia, and thus would be a good point for him to take off in his flight westward.

Accordingly, he turned to the right until he topped the mountain range, then turned to the left again, and followed the range southward.

But a tropical thunderstorm forced him to descend in a cleft of hills. Myles hoped that this rain extended to Vairkingi, and would serve to quench its fires.

After several hours, the weather cleared once more. The two companions compared notes on the adventures which had befallen them since their first hop-off that morning. Then they embarked once more, and continued their course southward. Soon they passed over the smoking ruins of the once-impregnable Sur, and at last came to the little radio hut of the Formians.

This, too, was in ruins; Otto had received his note. Wireless communication between Cupia, and Vairkingia and New Formia was at an end. Yuri would now believe the worst that Cabot had told him over the air. And that worst was likely to prove to be the truth after all.

Swinging to the westward, Myles passed over the deserted city of the ants, patrolled by a handful of Otto's Roies; and thence on and on until there loomed before him a solid wall of steam. It was the boiling sea, over which he must pass in order to rejoin his loved ones.

Hovering gently down on a little silver-green meadow about five miles inland, the two fugitives prepared for the trip. First they pulled off some of the tapestries to pad the fuel tank.

And there before them lay a figure in leather Vairking armor, a golden figure smiling up at them, little Quivven, whom they thought they had left behind.

"You!" Myles exclaimed, scowling.

"Yes," she replied. "I usually accomplish what I set out to do. When you sent me away, I persuaded one of the guards to lend me his suit. Then I returned, helped with the loading, and hid myself while you and Doggo were writing notes to each other. But I nearly died of fright when you were turning me over and over, up there in the sky."

Myles sighed resignedly. "I can't send you back now," he said, "though what I shall do with you in Cupia, the Builders only knows!"

So the three friends completed the preparations, and then sat down together for a meal.

It was too late to start their flight that day and, besides, a rest would do them all good; so they encamped for the remainder of the afternoon and the night.

The next morning, as the first faint flush of pink tinged the eastern sky, they took their farewell meal on Vairkingian soil. Then, swathed in tapestries and with goggles in place, they took their stations in the plane, and headed straight for the bank of steam.

As they passed within its clouds, all sight was blotted out.

They had decked the fusilage over like an Eskimo kayack, only Cabot's well-wrapped head protruding. Within, Doggo manipulated the levers and watched the altimeter and gyro-compass by the light of a Vairking stone lamp; strange mingling of modernity and archaism. Cabot's vigil was for the purpose of guarding against flying too high, and thus piercing the cloud envelope and exposing them to the fatal glare of the sun.

On and on they went. Cabot could see nothing. The hot vapor condensed on his wrappings, seeped through, and scalded his head and shoulders unbearably. Finally, he could stand it no longer. He pulled in his head and tore off the bandages. The relief was instantaneous. He seized the levers, and Doggo took his place at the opening.

But at last even Doggo succumbed. Having braved the heat too long, he collapsed weakly on the floor of the cockpit.

"It's my turn," Quivven shouted, above the noise of the motors. "Now aren't you glad you brought me along?"

And in spite of Cabot's remonstrances, she swathed her golden head and stuck it through the opening.

By this time, scalding water was leaking through all the covering of the cockpit. It was only a question of minutes before it would soak through the body-coverings of those within.

But just then the girl cried out, "Land. Land, once more; and clear silver sky."

Doggo revived and tore off the covers. True, the steam bank of the boiling seas lay behind them. Below them was the silver-green land.

What did it hold in store?

CHAPTER XX
THE WHOOMANGS

Thoroughly exhausted by their flight across the boiling seas, the Radio Man and his two strange companions—the huge ant-man, Doggo, and the beautiful, golden-furred Vairking maiden, Quivven—wished to land at once, without waiting to ascertain what particular section of Cupia lay beneath them. But the entire area below appeared to be thickly wooded.

Accordingly the fugitives hovered down to a short distance above the ground and then just skimmed the treetops at a slow rate of speed, keeping a careful watch for a landing place. They had not long to wait, for presently they espied a road running beneath the trees; and, after putting on more speed and following this road for a couple of stads, they finally came to a sufficiently large clearing a short distance from the road, to enable them to settle down quietly to the ground.

The party quickly disembarked upon the silver-green sward, and the three companions then broke through the bushes to the road, which proved to be of dirt, although well-traveled.

Myles remarked, "This must be some very out-of-the-way part of my country; for practically all of our roads are built of concrete,

a material similar to the cement with which I fastened the bricks together in making our furnaces in Vairkingi."

Quivven shuddered. "Please don't remind me of my poor city,"
she begged piteously; then in a more resigned tone: "But that is behind us. Let us forget it and face the future. You were speaking of
cement roads?"

"Yes," Myles replied. "The fact, that this road is not made of
concrete indicates that it is not a main highway, but the fact that it
is well-worn shows that it is traveled considerably. Let us therefore
wait for some passer-by who can tell us where we are."

At this point Doggo produced a pad and stylus, and wrote, "Let
me in on this."

Cabot obligingly transcribed, in Porovian short-hand, an account
of the conversation. Meanwhile the golden girl abstractedly examined the foliage beside the road.

While Doggo was reading the manuscript, Quivven called Cabot's
attention to the trees and shrubs. "How different they are from those
in Vairkingia," she remarked.

"That is to be expected," Myles answered, "for your land and
mine are separated by boiling seas across which no seeds or spores
could pass and live. Thus it is surprising that the two continents support even the same general classes of life. Come, I will point out to
you some of the more common forms of our flora."

He had in mind to show her the red-knobbed gray lichen-tree;
and the tartan bush, the heart-shaped leaves of which are put to so
many uses by the Cupians; and the saffra herb, the roots of which
are used for anaesthesia; and the blue and yellow dandelionlike wild
flowers. But although he searched for a hundred paces or so along the
road, he was unable to locate a single specimen of these very common bits of Porovian vegetation.

"It is strange," he muttered half to himself. "When I want to show
the common plants of Cupia, I find nothing but unfamiliar plants, and
yet I'll bet that if I were to go out in search of rare specimens for my
castle garden at Lake Luno, I should find nothing but tartan, saffra,
lichen-trees, and blue dandelions."

The mention of Luno Castle turned his thoughts homeward with
a jerk. Here he was at last, after many adventures, on the same continent with his Lilla and his baby Kew. He had come here to rescue
them, if it were not too late, from Yuri the usurper and his whistling

bees. Now that he was apparently within reach of his loved ones, he began to worry about their safety a great deal more than ever before.

But this fear *for* Lilla was completely out-weighed by a growing fear *of* Lilla. What would she say to his two allies? Doggo, the ant-man, was a representative of a race which Cabot had vowed to exterminate from the face of Poros; for, as he had repeatedly asserted, there can be no lasting peace on any continent, which is inhabited by more than one race of intelligent beings.

And Quivven, the golden-furred Vairking maiden, would be even more difficult to explain. She was beautiful, even by Cupian standards. She was more nearly the same race as Myles than was his own wife, Lilla. She and Myles could talk together, unheard by the radio-sense of Lilla. In these circumstances, it was hardly possible that the Princess Lilla would receive Quivven with open arms, or even be passably decent to her.

At this point, his reveries was interrupted by Doggo handing him the following note:

> If we are to await passers-by, do you not think it would be well to return to the plane and secure our rifles, so as to protect ourselves in case the passers-by should prove to be hostile?

Myles nodded his assent, and informed Quivven of their intentions. She, being nearer to the point where they had entered the road, plunged through the bushes at once, and they hastened after her.

Just as Myles and Doggo were breaking through the bushes in the wake of the golden one, they heard an agonized scream ahead. Redoubling their efforts, they reached the clearing in an instant, and beheld a most unexpected sight!

Perched upon the airship, like a flock of enormous vultures, were about a dozen huge, bat-winged, pale green reptiles, each with a wing-spread of fully ten-feet; and one of these loathsome creatures held the writhing form of Quivven tight in its claws.

Without a moment's thought for his own safety, the intrepid earth-man drew the Vairkingian sword which hung at his side, and rushed straight at the beast which held the girl. Doggo followed close behind, clicking his mandibles angrily.

But before they could reach the plane, the noisome flock flapped heavily into the air and disappeared over the trees to the northward, Quivven's childish face an agony of despair, and one little furry paw waving a forlorn farewell.

The next move was obvious. Myles and Doggo sprang to their places in the aircraft and soared after. It was an easy matter to overtake the clumsy-winged saurians, but not so easy to decide what to do after reaching them. The reptiles flew so close together their pursuers were afraid to fire on them for fear of hitting Quivven. The girl was as yet apparently unharmed, so the only thing to do seemed to be to follow and watch for some opportunity to effect a rescue.

Thus the chase continued for several stads without event. Myles was in an agony for the safety of his little friend, but even his deep concern did not keep his scientific mind from speculating about the pale green dragons which he was following. He had read about such beasts in books on paleontology as a child. These were undoubtedly pterodactyls.

He had seen somewhat similar stuffed specimens in the imperial museum at Kuana, capital of Cupia. He had encountered swarms of tiny pterosaurs, the size of sparrows, in the caves of Kar. But he had been informed by Cupian scientists that the larger species had long since become extinct on Poros.

Whence then these captors of Quivven?

While engaged thus in speculations, he flew a bit closer to the flock, whereat two of them suddenly turned and simultaneously attacked the plane from both sides. Doggo instantly dispatched *his* assailant with a rifle shot; but Myles did not dare let go of the control levers, as he was flying too close to the tree tops for safety as it was. Accordingly *his* assailant got a clawhold on the side of the fusilage, furled its wings and started to crawl in.

But the earth-man steered the machine high into the air, as his companion swung around and fired at the intruder, which promptly let go its hold, and, falling with a shriek of pain, crashed through the tree tops and disappeared from view.

Myles drew a deep breath of relief, and once more swooped down on the flock of pterosaurs. But this time he kept at a safe distance from them; and they, warned by the fate of their two comrades, did not attempt any further sallies at the plane.

So the pursuit continued. Occasionally, between the green wings, the two in the airship could catch a glimpse of the form of Quivven, held fast in the talons of her captor. She was still alive. She did not seem to be in pain. Once she waved feebly to her friends above. What would those beasts do with her?

The question was soon to be answered. But first it was to be succeeded by many other questions, for a large and prosperous looking
city loomed ahead. Its appearance was unfamiliar to Cabot. Strange,
he thought that he knew all the principal settlements of Cupia! Its
architecture was of an unknown type, not the pueblolike piles of ex-
aggerated toy building blocks affected by the Formians, nor the red-
tiled spires and minarets of the Cupians, but rather a style somewhat
resembling classical Greek or Roman.

The architecture was immaterial, however, compared with the
fact that this was a city of some sort, a city of a high degree of civilization. The beasts were apparently headed straight for it, and thus
there was every prospect of the inhabitants—presumably Cupians—
rescuing Quivven.

Suppose, however, it was a deserted city. Its unfamiliar style and
remote location suggested as much. Perhaps this was the long forgotten court of some Cupian Jamshyd, now kept by lion and lizard, or
rather by woofus and pterodactyl.

This was not so, however; for, as Cabot drew nearer, he could
clearly see that the buildings were in an excellent state of repair, with
not a crumbling ruin among them. No, this was an *inhabited* city, to
which the green dragons were bringing their prey. Could it be that the
Cupian inhabitants kept these creatures as pets, and that this fact was
unknown to the scientists at the Cupian metropolis?

Cabot's cogitations were again cut short by his arrival over the
city. The dragons made straight for an imposing centrally-located
domed edifice, which they entered by one of the upper windows. The
plane promptly dropped into a near-by plaza. Making a sign to the
ant-man to guard the ship, Myles seized a rifle and cartridges, and
rushed down a street which led toward the building which the green
beasts had entered.

On the way he met several pterosaurs, four or five four-legged
slate-colored reptiles ranging in size from that of a small dog to that
of a horse, one large snake about thirty feet in length, various sorts of
insects, and a few cat-like furry creatures; but not a single Cupian. If
these were the pets of the city, where were their masters?

The strange creatures did not offer to molest him. In fact, they
gave way to him with every indication of respect and not a little fear.
This seemed to indicate that they were all thoroughly domesticated,
so he made no effort to hurt them.

At last he arrived at the building which he sought. A wide incline led from the street up to its arched doorway. This smacked of Formia, for the ant-men before they were driven off the continent had used ramps everywhere instead of the flight of stairs employed by the Cupians.

Over the door was an inscription in unmistakable Porovian characters: "The Palace of the City of Yat."

This must be Cupia, or old Formia—now occupied by the Cupians—for this was the language of those two races. But then, he reflected, it had also been the *written* language of the Vairkings, far across the boiling seas.

Putting an end to his speculations, he rushed up the ramp and entered the building.

The splendidly arched and vaulted interior was crowded with the strangest assortment of animals the earth-man had ever set eyes upon. Picture to yourself Frank Buck's circus, the New York zoo, and the gr-ool of Kuana, all turned loose in one hall, and then you wouldn't imagine one-half of it; for very few of these assembled beasts bore the slightest resemblance to anything which you, or even Myles Cabot, had ever seen. He paused aghast and surveyed the assemblage. There was not a human or Cupian present, not even an ant-man!

At the farther side of the chamber, on a raised platform, there sat—or, rather, squatted—a gigantic pterosaur, whose wingspread must have been at least twenty feet from tip to tip. This beast, unlike those which had kidnapped Quivven, was pale slate-blue rather than green. His head was square, with a sharp crested beak, large circular lidless eyes, and earholes, but no ears.

Four legs he had, very much like those of a toad, except that the fifth finger of each hand, the finger which should have been the "little" finger, extended backward over his hips to a distance of about six feet, and served as the other supporting edge of his leathery wings, which now lay furled at his side.

In front of this creature stood Quivven the Golden Flame, guarded by two of the smaller pterodactyls, and seemingly unhurt and unafraid. None of the animals appeared to have noticed Cabot's entrance, so he decided to wait a few moments and size up the situation before doing anything rash.

As he watched the scene, a huge snake some thirty feet in length and at least half a yard in diameter squirmed on to the platform be-side the slate-colored dragon. This snake had two rudimentary legs and two small arms, none of which it used to help its progression; but in one hand it carried what appeared to be a sheet of paper, which it handed with a hiss to the dragon, who hissed in reply, and taking the paper appeared to read it.

This called the attention of the earth-man to the fact that each of the Alice-in-Wonderland animals about him was equipped with a pad and stylus. Occasionally one would scratch something on its pad, and then make two sharp clicks with its mouth, at which a small winged lizard would take the missive and fly with it to some other part of the chamber.

Standing very near Myles there was a small and particularly inof-fensive-looking furry animal somewhat resembling a beaver. In Cu-pia Myles would have assumed that it was some species of mathlab, except for its lack of antennae.

This looked like a good safe specimen to experiment upon, so he reached for its pad, which, to his great surprise, the creature promptly handed him without demur, together with its stylus.

Remembering the inscription above the arched doorway, Myles wrote in Porovian shorthand: "Most Excellent King—Myles Cabot, a weary sojourner, craves protection for himself and the golden one who now stands before you. We are from Cupia and Vairkingi re-spectively. What country is this?"

Then he folded the paper and clicked twice with his tongue against the roof of his mouth. Instantly a fluttering messenger was at his side. Indicating the platform with a gesture, he handed the note to the little winged reptile, who flew away with it. Myles passed the pad and stylus back to the furry creature from whom he had borrowed it, and then watched the great dragon to whom he had written.

This beast received and read the note, while the messenger hov-ered nigh. Then, steadying a pad against the floor with one front claw, he wrote on it with a stylus held in the other. What he had written he showed to the snake which lay coiled beside him, and upon obtaining a hiss of approval, folded the note and gave it to the little bat, who flew back with it to Myles.

On the paper, written in unmistakable Porovian characters, were the words: "Welcome to Yat, Myles Cabot. You and your mate are our guests. We know of no country of either Cupia or Vairkingi. This is the land of the Whoomangs, and I am Boomalayla, their king. You have permission to approach the throne."

So *that* explained the strange plants, the dirt roads, the unfamiliar architecture, and the absence of Cupians and Vairkings! This must be a *third* continent intermediate between the other two. Well, the plane was intact, and King Boomalayla had assured him that they were guests, so that it was just as well that they had landed on this Azores of the boiling seas. Reassured, the earth-man made his way through the strange throng to the foot of the throne where he bowed low before the hideous reptile monarch.

Little Quivven, with a cry of glad surprise, rushed over to him and nestled confidingly by his side. Placing one arm protectingly around her, he boldly confronted the winged king.

This beast, after some penciled conversation with his serpent adviser, handed Myles a note reading as follows: "Our nation was founded many years ago by a creature closely resembling yourself. Therefore you are an honored guest among us. We have long awaited this day. It is true that you have killed the bodies of two of my subjects, and thereby subjected their souls to a premature birth. The penalty for this would ordinarily be to have a similar death imposed upon your own body. But because of your resemblance to our great originator, Namllup, I shall spare your body. Furthermore, I fear that, like him, you may perhaps have no soul, although this deficiency can easily be supplied."

Myles read the note and handed it to Quivven, then pointed to the writing materials of the saurian. Instantly two of the tiny winged messengers brought him a pad and stylus.

Thus supplied, he asked the king: "Great ruler, does your offer of protection include my wings and the black creature who guards them in the public square outside?"

"And how about little me?" asked Quivven, reading over his shoulder.

"He has already pledged his friendship to both of us," replied Myles, handing the note to one of the tiny pterosaurs.

Back came the answer from the king: "You and yours shall all be protected. I will now send guards to relieve your guard at the wings, and to summon him into my presence."

But the earth-man held up one hand in a gesture of protest, and hurriedly wrote: "Better not, your majesty, unless you wish a fight. I will send a note, explaining all. You can then follow it in a few paraparths with your detachment of guards."

To this proposal the huge saurian assented, so Myles dispatched to Doggo by one of the tiny pterosaurs a long written explanation of the situation. A few minutes later, under orders from the reptile king, the flock of green pterodactyls who had been the original captors of Quivven departed with much leathery flapping through one of the windows overhead, and presently one of them returned on foot with Doggo.

"What kind of a gr-ool is this we have got into?" were the ant-man's first words, as Cabot handed him the pad and stylus.

"The Great Builder only knows," his friend replied. "Anyhow they claim to possess souls, and have offered us protection."

Doggo looked skeptical. Just then a messenger flitted over with a note from Boomalayla, reading: "The session is at an end. You will please follow me to the royal apartments for a conference."

The king clicked sharply. Instantly all was silence in the huge hall. Solemnly the king clicked three times. In unison the assembled Whoomangs clicked back a triple answer. Then all was bustle and confusion as those without wings crowded through the doors and those with wings departed through the windows in the dome above.

Boomalayla and his snake adviser, and the three travelers from Vairkingi were the only persons—if you can call them all "persons"—left in the vaulted chamber. Whereupon the snake, gliding ahead, led the way to an anteroom, gorgeously jeweled and draped. There the five reclined on soft tapestries, attended by a swarm of little messengers and engaged in the following written conversation. Due to the speed of Porovian shorthand, the "talk" progressed practically as rapidly as if it had been spoken, although Doggo was somewhat handicapped by not having a stylus which was properly adapted to his claw.

"Who are your companions?" the king asked.

So Myles introduced Quivven the Vairking maiden, and Doggo the Formian. Boomalayla explained that the snake was Queekle Mukki, prime minister of the Whoomangs, and wise beyond all his countrymen.

"His soul is brother to my soul, although our bodies are unrelated," the king wrote.

Myles was much perplexed. "How is it," he inquired, "that such diversified animals as you Whoomangs are able to live at peace with each other?"

"It was not so before the days of Namllup," the huge pterosaur replied, "but he gave us souls and made us one people. Our bodies may be unrelated, but our souls are the same. You and your two companions are as unalike as any of us; perhaps the three of *you* have a common type of soul."

Myles was even more perplexed. "Who was Namllup?" he asked. "And what means all this talk of souls?"

CHAPTER XXI
SOULS?

In reply to Cabot's question, the huge winged saurian, Boomalayla, King of the Whoomangs, wrote the following reply, "All that I am about to tell you of the traditional beginning of our race is shrouded in the mists of antiquity. The legend is as follows:

"Many hundreds of years ago this fertile continent was inhabited by warring beasts of every conceivable size and form; and they were but brute creatures, for they had no souls. Souls existed, it is true, but inasmuch as they inhabited no bodies, they had no learning, experience, or background. They were of but little use to themselves, each other, or the planet.

"Then one day there was born out of the ground a creature much like yourself. His name was Namllup. He it was who discovered how to introduce souls into bodies by making a slight incision at the base of the brain and inserting there a young soul.

"First he captured some very tame wild creatures and gave them souls. With their aid he captured others, more fierce, and so on, until there was hardly a beast left soulless on this continent. Thus did he make of one race all the creatures of Poros to dwell together on the face of the continent. This industry we have kept up to this day.

"It is reported, however, that Namllup himself had no soul. There was no scar at the back of his head, and no soul issued from his body after death. Others he gave soul to, himself he could not. This is the general belief."

All this was as clear as mud to Myles Cabot. He could not make head nor tail out of it. Boomalayla appeared to be talking in riddles, or allegories.

Nevertheless, Myles determined to try and make a beginning

somewhere in order to understand what this mass of verbiage was all about, so he wrote, "How can you tell? Surely you cannot *see* souls!"

"Surely we *can*," the reptile king replied, "for souls are creatures just as real as we are, and have an independent existence from the day they hatch until they are inserted in the brain of somebody. From the way you talk, I cannot believe that *you* have any soul."

"Of course I have," Myles remonstrated.

"Prove it to me," Boomalayla demanded. "Let me see the back of your head."

Myles complied.

"No," the winged king continued, "you have no soul. There is no scar."

This conversation was irritating in the extreme. It led nowhere. Quivven and Doggo read all the correspondence, and were equally perplexed.

The huge pterosaur continued writing. "I can see that you do not believe me," he wrote.

"This is not to be wondered at, since you yourself are soulless. Though I cannot understand how a beast like you, without a soul, can be as intelligent as you seem to be. Come to our temple, and I will show you souls."

So saying, Boomalayla, accompanied by Queekle Mukki, the serpent, led Cabot and his two companions out of the buildings and through the streets of the city to another edifice, which they entered.

What a travesty on the lost religion of Cupia!

Within the temple there moved about a score or more of assorted beasts—pterodactyls, reptiles, huge insects, furry creatures, and so forth—bearing absolutely no resemblance to each other except the fact that each and every one of them wore a long robe emblazoned with a crimson triangle and swastika, emblem of the true religion of Poros.

Among them was one enormous slate-colored pterosaur, almost the exact counterpart of Boomalayla, the king, who introduced this beast to his guests by means of the following note: "This is the chief priest of the true religion. She is my mate. But come, let me show you some souls."

The chief priest then led the party into an adjoining room, the walls of which were lined with tiny cages, most of which contained pairs of moths.

The dragon king explained as follows: "When a Whoomang dies, his body is brought to the temple and is watched day and night by a priest, net in hand, to catch the soul when it emerges."

What it had to do with *souls* Cabot couldn't see for the life of him. Neither could Quivven nor Doggo.

Having made a complete tour of inspection the party then returned to the palace, where they discussed the glories of Vairkingi and Cupia with the king and Queekle Mukki, and then dined on cereal cakes and a flesh resembling fish.

"Be not afraid to eat this," Boomalayla urged. "It is fresh flesh. We breed these water reptiles especially for food."

After the meal the three travelers were assigned rooms in the palace.

At Cabot's request, tapestries were brought from the plane, and the party severally retired for the night.

The next morning they were up early, and assembled in Cabot's room. The night had proved uneventful, but Doggo wrote in great excitement that he had talked with the green guards, who had refused to disclose the whereabouts of the plane, and had said that this was the king's order.

Immediately after breakfast, which consisted of cakes and sweetened water, they requested an audience with the king—and, when it was granted, demanded news of the plane. But Boomalayla waved them off with an evasive answer.

"Tarry but a day or so," he wrote, "and then your wings shall be returned to you, and you shall be permitted to depart. I promise it, on the word of honor of a king."

So there was nothing but to wait, for it would not do to antagonize this powerful beast, and thus perhaps lose forever the chance to return which he had promised them.

The day was spent in a personally-conducted tour of the city, with Boomalayla as a most courteous and attentive guide and host. The Whoomangs appeared to be a highly cultivated race, if you can call them a "race"—a "congeries" would perhaps be the most accurate term. Objects of all the arts abounded, and the tour would have been most pleasurable if the three travelers had not been so anxious to be on their way once more to Cupia.

The night was spent as before, uneventfully, but the next day Doggo was missing. In reply to all inquiries, the Whoomangs returned evasive answers.

"He is gone on business of his own," was all they would say.

This day Queekle Mukki, the serpent, was their host and guide. He used every effort to outdo Boomalayla in courtesy, but his two guests were strangely uneasy. Some impending calamity seemed to hang over them.

Late that evening, when they were in their quarters, Doggo rushed in bristling with excitement. He had something to tell them, and wanted to tell it quickly, but had mislaid his pad and stylus. Strange to relate, Cabot could not find his own writing materials either. Quivven finally found her stylus but no pad.

Seizing the lead-tipped stick, Doggo scratched on the pavement of the room, "Quick, give me paper! Quick! Your lives depend upon it! Quick, before it is too late!"

Cabot rushed into the hall and clicked twice with his tongue against the roof of his mouth, but nothing happened. Again and again he repeated the call, until finally one of the little winged messengers flitted into sight. To him the earth-man indicated his wants by going through the motions of writing with the index finger of his right hand upon the palm of his left. The little creature flitted away, and after what seemed an interminable wait returned with pad and stylus.

Myles snatched them and rushed back to Doggo. "What is the matter?" he wrote.

But Doggo replied, "Nothing. It was just a joke, to frighten you. We are all perfectly safe here, and Boomalayla has a wonderful plan to facilitate our departure three days from now."

It was not like Doggo, or any other member of the serious minded race of ant-men, to play a practical joke like this. Myles could swear that his friend had been genuinely agitated a few moments ago. What could have happened in the meantime to change him?

The earth-man looked at the Formian steadily through narrowed lids. His friend appeared to act strangely. Could this, in truth, be Doggo?

If they had been on any other continent Myles would have sworn that some other ant-man, closely resembling his friend, was attempting an impersonation, but that could not be the case here, for Doggo was certainly the only Formian on this continent.

It was Doggo's body, all right, yet it did not act or look like Doggo.

Even Quivven noticed that something was wrong. Nervously she said good night, and Cabot followed shortly after.

Instead of retiring he went to Quivven's room, where the two puzzled together for some time, trying to guess what had come over their friend. What at last they parted for the night the mystery was no nearer solution than before. In fact, they had practically made up their minds that no mystery existed, after all; and that the strange surroundings, and strange events, and strange talk of souls, had merely cast an aura of strangeness even over their friend.

The next morning Doggo was on hand bright and early, but this time it was Quivven who was missing.

"My turn next," thought Myles, "and then perhaps I shall find out what it is all about."

As before, the Whoomangs were evasive as to the whereabouts of the golden one, and even Doggo was singularly unresponsive and devoid of ideas on the subject.

This day the she-dragon high-priestess was their guide, but although she outdid both Boomalayla and Queekle Mukki, Cabot fretted, and worried, and merely put on an external show of interest.

Late that afternoon—the fourth—of their stay among the Whoomangs—as soon as the tour was over, Cabot left Doggo and withdrew to his own room.

Where was Quivven all this time, he wondered.

His question was answered by the Golden Flame herself bursting into the room full of excitement.

"Thank the Builder I can talk to you with my mouth, and do not have to wait for pencil and paper," she exclaimed. "The Whoomangs overlooked our powers of vocal speech when they hid our writing materials as before."

It was true; their pads and styluses had miraculously disappeared again.

"Where have you been?" Cabot asked, somewhat testily. "I suppose that in a few moments you will say that all *your* excitement has been a mere practical joke on me, the same as Doggo's was."

"Yes," she replied seriously. "I shall—undoubtedly. And therefore listen while there is yet time—while I am still Quivven."

"What do you mean?" Myles exclaimed, staring at her.

"This," she said. "In a few moments I shall be Whoomang."

He started to interrupt, but she stopped him with a peremptory gesture, and continued; "Know, then, the secret of all this talk of souls. The grubs which they breed from their moths are strong personalities, potential devils, needing only a highly-developed body in order to become devils incarnate. Namllup, whoever he was, discovered this, ages ago.

"By a simple operation, the Whoomangs can insert one of these larvae at the base of a creature's brain, where in a few hours the personality of the larva overcomes the proper personality of the creature, and henceforth rules the creature until the creature dies. The larva then flutters free, a moth, to propagate other devil-souls for this nefarious usage.

"Yesterday these fiends operated upon Doggo. For a time, his own soul and this brain-maggot struggled for supremacy. While his own personality remained ascendant, and yet had imbibed sufficient knowledge to understand the situation, he tried to warn us of our danger. Would that he had been in time! But when the pad of paper had arrived, dear old Doggo was dead. His body had become a Whoomang, dominated by one of their moth-grubs, 'souls' as they call them.

"This afternoon they operated on me!"

Myles shuddered, but Quivven went relentlessly on: "Two personalities are now contending within me for mastery. There can be but one outcome. Quivven must die, and her brain and body must become the vehicle for the thoughts and schemes of an alien mind. My will is strong. At present it is in control. But any moment now, it may snap. So I adjure you, by the Great Builder and your loved ones, refuse stonily and absolutely to listen to any denial which my mouth may give you.

"Now, while there is yet time, I must tell you their plans. Boomalayla sighs for more worlds to conquer. He was captivated by your tales of your country. To-morrow he will operate on you. Then, when the bodies of you and Doggo and I are all Whoomangs, and yet retain a certain amount of our own knowledge and skill, he plans to send us on to Cupia with a plane-load of moths, to operate on your countrymen, and build up a second empire of Whoomangs there."

Myles gasped at the dastardliness of the plan, a plan which might yet succeed; for, even if he escaped, Doggo's body might still carry the plan into execution.

"Where is our plane?" he asked.

"Yes," Quivven sadly replied, "I must lead you to the plane, while I am yet me. Come quickly."

"But can we leave Doggo?"

"Yes," she replied. "Not only must you leave Doggo, but you must leave me, too; for Doggo is no longer Doggo, and I shall not be Quivven in a few minutes from now, for I feel the Whoomang-soul struggling for ascendency within me. Come!"

Quickly she led him out of the room, and down several hallways to a courtyard of the palace, where stood the plane, guarded by a green dragon. This beast interposed no objection to their approach. Quivven smiled wanly.

"He will not stop you," she said, "for already they regard me as one of them, and count on me to inveigle you. And now, Myles, good-by. I feel myself slipping. In a minute or two your Quivven will be no more. Whether my own soul will then go to the happy land, as though I had normally died, or whether it will simply be blotted out, I know not; but one thing I *do* know, and that is that I love you with all my heart."

She flung her arms around his neck and kissed him.

Then suddenly she cried, "I've won! I made you love me. It was all a scheme, cooked up by Doggo and myself to trap you out of your complacency and force you to admit your love. The story of the moth-grubs souls is a lie, woven out of the weird philosophizing of Boomalayla. From now on, I know that you love me. From now on, I am confident that I can compete with that Lilla of yours."

He stood aghast. Could this be so? He was half inclined to believe. Then he remembered her words: "*Refuse stonily and absolutely to listen to any denial which my mouth may give you.*" Also he reflected that Doggo certainly would never have been a party to a trick to betray Lilla.

So he thrust the golden maid to one side, and strode toward the plane.

But she rushed after him and clung to him, wailing piteously, "Myles, Myles, surely you aren't going to desert us just because of this trick which we played on you. Surely you don't intend to leave us to the mercy of these terrible beasts."

He did not know what to believe. There was a possibility that her story about the souls was the truth. If so, then the safety of the whole continent of Cupia was at stake. And yet, if not, what an awful country to leave her and Doggo in!

He vaulted into the plane, then stood irresolute at the levers. He looked intently at the golden maid, who clung to the side of the car. There was something strange about her face, something clearly un-Quivven. And yet, as he gazed, he became certain that it was Quivven after all. And he was right.

"Myles," she shouted, letting go the plane, "Quick! By the grace of the Builder, my own spirit is again in the ascendency for an instant. The story I told you is true! Flee, before it is too late." Then suddenly she changed again and shouted to the guardian pterosaur, "Quick, stop him!"

Her expression altered as she spoke, but Myles slammed on the power, and the machine rose quickly, leaving behind the frantic golden form of little Quivven.

After him trailed a swarm of winged creatures of all sorts, but his fast airship soon outdistanced them as it sped due west toward a sky that had already begun to turn pink with the unseen setting sun. On and on he sped until his pursuers dropped from view. Then he turned northward to throw them off the trail; and then, after a while, due west again, until, as night was about to fall, the steam-bank of the boiling sea loomed ahead.

Whereupon he landed. He must wait until morning before attempting the passage. But as he prepared to spend the night he noticed that all the tapestries were gone from the cockpit.

How could he brave the steam clouds without wrappings of some sort? And was he certain, after all, that he was not leaving two perfectly good friends in the lurch?

CHAPTER XXII
FLIGHT

There must be *something* in the airship in which he could swathe himself for the trip across the boiling seas. With this in view he made a frantic search of the entire cockpit. Doggo's rifle and the ammunition were still there, but his own he had left in his room on his hurried departure. Here, too, was the little stone lamp, by the light of which they had watched their instruments beneath the kayack covering. Even some of their provisions were left.

Finally he came upon some boxes which he did not recognize.

A rank smell became evident upon closer examination. Gingerly he opened one of those boxes.

It contained flesh, finely ground and putrid. And in this carrion there wriggled and swarmed scores of small white grubs! The last of Cabot's doubts vanished. These were the devil-souls which he and Doggo and Quivven had been expected to carry to Cupia, to found there a new empire of Whoomangs. Evidently his hosts had expected some possible trouble from him, and therefore had prepared the plane for a quick get-away by Doggo and Quivven.

Indignantly the lonely earth-man emptied out box after box onto the ground, and mashed the contents into the dirt with his sandaled feet.

By this time it was nearly pitch dark, but of course, this would make no difference while flying through steam clouds, for visibility under such circumstances would be impossible even in daylight. If he only had some covering for the cockpit to keep out the steam, he could fly just as well at night as by day, except for one danger; how could he be warned of flying too high, passing through the circum-ambient cloud envelope, and being shriveled to a crisp by the close proximity of the sun.

In despair the earth-man sat beside his beached airship, as the velvet blackness crept out of the east and enveloped the planet. So near, and yet so far! He had successfully transmitted himself through millions of miles of space from the earth to Poros. He had escaped the clutches of the Formians and the Roies.

He had built a complete radio set out of nothing, and had talked with Cupia across the boiling seas. He had traversed those seas once without accident. He had eluded the machinations of the Whoomangs, with their moth grub "souls". And yet here he was, with only a few miles of ocean separating him from his loved ones, and, nevertheless, blocked effectually by the lack of a few yards of cloth. What fate!

As the last purple flush died on the western horizon, Myles suddenly jumped to his feet, and laughed aloud. The solution was so obvious that it had completely escaped him until now. It was the setting sun that had suggested the escape from his dilemma.

There is no sun at night!

Of course not!

Therefore why not soar straight up, pierce the cloud envelope and fly above it to Cupia, letting the clouds protect him from the heat of the boiling seas, as they normally protect the planet from the light and heat of the sun? At any rate, it was worth trying. To remain where he was would mean either eventual starvation, or recapture by the terrible Whoomangs.

So, by the light of his little Vairking stone lamp, he made a hasty lunch from his few remaining provisions, and then took his stand at the levers for a new experiment in Porovian navigation.

Up, up, he shot through the dense blackness, up to a height which in earth would have filled his blood with air bubbles, and have suffocated his lungs. But on Poros, with its thicker atmospheric shell and its lesser gravity, the change was not so evident.

Far to the eastward he saw the lights of Yat, the city of the beasts; but this was his only landmark. There was nothing but his gyro-compass to tell him exactly which was north, and south, and east, and west; nothing but his clinometer to indicate whether he was going up or down; nothing but his altimeter to indicate his approximate height above the surface of the planet. And these instruments he must read by the flickering light of a primitive open wick stone lamp on the floor of the cockpit.

What if this faint illuminator should become extinguished? He certainly could not leave the controls for long enough to use flint and steel to rekindle it.

During the early part of his stay in Vairkingi he had always gone to some one of the constantly burning lamps which were the primitive fire source of the furry Vairkings. Later he had found several pieces of flint, when investigating a small chalk deposit as a possible alternative for limestone in his smelting operations. After the manufacture of steel had begun he had practiced striking a light in this more modern method, and thereafter had always carried flint and steel and tinder with him in one of the pouch pockets of his leather tunic. It was with these crude implements that he had kindled his oil lamp for the present flight.

But this fire source would avail him little if a gust of wind should extinguish his primitive lamp. In such event, what could he do?

This question was immediately put to the test, for his ship struck a small air pocket and dipped. Out went the light! Now he could no longer read his compass nor his altimeter, but—happy thought—he could determine the inclination of the plane from time to time by *touching* his clinometer. So, on upward he kept.

Presently he found it difficult to breath, and this difficulty was soon increased by a damp fog, which choked his nostrils and windpipe, causing him to cough and sneeze. The water condensed on the airship, and dropped off the rigging onto the matted hair and beard of the earth-man. Yet still he kept on up.

Finally he breathed clear air once more. He pushed back the dripping locks from his forehead, and wiped out his water-filled eyes with the back of one wrist. All was still jet darkness, yet in front of him and above him there glowed some tiny points of light. Rubbing his eyes, he looked again. Stars! The first stars he had ever seen on Poros—a sky full of stars!

With some surprise Myles Cabot noted that above him were swung the same constellations with which he had been familiar on earth, among them the two dippers, Orion and Cassiopea.

He strove to recall the inclination of the axis of Venus to the ecliptic, but all that he could remember was that it did not differ appreciably from that of the earth. This information was enough for his present purposes, however, for it meant that the star which we call the pole star on earth was approximately north on Poros, and that its altitude above the northern horizon would give approximately the latitude of the location of the observer.

The pole star, which he readily identified by means of the two pointers of the great dipper, now hung about twenty degrees above the horizon, thus showing that Cabot was opposite the southern tip of that part of the continent of Cupia which formerly was Formia; so he leveled out the plane and, turning its nose northwest by the stars, scudded along above the cloud envelope of the planet.

It was not long before he noticed a quite appreciable increase of temperature. Gusts and swirls of hot vapor assailed him from below; so that if it had not been for the gyroscopic steadying apparatus, he must surely have foundered. Even as it was, it took all his efforts to control the ship. He suffered fearfully from the heat, but it was not absolutely unbearable.

Navigation so compelled his entire attention that he lost all track of time; he struggled on as in a dream, and had not the slightest idea whether he had been flying for hours or only for minutes.

On and on he drove through the terrific heat until at last he got so used to it that it actually seemed cooler. By Jove, he could almost believe that the air really was cooler!

So cautiously he tipped the nose of the plane downward, and entered the clouds below him. Feeling his way at a low rate of speed, and ever ready to slam on the full force of his trophil engines and shoot upward once more, he gradually penetrated the cloud envelope which surrounds the planet. Yet the heat did not increase.

At last he was through. And below him twinkled lights, the lights of a small city or town. Throwing the plane level once more, he hovered down in true Porovian fashion.

The light of the town showed closer. Cabot's heart beat fast, there was a lump in his throat, and his hands trembled at the controls. Was this Cupia, his own kingdom of Cupia at last? Was he home?

Or—and his heart sank within him—was this some still new continent, with other nightmare beasts, and horrible adventures?

Whichever it was, he ought not to land too near the town. His trophil-motor was making a loud racket, but he was not afraid of being heard, for Cupians have no ears, and their antennae can receive only radio waves. So he skimmed low over the houses, straining his eyes to try and make out their style of architecture. But it was no use; the jet blackness of Porovian night obscured all below. Accordingly he planned to land about half a stad from the village, and then reconnoiter at daybreak.

This was to be accomplished as follows. His distance from the ground he could gauge from the lights of the houses. Therefore he would hold his craft as nearly as possible level, and hover softly down, taking a chance of landing on some bush or tree.

The plan worked to perfection. After just about the expected drop, he felt the skids grate on solid ground. Land once more, after his sensational flight above the clouds! Exhausted and relaxed, he shut off his motor, and proceeded to crawl over the edge of the cockpit.

Of course he could not even see his own machine in the intense darkness. As he started to clamber out the plane suddenly tilted a bit under his weight, then gave a lurch, and slid out from under him, dislodging him as it did so.

He struck the ground, but it crumbled beneath him, and he felt himself slipping and sliding down a steep gravel bank until finally some sort of a projection stopped his descent. To this projection he frantically clung. During his slide he had heard the loud splash of the airplane below him, so he knew that there was water there.

As he hung to the projection on the side of the steep sand bank, he looked about him in the jet black night; and, as he looked, he noticed the edge of the bank above him, just showing against the sky. The edge became more and more distinct. The sky above turned to slate, then purple, then red, then pink, then silver. Day had come once more.

Cabot found himself clinging to a sharp spur of rock which stuck out from the bank. So he hauled himself into a comfortable position upon it and stared around at his surroundings.

His location was halfway down the precipitous side of a crater-like hole about a quarter of a stad in diameter and three parastads deep, the banks of which were of coarse black sand. At the bottom a clear pool of water reflected the silver sky. There was no sign of either his rifle, his cartridge belt, or his plane. He possessed nothing save his leather tunic, his wooden Vairking sword, a steel sheath knife which he had made in his foundries at Vairkingi, and the contents of his pockets.

Even his leather helmet was gone. He espied it, floating like a little boat, far out upon the pond; but even as he looked, some denizen of the deep snapped at it, and it disappeared beneath the surface. This was a forewarning of what might happen to Myles if he should have the misfortune to slip into the pool below.

Well, he must risk it in an attempt to get out, for even a sudden death beneath the waters was preferable to starvation on a rocky perch. So, carefully and laboriously, he attempted the ascent. Many times he slipped back, losing nearly all that he had gained; but fortunately the bank was rather firm in spots and was dotted with large jagged rocks which afforded a good handhold, so that eventually Myles reached the top.

Here he found a flat plateau, flanked by a continuous hedge of bushes about thirty paces from the edge. These bushes were too high to see over, and grew so thickly together that Myles was unable to penetrate them. Round and round the top of the pit he walked, repeatedly trying to force his way out, but with no success.

The day wore on. Myles became tired, and hungry, and thirsty, and disgusted. By placing a small pebble in his mouth, he relieved the thirst for awhile, but this had no effect on his other symptoms. Finally even his thirst returned.

The thirst was aggravated by the presence, almost at his feet, of the clear pool of water within the pit. He almost decided to slide down and try it, until he remembered what had happened to his leather hat.

So instead he began systematically to hack at the bushes with his knife and tear them up by the roots at one given spot. At the end of an hour he had progressed only about a yard, so he gave this up, too. He sat down, wrapped his arms around his knees, gazed at the silver sky, and thought of nothing for a while.

Then he thought of Lilla and the Baby Kew. Here he was, presumably in Cupia, perhaps within a few stads of them; and yet what good did it do him?

It seemed to him as though the nearer he got to his loved ones, the more effectually he was separated from them. On the Farley farm, in Edgartown, Massachusetts, when he had received the S O S message from the skies, it had appeared but a simple matter to step within the coordinate axes of his matter-transmitting apparatus, and throw a lever, in order to materialize on Poros.

In Vairkingi there had been the more difficult task of securing an ant plane, before essaying to cross the boiling seas. In the land of the Whoomangs, he had been confronted with the almost insuperable lack of swathing materials for such a flight. And now, in Cupia at last, he was hemmed in by an impenetrable wall of trees.

Yet, he reflected, he had surmounted in turn each of these successively more difficult difficulties; so why not this? With renewed determination he arose, and resumed his grubbing operations. Another hour passed and another yard of path had been completed. This was encouraging, and yet he had no means of knowing how much farther there still remained for him to go.

As he paused for breath, he heard a crashing noise almost directly across the pit. Concealing himself as well as he could in the recess which he had formed in the bushes, he watched expectantly. Presently the thick growth on the other side parted neatly, and the sharp edge of a wedge appeared. This wedge continued to divide the bushes until finally it came completely through. All curiosity to see what was pushing the wedge, Myles craned forward, but there was *nothing* behind it; it had been pushing itself.

As the bushes slowly closed together again, the wedge stood up on six sturdy legs and trotted around the top of the pit, until it came to a stop directly opposite the hiding place of the earth-man. This gave him a good opportunity to observe it.

Apparently it was some sort of insect. Its head came to a sharp cutting edge in the front about five feet high; and lateral projections extended diagonally backward from the edge, like the wings on a snow-plow, to a point well beyond the rear end of the animal.

These two sides were covered with stiff backward-pointing bristles, which evidently served to catch on the bushes through which the creature passed, and thus to hold whatever gains it made. Its eyes, like those of a crab, were located on long jointed arms, which it could raise whenever it wanted to look around. The lower edge of the sides of the wedge were serrated, and Myles soon learned what this was for. After wiggling its eyes about for a while, the creature walked to the edge of the bank, thus giving the watcher a good view of the body and legs within the projecting wedge, and slid off into the pit, where a splashing sound indicated that it was probably drinking.

Soon it reappeared over the top of the pit. Evidently the saw teeth on its sides were to hold its progress up the face of the sand bank in much the same way as its spines held its progress through the bushes.

The wedge insect, upon topping the bank, made a beeline for the edge of the clearing, thrust its nose between two saplings, furled its eyes, braced it feet against the ground, and started forcing its way through. Quick as a flash, Myles Cabot darted from his hiding place and followed.

The creature, rolling its eyes to the rear, saw him and tried to back out; for what purpose he could not tell, but probably either to attack him or at least to prevent him from attacking its vulnerable body. But it was already in too far, and its spines held it securely.

It tried to kick at him, whereat he followed not quite so close. Then it stubbornly stopped moving, pulled in its eyes and its legs and lay down within its projecting head-piece, whereat he gave it a prick in the tail with his Vairking sword. The effect was immediate and sudden. The creature leaped to its feet and tore its way through the trees like a cyclone, plunging high in air like a frantic horse. This left such an erratic and only partially spread path that the earth-man had difficulty in following, and soon fell far behind.

But just as he was about to despair, the branches which he parted ahead of him revealed a meadow of silver-green sward. He had reached the end of the wood.

Beyond the field was a grove of gray-branched lichen trees, through which he could see the steep red-tiled roofs of a village. Just short of the grove there grazed a herd of those pale-green aphids, the size of sheep, which the Cupians call "anks," and which Myles was wont to call "green cows." Close by his right hand was a large shrub with heart-shaped leaves, unmistakably a tartan bush.

Steep red roofs, gray lichen trees, anks and tartans! This must be Cupia! He was home!

Myles quoted aloud:

> *"Breathes there a man with soul so dead*
> *Who never to himself has said*
> *'This is my own, my native land'?"*

Cupia might not be his *native* land, but it was his *own*, the land of his wife and child, the land of which his son was rightful king, the land whose armies he had twice led to victory. And now he had returned to lead them yet again.

Drawing a deep breath of Cupian air into his lungs, Myles raced across the meadow to the shelter of the grove of trees. From that point of vantage he inspected the village. The architecture was undoubtedly Cupian. In fact, its character was so clear he was even able to judge by it just what part of Cupia he was in, for this architecture was typical of the southeastern foothills of the Okarze Mountains, a thousand stads or so north of Kuana, the capital city.

These foothills held, among other spots of interest, Lake Luno, on an island of which he and Lilla had built their country home. And the inhabitants of these mountains had always been intensely loyal to the earth-man, his golden-haired wife, and royal son.

On the outskirts of the village Cabot could see figures moving— figures in white togas with colored edges, figures with tiny vestigial wings projecting from their backs, figures with butterflylike antennae rising from their foreheads. These were Cupians, his own adopted countrymen.

Yet they never would recognize him in his present condition, with shaggy hair, massive beard, and leather tunic, and without the artificial wings and antennae which he had been accustomed to wear among them. Therefore he could not yet reveal himself. He must first restore his appearance to normal and also find and put on one of the small portable radio sets which he had contrived years ago in his laboratories of Mooni, in order to talk with these folk who have neither ears nor voice.

So, turning his back on the alluring village, he made a meal of the green milk of the grazing anks, and then set out to circle the settlement and find a road.

When he did reach the road he recognized it. And now he knew exactly what village that was. For the moment he could not recall its name; but he knew it to be a little town which he and Lilla had often visited, scarcely twenty stads from Luno Castle.

As he strode on toward Luno Castle, his thoughts raced ahead of him, sometimes picturing a happy homecoming with Lilla and Baby Kew standing in the great arched doorway to greet him, and sometimes desolation and destruction with Prince Yuri, the murderer of the baby king, and the kidnaper of Princess Lilla.

What would Myles Cabot find on the beautiful island in Lake Luno?

CHAPTER XXIII
LUNO AND BEYOND

With no weapons except a steel knife and wooden rapier, the unkempt and bearded earth-man set out resolutely along the twenty-stad road which led to Lake Luno. All the rest of the afternoon he tramped along, avoiding the towns, and taking cover whenever a kerkool approached.

Night fell—the velvet, fragrant, tropic-scented night of Poros; yet, still he kept on, for he knew the road.

As he trudged along he tried to picture to himself the state of affairs in Cupia. Back in Vairkingi, when at last he had succeeded in getting the Princess Lilla on the air, she had mentioned the whistling bees, just before Prince Yuri had cut her off.

These bees were called "whistling" because of the heterodyne squeal with which they appeared to converse; but Myles had discovered, by means of the greater range and selectivity of his own artificial radio speech-organs, that this whistle was due to the bees sending simultaneously on two interfering wave lengths, for signal purposes. When simply talking they used a wave length beyond the range of Cupian speech!

Cabot had been able to adjust his portable set to this wave length, and had talked with the bees. As a result of this conversation an alliance had been formed between Cupia and the Hymernians—as the bee-people called themselves—which had driven Yuri and his ants from the continent. Thereafter the bees had lived at peace with the Cupians, a special ration of green cows being bred for their benefit.

What, wondered Cabot, had the returned Yuri done to disturb this state of affairs? If Portheris, the king of the bees, still lived, Cabot could not imagine him siding with Yuri.

But, whatever had happened, it was clear that the bees were at the bottom of it. Time would tell very speedily.

Traveling on foot at night on the planet Poros is necessarily slow and tedious, for the blackness of the Porovian night is dense beyond anything conceivable on earth. On earth even the light of a few stars would enable a man to distinguish between a concrete road and the adjoining fields and woods and bushes, but on Poros no stars are visible. Accordingly Myles had to feel his way with his feet, and fell off the road many times before he reached his destination. Due to the mountainous character of the country, most of these falls were extremely painful, and some were positively dangerous.

Yet on he kept, and before long the lights of Luno village loomed ahead. Even here it would not do to reveal himself in his present state of appearance, so he skirted the town and made his way down the steep path which led to the shore of the lake.

If his island dwelling had been disturbed, he half expected to find that his boats were gone from this landing place; but upon groping about in the dark he came across several of them, tied up just where they ought to be. This cheered him immensely.

But when he stared across toward the island and saw no sign of any light there, his spirits fell again. It was not the custom at Luno Castle to go through the night totally unillumined.

He would soon find out what the trouble was. So stepping into one of the boats he cast off, and paddled vigorously toward the middle of the lake. Keeping his bearings was difficult in the jet-black darkness, but he was guided somewhat by the faint illumination sent skyward by the little village.

Finally he bumped against the rocky and precipitous sides of the island, but misjudging his location he had to paddle nearly clear around the island before he came to the landing beach. This gained, he pulled his craft ashore, and groped his way up the narrow path to the summit, thence across the lawns, which sloped gently down toward the center of the island, where lay a little pond with Luno Castle standing beside it.

Myles ran into several shrubs, got completely mixed up as to his directions, and finally fell into the pond. This gave him a new starting point from which to orient himself. Walking around its edge, with one foot in the water, he would diverge outward from time to time, until at last his groping hand touched a wall of masonry. It was his castle! He was home! But what did that home hold? His heart beat tumultuously with anticipation.

Feeling his way along the wall, he came to the steps, and crawled up them to the great arched doorway. The door was closed, but not locked. Myles flung it open softly, and entered, closing it behind him. Then closing his eyes, he turned an electric switch, flooding the hall with the light of many vapor-lamps.

Gradually opening his eyelids, he glanced around him. Everywhere was the musty odor of unoccupancy. He had expected either his family or a sacked and ruined castle; he had found neither.

It would not do for the surrounding populace to discover his return until he was ready; so he hastily found a flashlight, and then switched off the vapor-lamps again.

Flash-light in hand, he made a tour of the castle. Everything was in perfect order. Lilla was a good housekeeper, and had evidently been given plenty of time by Yuri to prepare for her departure. This spoke volumes for her safety and that of the baby king.

Myles even found his own rooms undisturbed. This surprised him greatly. He had not expected this much consideration from Yuri. But then he reflected that Yuri must have been pretty sure that he would not return from the earth, and had wanted to do nothing to antagonize Lilla any more than absolutely necessary. This time Yuri had been playing the game of love-and-empire with a little more finesse than usual.

Myles, in his own dressing room, switched on the light; this was safe, as its windows opened only onto the courtyard. Then he bathed, shaved, trimmed his hair, and donned a blue-bordered toga, in place of his leather Vairking tunic. On his head he placed a radio headset of the sort which he had devised shortly after his first advent on Poros, to enable him to talk with the earless and voiceless Cupians and Formians.

Artificial antennae projected from his forehead. His earphones and ears were concealed by locks of hair, his tiny microphone—between his collar-bones—by a fold of his toga. Artificial wings strapped to his back protruded through slits in his garment. Around his waist, beneath his gown, was the belt which carried his batteries, tubes, and the sending and receiving apparatus itself.

Thus equipped, he surveyed himself complacently in the glass. Barring the absence of a sixth finger on each hand and a sixth toe on each foot, he looked a Cupian of the Cupians.

Then he proceeded to the radio room. The long distance radio-set was in perfect condition, but there was nothing on the air. One of the three-dialed Porovian clocks showed the time to be 1025; that is, a half hour after midnight, earth time. There was nothing further he could do before morning; so he lay down for a few hours of much needed rest.

When he awoke it was broad daylight, 310 o'clock. The pink flush of sunrise was just fading from the eastern sky. Less than three parths—six hours—of sleep! And then he realized that he must have slept the clock around, and more. A day's growth of beard confirmed this. It was now the beginning of his *third* day in Cupia. He had been dead to Poros for fifteen parths.

So he shaved, bathed, and breakfasted on some dried twig knobs—which was all he could find in the house. The courtyard garden was full of weeds. The lawns which surrounded the castle and the pond were uncut. Everything bespoke an abandonment many sangths ago.

After a complete tour of the premises Myles hastened to the radio room, and tuned-in the palace at Kuana. The result was the voice of the usurper Yuri, testily calling the ant-station in New Formia, far across the boiling seas. From time to time there would be silence, during which the prince was evidently waiting for a reply; but none came. Otto the Bold had done his work of destruction too well.

Myles chuckled. Yuri's frantic voice, coming in over the air, was a radio program much to Cabot's liking. Even the best earth-station of Columbia, National or Mutual could not surpass it. The only thing he would rather hear would be his own sweet Lilla.

His recollection of Otto the Bold led him to wonder how the battle for Vairkingi had progressed. Roies and Vairkings on one side against Roies and ants on the other. It was a toss-up.

It seemed years since he had left the land of the furry ones—Otto, Grod, Att, Jud, Theoph, Crota, Arkilu. They all resembled mere shadows of a dream. The only real feature that stood out in his memory was the radio set which he had fabricated.

Then his thoughts flew to Yat, the city of the Whoomangs, with its strange assortment of creatures, including Boomalayla, the winged dragon, and Queekle Mukki, the serpent. Cabot shed a tear for Doggo and little golden furred Quivven, and then came down to the present with a jerk.

He was back in Cupia, clean, clothed, shaved, equipped, fed, and rested. It was now up to him to rescue the Princess Lilla from her traitor cousin. First he must find firearms. But of these the castle had been looted; for not a trace of a rifle, an automatic, or even a single cartridge could he find, though he searched high and low. So reluctantly he strapped on merely his Vairking sword and knife, and ran down the path to the beach.

In the boat once more, he paddled rapidly toward the shore. At the landing place, sitting on one of the boats was a Cupian, but as this man seemed to be unarmed, Cabot approached him without fear. As he came within antennae-shot the man sang out: "Welcome back to Cupia, Myles Cabot, defender of the faith!"

Myles shaded his eyes from the silver glare of the sky. "Nan-nan!" he exclaimed; for the Cupian before him was none other than the young cleric of the lost religion who had helped rebuild his radio head-set in the Caves of Kar during the Second War of Liberation.

As the boat grated on the beach the earth-man leaped out, and the two friends were soon warmly patting each other's cheek.

These greetings over, Cabot asked: "What good fortune brings you here?"

He found it easy to slip back again into the language of this continent.

"The Holy Leader detailed two of us," Nan-nan replied, "to watch Luno Castle, for you know he must be kept informed of everything, as he waits within his caves for the promised day. Night before last my colleague saw lights for a night, so this morning I decided to reconnoiter."

"Is Owva still Holy Leader?" Myles asked politely.

"Yes," the cleric replied. "The grand old man still lives."

"The Builder be praised! But," changing the subject, "how are my family?"

"Both well," Nan-nan answered, "though for the past six or nine days the princess has not been permitted to communicate with any-one."

Myles smiled. "Why?" he innocently asked.

"I know not," the young cleric admitted.

Myles laughed. "I thought that the Holy Leader knew every-thing," he said. "Well, as it happens, *I* can tell *you*. It is because I communicated with her a few days ago and informed her that I was about to return. Has no news of this got out from the palace?"

"No," Nan-nan replied, "but it explains why Yuri has kept a large squadron of whistling bees patrolling the eastern coast all day long every day. How did you get by them?"

"Came over at night," the earth-man answered. "But what about the bees?"

"I'll tell you," Nan-nan said. "Shortly after you left on your visit to your own planet Minos, Prince Yuri flew back alone from his exile with the Formians beyond the boiling seas. This was the first that we of Cupia had known that any of them survived.

"Yuri kept his return a secret for some time, but got in touch with some old supporters of his. First he contrived to cut off the allowance of anks which are doled out to the bees for food. Then he stirred up trouble among the bees because of this.

"The bees imprisoned Portheris, their king, and, under promise of an increased allowance of food, seized the arsenal at Kuana, the air base at Wautoosa, and Luno Castle. As you know, the air navy has been practically disbanded, because there was nothing for it to fight. The rifles of the marching clubs had fallen into disuse because other newer games had superseded archery. Most of the rifles were stored at various central places, which the bees succeeded in seizing.

"Some of the hill towns still had arms, but they surrendered these under threat of Yuri to kill the Princess Lilla and the little king.

"All the arms are now stored in the arsenal at the capital under guard of Yuri's most trusted henchmen. A new treaty was made with the bees, giving them an increase in food. But even so they are res-tive and are held in check merely by fear of the anti-aircraft guns at Kuana.

"The general belief of the populace is that you are dead. Yuri is ruling strictly, and has dissolved the Popular Assembly. The pinquis everywhere are his personal appointees. These facts and the burden of supplying anks to the Hymernians irk the people; but they are im-potent. 'Can a mathlab struggle in the jaws of a woofus?'

"Lilla he treated well. If he had not done so, the populace would rise against him, bees or no bees. And he has promised the succession to little Kew, if Lilla will marry him. But your dot-dash message many sangths ago stopped that, for it showed that you still lived and had returned to Poros, although not to this continent.

"That is all. Now tell me of your adventures."

But before complying with this request, the earth-man asked: "What has become of the loyal Prince Toron and my chief of staff, Hah Babbuh, and Poblath the Philosopher, and all my other friends and supporters?"

"Every one of them, so far as I know, is safe," the young cleric replied. "Most of than are hiding in the hill towns. Yuri has not risked the wrath of the populace by molesting them, and in fact has given notice that so long as they behave they will be let alone."

Then Cabot related all that had occurred to him from the time he transmitted himself earthward through Poros down to the present date.

When he concluded he remarked: "That will be an antenna-full for the Holy Leader. But now to get to work. On whom can I best depend in this vicinity?"

"On Emsul, the veterinary," Nan-nan replied. "He lives in the village now. Return to the island, and I will bring him to you."

Myles did so, and in a short time the three were in conference in the castle. It seemed to Myles that the first thing to do was to recover his airplane, rifle, and ammunition from the waters of the pit, but Emsul demurred.

Said he: "Huge dark-green water-insects inhabit the pool. They are very like the red parasites which cling to the sides of the anks, and which we roast for food, but they are much larger and the bite of their claws means death."

The parasites to which the veterinary alluded had always tasted to Cabot exactly like earth-born lobsters. The description of these new beasts were further suggestive of lobsters. He asked Emsul for a more detailed description, and found that this tallied still further with the earthly prototype.

This reminded Myles of an interesting experiment which he had seen tried in the Harvard zoological laboratory, and which he now hoped to put to a practical use.

So he asked: "Have these creatures a gravitational sense organ?"

"Yes," the Cupian veterinary replied, "although it is unlike ours.

We Cupians, and I suppose you Minorians, have inside the skull on each side of the head, a group of three tubes like the spirit levels of a carpenter.

"The corresponding organ of the scissor-clawed beast is different, although serving the same end. On each side of the thorax of these creatures there is a spherical cavity, with a small opening to the outside. This opening is just large enough to admit a grain of sand at a time.

"The membrane which lines the cavity, exudes a liquid cement which unites into a little ball the grains of sand which enter. The cavity is lined with nerve ends; and, as the ball always rolls to the bottom side of the cavity, the beast is able to tell which direction is up, and which is down."

Cabot clapped his hands in glee. This was exactly as in the case of earth-born lobsters.

"They won't know which is up and which is down when I get through with them," he exclaimed cryptically.

It was quickly arranged that Nan-nan should go at once to the village near the lobster pool, and engage a gang of Cupian men to cut a swath through the thick woods which hem in the pool. When this was completed, he was to send a messenger to Luno Castle to summon Cabot, who, meanwhile, would be engaged in preparing certain mysterious electrical apparatus. For the present, the earth-man's return was a secret.

The plan worked to perfection. Only one day was consumed in chopping the path through the woods. On the second day after his meeting with Nan-nan and Emsul, Myles proceeded to the lobster pool by the kerkool, with his electrical equipment and several boats.

CHAPTER XXIV
THE LOBSTEROID CIRCUIT

Myles could not help comparing his present ease of passage down the swath cut by the Cupians with his difficult grubbing through the shrubs a few feet an hour, or even with forcing his way behind the wedge-faced insect.

Upon his arrival at the brink of the abyss, his first act was to test the black sand with an electric coil. As he had expected, it was magnetite, the only iron ore which will respond to a magnet. It was the same ore as he had used in his crucibles while making his radio set in Vairkingi.

This preliminary disposed of, cables were quickly stretched back and forth across the pit, and from these cables large electro-magnets were hung close to the surface of the water. Wires were run from the lighting system of the near-by town to a master controller at the top of the cliff.

When all was in readiness, the earth-man threw the current into all the circuits. The result was immediate. To the surface of the water there floated bottom side up, a score or more of lobsterlike creatures, each the size of a freight car. Poor beasts!

The pellets of sand and cement, in the cavities of their gravity-sense organs, were composed of magnetite; and this being attracted upwardly by the suspended electro-magnets, gave the poor creatures the impression that up was down, and down was up. Consequently, reversing their position and floating to the surface, they imagined— with what little imagination their primitive brains were capable of— that they were resting peacefully at the bottom of the lake.

Next there were turned on, in place of the suspended magnets, a number of magnets lying against the steep side of the pit near the surface of the water; and instantly all the lobsteroids rolled over, with their bellies toward that side of the pit. The experiment was a complete success.

Grappling hooks and blocks and tackle were then brought, and dragging was begun for the airplane, the ant-rifle, and the bandoleer of cartridges which Myles had lost on the night of his landing in Cupia.

The radio man himself, stationed at his switchboard, manipulated the instruments. Presumably all three of the sought articles were near the bank where Cabot had landed, so fishing was begun at that point, while energized magnets, across the pond, drew the huge crustaceans away. Even so, several of them swam back and snapped at the grappling hooks.

This gave Myles an opportunity to practice his controls. Whenever one of the monsters of the deep would approach any of the dredging apparatus, the radio man would close the switch which controlled some near-by magnet, whereat the bewildered beast would be thrown completely off his balance, and would require several paraparths before he could orient himself to the new lines of force. By the time that this had been accomplished, Cabot would have switched on some other magnet, thus again upsetting the beast's equilibrium.

It was truly a weird and novel tune which this electrical genius of two worlds played upon his keyboard, while huge green shapes moved at his command.

Finally Myles got so expert at this strange game, that it became safe for his workmen to descend into the pit without fear of the denizens of the deep. At last the ropes were securely fastened to the ant-plane, and it was drawn up the bank to safety. The fire-arm and ammunition followed shortly thereafter.

The forces of the true king—Baby Kew—were now armed with one small airship, one rifle, and one bandoleer of cartridges.

"You must attack at once!" Nan-nan asserted.

The earth-man looked at the Cupian in surprise.

"Why?" he asked.

"Because," the young cleric explained, "if you don't some one of this village is going to get word to Prince Yuri of your return. Although no announcement has yet been made of your identity, this feat of yours of overcoming the scissor-beasts is as good as a verbal introduction. Runners will soon be notifying the usurper."

"Why runners?" Myles asked. "Why not radio?"

"Because," Nan-nan replied. "I took the precaution to throw an adjusting-tool into the local motor-generator set early this morning. One of the solenoids is hopelessly jammed, and it will take several days and nights of steady work to restore it."

"Great are the ramifications of the lost religion," Cabot murmured approvingly.

But the young cleric pouted, in spite of the tone of approval. Said he: "There were no ramifications to *this* accomplishment. I did it all myself."

"Have it your own way," Myles returned conciliatorily. "But to get back to what we were discussing, how am I to attack the usurper with no troops, and only one plane, and one rifle?"

"But you *must* attack!" Nan-nan objected. "As for planes, every plane in the kingdom, save only yours, is under lock and key at Wau-toosa, the old naval air base, which now is the headquarters of the whistling bees. Every firearm, save two, your rifle and Prince Yuri's automatic, is under heavy guard at the Kuana arsenal. Only the pretender himself and the arsenal guards—who are trusted henchmen of his—are permitted to be armed."

"And I suppose," the earth-man interjected, with a shrug, "that you expect me, alone and single-handed, to seize the Kuana arsenal, and distribute arms to my people."

"Not exactly," the priest replied. "You see—"

At which point the conversation was interrupted by a body of troops, four abreast, which came marching toward them down the aisle which had been cut through the trees.

Cabot stepped back aghast. Trapped! The soldiers swung along in the perfect cadence which had been taught them by generations spent in the marching clubs—or "hundreds"—of Cupia. True, they were unarmed, but what could one armed human do against such numbers? Cabot glanced down the path, and saw hundred after hundred turn into it at the farther end.

There was only one possibility of escape, his plane. But the plane was still dripping from its submergence in the pond. Would its trophil-engine start while wet? Had enough water leaked into the alcohol tanks to damage the fuel? He would see.

Shouting to Nan-nan and Emsul to follow, he started toward his craft; but the young cleric blocked his way. Treachery.

No. For the young priest cried: "Fear not, defender of the faith. These be friends! They are the armies which you are to lead against Yuri. They are marching clubs of the loyal hill towns, which have been called together here, ostensibly for an athletic tournament."

Cabot stopped his mad scramble of retreat, and smiled. With such men he would reconquer Cupia, Yuri or no Yuri, bees or no bees!

The foremost hundred debouched and formed in company-front. Then from the ranks there stepped a Cupian, who snatched off his blond wig, revealing ruddy locks beneath. Onto his own right breast he pinned a red circle, the insignia of Field Marshal. It was Hah Babbuh, Chief of Staff of the Armies of Cupia, who had been Cabot's right-hand man in the two wars of liberation.

Facing the troops he gave a crisp command. Up shot every left hand. Then, wheeling about, he held his own hand aloft and shouted: "Yahoo, Myles Cabot! We are ready to follow where you lead!"

"Yahoo!" the troops echoed in unison.

Then, giving his men the order "at ease," Hah strode up to the earth-man. Warmly, the two friends patted each other on the cheek. It was many sangths since they had seen each other, and much had happened in the meantime.

A council of war was immediately held between Myles, Hah, Nan-nan, and Emsul, at the plane.

"Won't this gathering come to the attention of Yuri?" Myles asked. "And won't he at once suspect its cause, in view of its nearness to Luno Castle, and in view of my recent radio announcements from Vairkingi?"

"I doubt it," the Babbuh replied, "for we have wrecked every radio set in the vicinity."

But, this did not reassure the earth-man as much as it might.

"It would seem to me," he asserted, "that this very fact would put Prince Yuri on his guard."

"Possibly so," Nan-nan ruefully admitted, "but it will take four days for investigators to cover the thousand stads from Kuana to here by kerkool, two days by bee."

"And in the meantime," Myles countered, "it will take our plane two days to reach Kuana, and our kerkools four."

"Then," Emsul suggested, "had we not better march openly and at once?"

This suggestion was accepted, with the reservation, however, that the return of Cabot and the existence of their plane were to be kept as secret as possible.

Accordingly the main body of the troops were put on the march toward Kuana, under Emsul, with instructions to requisition every available kerkool, wreck every radio set, and place every settlement under martial law. The kerkools, as fast as seized, were to be manned by the best sharpshooters, and sent ahead.

The local village and the lobster pond were placed under heavy guard, and the earth-man with his plane and rifle remained under cover.

That night, just at sunset, he started forth. The airship had been stripped to its lightest, and in it were crowded Myles Cabot, Hah Babbuh, Nan-nan, and half a dozen sharpshooters. Long before morning, they came up with the lights of the foremost kerkools, and so were forced to cease their advance, whereupon they landed, and encamped for the rest of the night and the following day.

All day long, kerkools passed them on the road, stopping to report as they passed. Apparently a surprising number of these swift two-wheeled Porovian autos had been captured.

The following night the plane again took wing, and continued until it caught up once more with the advance guard of the "taxi-cab army." These men reported that, at the last radio station seized, they had learned that Prince Yuri had put censorship on the air, thus showing conclusively that the usurper had learned something of what was going on. Then the kerkools swept ahead, and Cabot encamped as before. He was now halfway to Kuana, his loved ones, and Prince Yuri.

Toward the end of the day which followed, the advancing kerkools met a bombing squadron of whistling bees, and were forced to halt and take cover as best they could. Most of the men escaped, but many of the machines had to be left on the road, where they were demolished by the bombs of the enemy.

During all this confusion, a kerkool from the capital, bearing crossed sticks as a flag of truce, drew up at the vanguard, with the following message: "King Yuri cannot but regard the steady procession of kerkools toward Kuana as a menace directed against him. If it is not so intended, then let a delegation in one kerkool proceed under crossed sticks to convince him of your sincerity. From now on, if more than one kerkool advances, it will be taken as a hostile act, and Prince Kew, the heir to the throne, will be sacrificed as a hostage."

Upon receiving this message, Emsul at once directed his followers to stay where they were until Myles Cabot should catch up with them. Then, with a picked body of men, in one kerkool, under crossed sticks, he took up the road toward Kuana, preceded by the delegation which had brought the message from Yuri.

Not a word would he give them as to the purpose of the advance.

"Your message was from Prince Yuri," he said, "and therefore to Prince Yuri shall be the reply. But it does seem a bit thoughtless of the Hymernians to drop bombs on our men, before even attempting to ascertain whether or not our advance was intended to be peaceful."

To this, they in turn made no answer.

About midnight, Myles Cabot, in his airplane, reached the point where the kerkools had halted. He found the Cupians confused and more or less leaderless. He, as they, was horrified at the threat which the usurper Yuri held over the head of the little king.

But while he and Nan-nan and Hah Babbuh were conferring on the situation, word was brought in, by a party who had just demolished a near-by radio set, that they had picked the following unaddressed and unsigned message out of the air:

Fear not. Baby Kew has been kidnaped from the palace, and is safe.

Somehow this news carried conviction. The longer they considered it, the more authentic it appeared. Certainly, it could not have emanated from Yuri, for he could have no possible object in deceiving them into thinking that the little king was safe, and thus encouraging them to proceed with whatever they might have afoot.

But they could not imagine who was their informant. It might be any one of a number of the leaders in Cabot's two wars of liberation, Poblath the Philosopher, mango of the Kuana jail; Ja Babbuh, Oya Buh, and Buh Tedn, professors at the Royal University; Count Kamel of Ktuh, the ex-radical; or even the loyal Prince Toron, Yuri's younger brother, whom Cabot had left in charge as regent, upon embarking on his ill-fated visit to the earth.

All these loyal Cupians had been driven into hiding, when the renegade Yuri had returned across the boiling seas and had usurped the throne with the aid of the Hymernians. Where they now were, no one knew. This message might be from any one of them—or it might not.

Anyhow, it served to hearten Cabot and his two companions.

Said Myles: "Undoubtedly there were some of Yuri's Cupian henchmen on the backs of the bees which bombed our kerkools. These have probably reported by wireless that our advance has stopped. I do not believe that Yuri yet knows that we have a plane; accordingly, he will not expect immediate trouble, so long as our vanguard remains here, four hundred stads from Kuana.

"You, Hah Babbuh, remain here in charge of our troops. I seriously doubt if the usurper will attack you, for he does not dare trust enough Cupians with rifles for that purpose. Nan-nan and I and our sharpshooters will proceed as rapidly as possible in the plane, until daybreak, when we will encamp as usual.

"To-morrow afternoon, send scouts ahead to destroy the wireless and start your whole kerkool army on the move at sunset. Bend every effort to join me as soon as possible at the capital, where I expect to arrive some time to-morrow night. Beyond that, I have no definite plans. May the Great Builder speed our cause."

Then he said good-night, and took off once more in his plane. As he soared aloft with his noisy trophil-motor, earth-men would have heard it for stads in every direction, but these Cupians were earless and hence possessed no sense of hearing as we know it. The noisy plane could make no impression upon their antenna-sense, for its engines being of the trophil variety—or Diesel, as we call a somewhat similar device on earth—had no electrical ignition.

Throughout the remainder of the night the plane sped southward, deviating from its course only when whistling sounds warned them of the presence of bees. With the first faint tinge of pink in the east, they landed and hid their airship at the edge of a wood, two hundred and sixty stads from Kuana.

A small town lay near by. To it went several of the crew in search of food and information, while the rest took turns guarding the plane and sleeping.

During Cabot's turn at watch, he noted a figure slinking across a neighboring field. There was something strangely familiar about this figure, so Myles hid himself in a tartan bush and awaited its approach.

It walked with a peculiar limp, very much like that which had characterized Buh Tedn, ever since he recovered from the shell wound which he had received in the Second War of Liberation. But the face and the hair of the approaching Cupian bore no resemblance to that of Professor Tedn. Nevertheless, Cabot took a chance.

Stepping suddenly from his place of concealment, he shouted: "Buh Tedn!"

Thereat, the Cupian emitted a shriek of terror from his antennae, and started running away across the fields.

"Stop!" the earth-man called. "I am Myles Cabot."

The fleeing man halted abruptly and peered at Myles inquisitively; then he smiled and snatched off his wig, and straightened out his expression. It was none other than Buh Tedn!

"So you are the cause of all the rumpus," he ejaculated, returning and patting his friend warmly on the cheek.

"What rumpus?" Miles inquired with interest.

"Wireless won't work," the other replied, "and no messages on the air anyhow. Nothing but bees; the air is full of *them* anyhow—also full of vague rumors of all sorts. As Poblath would say: 'Where there's wind, there's a storm'."

"Speaking of Poblath," Myles said, "where *is* the philosopher?"

"Kuana, the last I heard," Buh Tedn replied. "Ja Babbuh and Oya

Buh are somewhere in the west. Prince Toron has disappeared completely. Hah Babbuh and Emsul are supposed to be in the northern part of the Okarze Mountains. Kamel Bar-Sarkar has gone over to Yuri. I am here. That about completes the list of our former leaders."

"Hah Babbuh is in charge of my unarmed forces one hundred and sixty stads north of here," Cabot answered. "Emsul is on his way to Yuri under crossed sticks. I am here in a plane, with one rifle, Nannan the cleric, and six unarmed sharpshooters."

"What is the idea?" Tedn asked.

"The idea is to fly to Kuana to-night," the earth-man replied, "and raise as much rough-house as possible for Prince Yuri. Will you come with us? There is one vacant place in the plane."

The Cupian looked at him admiringly, and said: "You are still the same old Myles Cabot! You propose to capture Kuana practically without arms and single-handed. And the joke is that you will probably succeed. How *do* you do it?"

"It's a gift!" Myles laughed. "But 'trees have antennae', as Poblath would say. Let us proceed to the plane and wait for evening."

At the plane, Cabot awakened one of the Cupians to take his place on guard. Then, in low tones, he and Buh Tedn each related to the other all that had occurred since the matter-transmitting apparatus had shot the radio man earthward.

Along toward night the absentees returned from the village, bringing provision, but scarcely any news except that the place was seething with suppressed excitement, and that they had succeeded in getting into the radio station and "pying" the apparatus.

"Let us start then at once," Buh Tedn counseled. "No one can now get word to Yuri, and perhaps they will mistake us for a Hymernian, anyhow."

But impatient as he was, Myles would hear none of this.

"They could easily dispatch a runner to some near-by town to send the message from there," he said. "Furthermore, a plane looks very little like a whistling bee."

So the group feasted, and waited until the last streaks of red had died in the west, before they shot into the air and southward. The plane was driven to its utmost, but it was later than 1:00 o'clock before the lights of Kuana loomed ahead.

Turning to the right, Cabot skirted the city and landed near the arsenal.

Nan-nan promptly left them.

"I have church affairs to attend to," he explained.

"Great are the ramifications of the lost religion," the earth-man replied, laughing, "and I hope that you pick up some useful information."

After the young cleric had gone Buh Tedn asked:

"Surely you don't plan for us to attack the arsenal? It is heavily guarded by the only men whom Yuri permits to carry fire-arms in this entire kingdom."

CHAPTER XXV

ALL KINDS OF TROUBLE

"We must reconnoiter first," Cabot replied, "for as yet I have no definite plans."

Accordingly they made their way to a grove of trees near the arsenal. Where they stood they were completely enveloped by foliage and tropical darkness, but the arsenal was in a flood of light which emanated from large floodlights on poles a short distance outside the surrounding wall. Along the top of the high wall walked sentinels armed with rifles.

Cabot quickly formed his plans.

Turning his rifle and bandoleer over to the best shot in the party, he instructed the sharpshooter as follows: "When I raise my hand so, then shoot the sentinel to whom I am talking. Follow that by a shot at the nearest light. Then, under cover of the darkness, slink across the plain and join me at the wall."

Without any further explanation he walked boldly out into the light.

As he approached the arsenal there rang out the cry of "Halt!"

He halted.

"Who is there?"

"Not so loud!" he cautioned. "You see I am unarmed. Let me approach near the wall so that I may explain my mission, which is for your antennae alone."

The sentinel signified his assent, and Cabot drew nearer.

"Halt!" The Cupian on the wall repeated, but this time in a low tone.

Cabot halted again, this time almost directly under the light.

"Stand where you are," said the soldier, "while I let down a ladder. Make any attempt to flee, and I shall fire."

Myles remained where he was, with every indication of extreme terror, as the Cupian let down a rope ladder from the top of the wall, and descended.

"Hold up your hands!"

Up shot Cabot's right hand. It was the signal agreed on with the concealed sharpshooter. *Ping!* The sentinel dropped to the ground without a sound. *Ping!* The light went out. Hastily the earth-man exchanged his white toga for the black toga of his fallen enemy, and picked up the latter's rifle and cartridge-belt. It felt good to have a real rifle-shaped rifle in his hands once more in place of the buttless firearms of the ants.

Just then a voice hailed him from the top of the wall. "What's the trouble?"

Out of the dim twilight below Myles called back:

"I shot a sutler, and just as I was about to search his body the light went out. Have you your flash light with you?"

"Yes."

"Then come on down and help me search."

The second sentinel, eager for a taste of sutler's food after weeks of garrison rations, started to scramble down the rope ladder; but as he neared the ground Cabot stepped to his side and put a single bullet through his brain.

Out of the semidarkness around him there arose seven forms. They were Buh Tedn and the six Cupian marksmen from the hills. Buh Tedn started to change clothes with the fallen guard, but Cabot stopped him, saying, "No; your limp would give you away. Let one of the others assume the personality of this sentry."

One of the others made the exchange.

Then said their leader: "Two of the posts of the guard are now cleared. Do you, marksman, ascend the ladder and walk this beat, impersonating Yuri's guardsman."

The man did so, while those below cowered close to the wall. Soon Cabot heard a shot to the extreme right of the beat. Then a voice from above called softly:

"One less guard, O Cabot. Three sections of the wall are now cleared. I have the body up here."

Myles and one more sharpshooter mounted the parapet; soon all three were walking post with the precision of old war-time practice, while the other five members of the party clung to the rope ladder under the shadow of the wall. Cabot himself walked the leftermost post, and took pains never to meet the adjoining sentry. Thus nearly half a parth of time passed.

Finally an officer with a squad approached along the top of the wall to the left. Cabot promptly crowded to the extreme right-hand end of his beat, and cautioned his own adjoining sentinel to remain close at hand.

As the squad drew near he sang out, "Halt!"

The squad halted.

"Who is there?" the earth-man demanded.

"Relief."

"Advance one and be recognized."

The officer stepped forward.

"Advance relief."

The officer brought the relief forward, halted it again, and called out, "Number four!"

Thereat one of the squad stepped from the ranks at port-arms. Cabot himself came to port in unison.

At this point the routine ended. Tilting his gun slightly from its position, Myles suddenly fired two shots, and the officer and the new Number Four sank down upon the parapet.

Instantly the whole squad was in confusion, but before they could raise their rifles to reply Myles and his companions riddled them with bullets.

One of them, more quick-thinking than the rest, dropped prone without being hit, and then cautiously drew a bead on Myles Cabot, who, seeing his enemies all down, had just paused to breathe. Neither he nor his companion saw his hostile move, and Myles's other man was walking his post, far to the right, in a military manner, so as to attract no attention from the guardsmen farther on.

Everything was all set for the tragedy which would forever put an end to the hope of the redemption of Cupia from the renegade Yuri and his bee allies.

But just as the soldier was about to pull the trigger, a brawny arm slipped across his throat and yanked him backward, so that his gun went off in the air. It was Buh Tedn, who had crawled to the top of the wall in the rear of the squad. A shot from Cabot's companion promptly put an end to this last enemy.

Then the seven conspirators searched the bodies and equipped themselves, Cabot pinning on the insignia of the officer. There were eight bodies, but some had undoubtedly fallen from the wall in the struggle. No time could be spared to hunt for these, and eight was more than enough for the present purposes.

Myles formed his men in two ranks, counted them off, faced them to the right, and proceeded along the parapet, picking up his one already posted man as he went.

Number Six was relieved in true military form. He was too glad of getting off duty to notice the unfamiliarity of the officer who relieved him. Similarly with Numbers Seven, Eight, Nine, and so on.

As he came to Number Eleven, Cabot began to worry for fear that his supply of new sentinels might run out. Why hadn't he made some arrangement to have his own men rejoin him after being posted? But then he reflected that that would never do, for it certainly would have been noticed by the others. He was in a fix.

Number Twelve was relieved, all seven of his own men were gone, and Myles Cabot found himself at the head of a squad composed entirely of the enemy. What could he do at Number Thirteen?

But just as he was frantically turning this question over in his mind, he came to a long ramp leading inward from the wall, down to a small building between the wall and the main arsenal. He stepped back as though to inspect the squad; and they, without command, marched past him, turned, and proceeded past Number One down the ramp. This was the guard-quarters; there were no more sentinels to relieve.

Inside the buildings he gave the commands: "Relief—halt! Left—face! Port—arms! Open—chambers! Close—chambers! Dismissed! Hands up!"

The last was not in the Manual. The tired men, on their way to the gun rack, stopped in surprise. Up shot their hands, some first dropping their rifles, but some retaining them.

"It is Cabot the Minorian!" one of them shouted.

The situation was ticklish in the extreme. The Cupians were scattered throughout the room, so that it was impossible for Myles to cover them all simultaneously with his rifle. They were desperate characters, thugs of the worst type, typical henchmen of Prince Yuri. If they started any trouble, Myles could expect to get one, or at most two, of the seven before the rest would get him. Furthermore, they knew it.

"Back up, all of you, into that corner! Quickly!" he directed.

But they did not budge. Gradually smiles began to break over their ugly visages. They realized that they had him at bay, rather than he them. And what a prize he would be for presentation to King Yuri! Why, the king might even blow them to a beefsteak party.

The earth-man confronted them, unafraid. He still had the drop on them, and he intended to press his advantage to the limit.

"You fat one over by the rack, back into the corner," he ordered, "or I'll shoot you first."

The Cupian addressed obeyed with alacrity.

"You with the scar! Lay down your gun! Now you back into the corner!"

The second soldier did so. Things were progressing nicely. One by one he could subdue the Cupians confronting him. But, just as he was exulting in his triumph, his gun was seized from behind. Turning, he saw Number One leering at him.

One blow from his fist in that leering face and the newcomer crashed to the floor. But before Myles could wheel to confront those in the guardroom, they had rushed him and borne him to the ground.

"Capture him alive!" some one shouted, and that was the last that he heard, for something snapped in his portable radio set, and from then on he was deaf to antennae-emanations. All that he could hear was an occasional rifle shot.

In spite of the overwhelming numbers upon him, he fought with feet and fists, until at last, the weight seemed to lessen. Finally he struggled to his feet and confronted his tormentors. Could it be that single-handed, he had vanquished eight brawny Cupians?

But no, for the figures he confronted were Buh Tedn and his own men. The eight enemies lay dead on the floor.

The mutual congratulations were silently given. A quick inspection showed that the head-set and the apparatus-belt were hopelessly damaged, so the radio man found a stylus and paper and wrote: "My artificial antennae and the accompanying apparatus were ruined during the fight. Luckily there is another set in the airplane. One of you go quickly and fetch it."

One of the party accordingly withdrew. The others, rifle in hand, proceeded to search the building, but not a soul did they find, although the couches had evidently been recently occupied.

It seemed likely that, during the struggle in the guardroom, the rest of the guard, being unable to reach the arms racks, had stealthily left the building.

So Myles and his party hurried on to the door which led from the building into the arsenal yard. As they emerged they were met with a volley from the arsenal, and three of their number went down. The rest beat a hasty retreat and barred the door.

Then they made their way to the windows which faced the main arsenal, but two more of them were picked off before they realized how perfectly they were silhouetted by the lighted rooms within. One of these two was Buh Tedn. Myles Cabot and one Cupian sharpshooter were all that were left of the party.

As rapidly as possible the two survivors extinguished all the lights in the guardhouse, and then mounted to the roof, which was flat and surrounded by a low parapet which protected them from showing themselves against the illumination of the surrounding vapor lamps.

Crawling along the roof to the edge nearest the arsenal, they peered cautiously over. The whistle of a bullet caused Myles to duck his head, and he pulled his companion to cover as well. With his artificial antennae gone, he could not explain orally and it was too dark to write. But the other followed him to the opposite edge, where they succeeded in potting the sentinels at Posts Two and Three, which were the only occupied posts within sight.

There appearing to be nothing further to be accomplished up there, they crawled down into the building and took up their station at windows of the upper story, from which they fired at every sign of movement in the direction of the arsenal, taking care to drop to the floor and then change windows after each shot.

Finally their ammunition gave out, and Cabot went down to the guardroom for more. But a long and careful search revealed only a few rounds.

Myles returned to the upper story and groped through the rooms to find his friend. But it was his foot, rather than his out-stretched hand, which finally found him. The Cupian sharpshooter lay dead.

Myles Cabot alone, with only about a dozen cartridges, was the sole remaining defense of the captured building. No life seemed to be stirring on the arsenal side, so he crossed the building and looked out at the wall.

Dark figures were stealthily creeping along where Post No. 12 should have been. The earth-man let them have it with rapid fire, and they quickly disappeared.

He now heard firing in that direction, and then the lights there went out, so that the wall no longer showed against the sky. From time to time he fired where he judged the wall was, so as to keep back the invaders, and thus soon entirely exhausted his ammunition.

"Thank heaven," he said to himself, "the downstairs door is barred!"

But as he said this he realized that he had omitted to bar the door which opened toward the wall; and even as he realized this there came a rush of many feet down the ramp which led from the wall to this door.

CHAPTER XXVI
THE DEBACLE

Myles drew his knife, crouched in a corner of the dark room, and prepared to sell his life dearly. He was ready for searchers who might come groping through the room, but he was wholly unprepared for the sudden switching on of the electric lights. As he sprang to his feet and rubbed his eyes, he saw before him Nan-nan and the sharp-shooter whom he had sent back to the plane to get his second radio set. Behind them in the doorway were a score or more of Cupians.

Snatching the new set he fastened it in place, while the others waited. Then, articulate once more, "You have come in the nick of time. How did it happen?"

The young priest replied, "Through spies of our religion I located Oya Buh; he rounded up a number of his followers, and we hastened hither. The wall we found unguarded, with a rope ladder hanging down, and at its foot six dead soldiers in black togas. We took their arms and mounted the wall, only to be driven back by shots."

"My shots," Myles interjected.

"Not all," Nan-nan replied, "for some came from the arsenal; we could tell by the flashes. Several of our party were hit—although not by you, so your conscience may feel clear—before we put a stop to this by shooting out all the outside lights. Then we rushed the guard-house, and here we are. But where are *your* men?"

"Dead—all dead," the earth-man sadly replied. "Even Buh Tedn."

Oya Buh then stepped forward and greeted his former chief.

"Yahoo, Cabot!" he cried. "May the dead rest beyond the waves. We, the living, have work to do. Look—the sky turns pink and silver in the east! Morning has come. What do you propose?"

"Morning means that the whistling bees will soon be upon us," Myles answered. "We must capture the arsenal before they arrive."

The party then took inventory of their supplies. There were thirty-eight rifles, forty Cupians, and Myles Cabot. One man was promptly sent to the roof with crossed sticks. When these were recognized, thirty-eight men under arms were marched up onto the roof as well. It was considered advisable for Cabot himself to keep under cover. Then Oya Buh unbarred the door and stepped out. An officer from the arsenal advanced to meet him. The two gravely patted each other's cheek.

The officer, whose rank was that of pootah, inquired:

"What is the idea of defying your king, professor?"

"The idea," Oya replied, "is that we have come to restore Kew XIII to the throne and the Cupians to their proper dominion over the bees. The guardhouse, as you see, is manned by sharpshooters, fully armed. A vast force, unarmed but determined, awaits outside the walls. If you surrender, we shall spare your lives. If not, we shall rush the gates while our sharpshooters pick off any one who opposes, and shall kill all whom we find within. What say you?"

The pootah shrugged his shoulders. "What is there to say?" he replied. "We surrender, provided we are given safe conduct."

"Safe conduct without arms?"

"Agreed."

So the guard, about a hundred in number, in their black togas, filed out of the arsenal, through the guardhouse, onto the wall, along it, and down the rope ladder. The ladder was then hauled up again. The pootah looked around him.

"Where is your vast army?" he asked.

"On the other side of the wall," Oya Buh replied, with a smile. "Now run along away from here, like a good little boy."

But the officer and his followers started circling the wall to investigate. Before he gained the main gate, however, it had been opened and, for all he could tell, the "vast army" had passed inside. A guard stationed there advised him to get out of rifle range as speedily as possible, and twelve sentinels, who by now had manned the wall, bore out this menace; so, grumbling somewhat the pootah led his men off toward the city.

Thus did Myles Cabot and forty-seven practically unarmed followers capture the Kuana arsenal from its hundred defenders.

Straggling Cupians now began to drift in from the city. These were put to work carting arms and ammunition out of the arsenal and stacking it up in widely separated piles wherever cover could be found. Every Cupian who reported was issued a rifle and a full bandoleer of cartridges.

"We may perhaps thus arm some enemies," Myles admitted, "but we must take the risk. The majority will be friends."

It was well that they removed all the ammunition which they could. It would have been better if they could have removed more. They all worked feverishly for half the morning, even taking the guards off the wall for this purpose, but they had scarcely made a dent in the supplies stored in the arsenal when a fleet of bees appeared on the southern horizon.

In spite of the approaching menace, Myles and his men continued to work. The Hymernians flew low straight at the arsenal, until a volley from Cabot's men brought down two of them and caused the rest to soar into the sky. Whereupon they started dropping bombs on the arsenal, and on the men carting materials therefrom.

Naturally, this put an abrupt end to Cabot's operations. His men scattered as rapidly as possible; and individually made for the city with small quantities of arms, keeping to cover as well as they could. Cupians from Kuana helped themselves to the rest, and by nightfall the captured supplies were pretty well distributed. The arsenal was a smoking ruin.

All through the afternoon the bees, flying low, harassed whoever they saw moving on the streets, especially such as were carrying rifles; but these retaliated by firing at all bees that came within range, in spite of which very few bees were killed. Night brought a cessation of this sort of warfare.

Emsul arrived and of course at once gave up the idea of his projected peace mission to Yuri. He and Cabot and Nan-nan and Oya Buh spent the night under heavy guard at separated points throughout the city, securing much-needed sleep. Under cover of the darkness, many of their followers foraged in the ruins of the arsenal and secured a surprising quantity of undamaged material, being joined in the morning by the army in kerkools from the north.

Before daybreak a resolute band of several thousand loyal Cupians had gathered in the streets and houses surrounding the palace, and promptly at sunrise they launched an attack. They had expected to find the palace guard unarmed; but evidently a large quantity of the rifles and ammunition, which had been distributed throughout the city, had found their way to the palace, for the assault was at once repulsed by heavy fire from the palace guards.

As Cabot's forces reformed for a second attack, they were deluged with explosives from above. The bee-people had evidently not returned to their base at Wautoosa, but had spent the night near by, so as to be on hand to protect the palace.

Whenever they sighted even a small group of Cupians, or wherever they had reason to suspect that some building was hostilely occupied, there they would drop one of their devastating bombs. Cabot's forces were completely at the mercy of the Hymernians. There was but one thing to do—flee.

In vain, the earth-man and his able lieutenants tried to rally their troops. What was the use in assembling, when assembly was the signal for a bomb from above? What was the use of attacking the invincible bees?

Myles Cabot stood irresolute in one of the public squares. He was as near to despairing as he had ever been in his many vicissitudes on the planet Poros, since his first arrival there five earth-years ago. Oh, if only he had airplanes with which to subdue the Hymernians as in the days of old! Almost was he tempted to return to the vicinity of the arsenal, ascertain whether his one plane was intact, and if so fly alone in a last desperate attempt to give battle to his winged enemies.

The more he thought of the plan, the more it appealed to him. There seemed to be no other way out. His bravely engineered revolution had crumbled. If he stayed where he was, he would undoubtedly be tracked down, and put to some ignominious end by the usurper. How much better, then, to die bravely fighting for his Lilla and his adopted country.

And his baby? He wondered where the little darling had disappeared to. At least the infant king was out of Yuri's clutches.

So, his mind made up, Myles set out on a run for the wood overlooking the arsenal. After a few paraparths he reached it. There stood his plane. Rapidly he went over all the struts, and stays, and engine parts. Everything appeared to be in first class order. The fuel tanks contained plenty of alcohol. How this machine had escaped capture or destruction was a marvel, but probably the bees had been too busy bombing groups of Cupians, to take the time to explore the apparently deserted grove.

Myles sprang aboard and was just about to start the trophil engine, when a familiar sound, smiting upon his earthborn ears, caused him to delay for a moment. From the southward came the purr of many motors.

Was the wish the father to the thought? His longing for an air fleet, with which to vanquish the bees, had been so intense; had it affected his mind and caused him to hear things which did not exist? Impossible, for the purr of the motors was unmistakable.

He strained his eyes toward the southern horizon, so that they might see what his ears heard; but there was nothing there. The radiant silver sky was untouched save by an occasional small cloud.

The bees still kept up their bombing of the city. He could see them flying low over the housetops, and up and down the principal thoroughfares, ferreting out any groups of Cupians who dared to gather in Cabot's cause, dropping bombs on any houses which presumed to fly the blue pennant of the Kew dynasty in place of the yellow of Yuri.

The bees did not heed the approaching planes from the south. Of course not! For the whistling bees of Poros had no ears. They heard with their antennae, and heard only radio waves at that, in fact only short-length radio waves.

The noise of a large fleet of airships swept on out of the south. Nearer and nearer it came, until it was right over the city, and still not a single plane appeared in sight. Meanwhile the bees continued their depredations, and the earth-man sat in his own plane and watched and waited.

As he watched, he saw one of the bees who happened to be flying higher than the rest, suddenly vanish in a puff of smoke. And then another and another.

The Hymernians, too, saw this and rose to investigate, whereat there came the shut-off whir of descending planes.

Fascinated, Myles stared into the sky, whence came these sounds, and saw occasionally, against gathering clouds, a glint of silver light.

Several more of the ascending bees exploded. And now Myles

was able to see from time to time, silhouetted on a background of cloud, the ghostly form of an airship. The bees, too, saw, and flew to the attack. What was this shadow fleet? Had the spirits of the brave Cupian aviators of the past returned to free their beloved country from Hymernian domination?

The two fleets, bees and ghostly planes, had now completely joined battle, and were drifting slowly to the southeast. Myles came out of his trance, started his engine, and rose into the air, intent on joining the fray.

On his way, he circled over the city, and gave it a glance in passing. Then he gave it a second glance, for the Cupians, relieved of the menace of the bees, were forming for a second attack on the palace.

Instantly his plans changed. What business had he running off to watch however interesting a sky battle when right here before him lay a chance to do what he had braved so many misfortunes to accomplish, namely free his Lilla from the unspeakable Yuri! Veering sharply, he landed on one of the upper terraces of the palace.

He still wore his bandoleer of cartridges, and still carried his rifle. Filling the magazine, he boldly descended into the building. No one guarded the approaches from the air, for they depended on their aerial allies to do that for them. The upper rooms were deserted, doubtless because the womenfolk were cowering in the basements and because the palace guards and Yuri's other henchmen were resisting the attack of Cabot's Cupians at the ground levels.

Cabot himself explored the place unimpeded and unchallenged. Here he was at last at his journey's end, but where was Lilla? Lilla the blue-eyed princess, Lilla of the golden curls, his Lilla!

The rooms which he and she had occupied showed every sign of continued and present occupancy, even to the crib of the baby king, emblazoned with the arms of the House of Kew. Cabot looked reverently around the living rooms of his wife and child, and then swept on into the lower levels of the palace.

Occasionally he would come upon groups of defenders; but they, naturally assuming that he was one of them—especially as he still wore the black toga of the arsenal guard—gave him but little heed. Whenever the group was not too numerous he would shoot them. He hated to do this, but he knew he had to in order to save his loved ones.

Thus he traversed practically the whole of the upper reaches of the palace without encountering his arch enemy Yuri, or any of the womenfolk. Yuri was no coward. However much of a scoundrel he might be, no one would ever accuse him of that. Therefore he was not in hiding. He was apparently not in command of the defense. Therefore he must be either away from the palace, or concocting some devilment.

Figuring thus, Cabot continued to descend to levels below the ground floor. While treading these subterranean passages, searching, ever searching for either Lilla or Yuri, he came upon one of the palace guards. The fellow was unarmed, so Cabot did not shoot.

Instead he ordered, "Up with your hands."

The guard promptly obeyed.

"Now," said his captor, "the price of your life is to lead me to your king."

"Indeed, I will with pleasure," the soldier replied with a sneer, "for King Yuri will make short work of one who turns traitor to his black garb."

The earth-man smiled. "I am no traitor," he announced, "and this black toga is mere borrowed fur. Do you not know Cabot the Minorian?"

The other blanched. "Good Builder!" he exclaimed. "We did not believe the story that you had returned from the planet Minos. But I am at your orders, for I am one of the old guard who served under King Kew the Twelfth, the father of Princess Lilla, may he rest beyond the waves."

"Lead on, and no treachery," Myles curtly replied. "I trust no one who has ever worn the livery of Prince Yuri."

So the guard led the way through many winding passages, down into the very bowels of the subterranean labyrinths of the palace. What could Prince Yuri be doing way down here unless he was hiding, which seemed unlikely? Cabot became very suspicious, and, rifle in hand and finger on trigger, watched his guide with eagle eye.

Finally they came upon a form in an elaborate yellow toga, huddled in a corner.

"King Yuri," said the soldier laconically.

At the sound of the voice the usurper looked around; and now it became evident that he was crouching there not for fear, but rather because he was engaged in repairing something with a set of typical Porovian queer-looking tools.

Apparently not at all surprised, he hailed his deadliest enemy and rival as though the latter were a long lost friend, "Yahoo, Cabot the Minorian. I rather expected you would turn up sooner or later. Just a minute until I fix this wire, and then I will be at your service. You see, one of my mines wouldn't explode; no one else seemed able to get at the cause of the trouble, and so I had to come down here in person."

And so saying he turned back to his work. Myles stepped forward to see what Prince Yuri was doing. For a brief moment the earth-man's scientific curiosity got the better of his caution. But that moment, brief as it was, proved long enough for the watchful soldier, who had led him hither, to snatch Myles' rifle from his hand, and cover him with its muzzle.

"Up with your hands!" the soldier peremptorily commanded.

Cabot obeyed. Not to do so would have been suicide.

Yuri, still unperturbed, remarked, "Well done, Tobo; you shall be promoted for this."

"Shall I shoot him, sire?" Tobo eagerly asked.

"N-no," the usurper ruminated, waving his antennae thoughtfully, "not just now. Wait until I finish with this wire. In the meantime you might let the Minorian lean against the wall, so that he will be more comfortable."

So Myles leaned against the wall and waited, his hands still held high, while the prince puttered around in the corner. Finally, after a seemingly interminable period, Yuri arose, slung his tools together, brushed one hand against the other, and looked at his victim with a cruel smile.

"Shall I kill him now?" asked Tobo.

"No. I am reserving that pleasure for myself," the prince replied. Then to Cabot: "At last, you are in my power. I intend to shoot you myself. I intend to shoot you down, unarmed."

Turning to Tobo, the prince asked, "How is our battle going?"

"Very well, sire," the soldier replied. "We are repulsing all assaults, in spite of the departure of the bees to the southward."

A momentary cloud of doubt spread over the sinister handsome visage of Prince Yuri. Then he smiled and said, "Doubtless the bees know what they are about, and will soon return to the fray. So let us proceed with the execution. Follow me!"

Myles followed. Almost was he tempted to spring upon his enemy and attempt to throttle him before the inevitable bullet from Tobo could do its work. It would be well worth the sacrifice of his own life to rid Cupia of this incubus. But what if Yuri should survive? No, it would never do to risk this. So he meekly followed.

The prince led the way up several levels, until they came to a small circular chamber hung with curtains. At one side was a dais. An electric vapor-lamp on the ceiling furnished the light.

Prince Yuri took the rifle from the guard, stood Myles in the center of the room, and sat down himself on the dais.

Then he directed Tobo, "Go and summon the Princess Lilla hither, for I wish her to see me kill this lover of hers, this beast from another world."

Myles winced at the mention of his beloved, and threat his tormentors smiled.

The soldier departed on his errand. Yuri toyed with the weapon, and watched his victim, with a sneer on his handsome lips. Myles returned his stare without flinching.

"You can put down your hands now, if you wish, you fur-faced mathlab," the prince remarked.

Cabot did so, and instinctively felt of his face. The insult was unwarranted, for he had shaved only that morning.

"Don't go too far!" he admonished his captor. "Remember Poblath's proverb: 'You cannot kill a Minorian'."

"I've a mind to kill you right now," the prince replied, "just to prove to you that your friend is wrong."

"Go ahead and try it," Myles challenged, half hoping that Yuri would take him at his word, and thus spare Lilla the pain of attending the execution.

A grim look settled on the usurper's face as he slowly raised the rifle and pointed it at the earth-man's right side.

"Left side," Myles admonished. "Remember that my heart is on the other side than is the case with you Cupians."

"My, but you are a cool one!" Yuri admired, shifting his arm as directed. "Now, are you prepared to die?"

"Yes," Myles replied.

It all seemed like a dream. It couldn't be possible that he was really going to die on the far-away planet Venus. Perhaps all his adventures in the skies had been a mere dream, and he was now about to be awakened.

"Thus do I bring peace to Poros!" the Cupian sententiously declaimed.

His finger closed upon the trigger.

The rifle spat fire.

CHAPTER XXVII
PEACE ON POROS

Myles felt a sharp warm pain in his shoulder. But he still stood erect. He was not dead. Could it be that Yuri had missed? Shaking himself together and blinking his eyes, Myles stared at the prince.

The prince stared back with an open-mouthed expression of surprise. His eyes were fishlike. His body was no longer erect. The rifle lay in his lap, and he seemed to be feebly trying to raise it and point it at Cabot.

Then, with a gurgle, some blood welled from the prince's mouth and trickled down his chin.

With one supreme effort his antennae radiated the words, "Curse you!"

Then the rifle dropped clattering from his nerveless hands, and his body slouched forward prone on the floor at the foot of the dais. From the right side of his back there protruded the jewelled hilt of a dagger.

Behind the couch, between parted curtains, stood a wild-eyed Cupian woman, her face hideous with pent-up hate and triumph.

For a moment Myles stood rooted to the spot; then, tearing his feet free, he rushed to his fallen enemy and plucked out the dagger. From the wound there gushed bright cerise-colored blood, foamy with white bubbles. Myles turned the body over, and listened at the right side of the chest. Not a sound. Then, the Prince's chest collapsed, with a sigh, a little more blood welled out of the mouth, and all was still once more.

Prince Yuri, the most highly developed specimen of Cupian manhood—but a renegade, traitor, rejected wooer of the Princess Lilla, pretender to the throne of Cupia—Prince Yuri was dead!

And such an ignominious death for one of his high spirit to die! Stabbed in the back by a woman.

Cabot rose and faced her, the jeweled dagger still in his hand. "Who are you?" he asked. "And why did you do it?"

"I am Okapa," she replied in a strained voice—"Okapa from the mountain village of Pronth. Do you remember how in the Second War of Liberation you found Luno Castle deserted and a slain infant lying on the royal bier?"

"Can I ever forget it?" he answered, his mind going back into the past. "Naturally I thought it was my baby son, whom I had never seen. Therefore I fought all the harder against the usurper Yuri until I drove him and his ant allies southward, rejoined Lilla in Kuana, and learned that little Kew was safe, and that the dead child was but an orphan baby whom Lilla had substituted for our own baby for fear of just such an outcome."

"It was no orphan!" Okapa shrieked. "It was mine—mine! The dead child was mine! Yuri stabbed my child and now I have stabbed him with the selfsame dagger. Yuri killed my baby, and I have slain him, and now I must die myself for killing a king."

So saying, her anger spent, she flung herself upon the couch and wept silently, as is the habit of Cupians.

Just then the Princess Lilla in a black gown swept into the room.

"They told me the king wished to see me here," she said. "Where is the king?"

She stopped abruptly as she saw the body on the floor. Then her eyes rose until they rested on Myles Cabot. With a glad cry she rushed toward his outstretched arms.

But a peremptory shout of "Hands up!" from the doorway caused her to halt. She was between Myles and the door. He still held the jeweled dagger in his hand. Stepping quickly to one side, he cast it straight at Tobo who stood by the entrance, a rifle in his hands; and before the Cupian soldier could raise his weapon to fire, the missile had penetrated his heart. Down he went with a crash.

While this had been going on, Okapa, the madwoman, had crept stealthily toward Yuri's body with a view to securing the rifle which he had dropped. Seizing it, she leaped to her feet with a shriek.

"You too!" she cried, pointing at Lilla with one skinny finger. "For it was you who took my babe from the orphanage and exposed him to danger. You are joint murderer with Yuri. Him I have slain, and now it is your turn."

But Myles stepped between her and the princess and wrenched the gun from her poor mad hands, whereat she flung herself upon him, clawing and biting like a demon. It was only the work of a few minutes, however, to get both her wrists behind her back.

Lilla, sensing the need, ripped some strips from the hanging draperies; together they tied the woman and seated her to one side. Then once more the long separated earth-man and his Cupian beloved started to embrace, while Okapa glared at them with baleful eyes.

This was too much for Myles.

"Just one paraparth!" he said; and, stepping over to Okapa, he spun her around until she faced the wall.

Then he clasped his princess to him in a long embrace.

But at last a pang intruded in his bliss. "Lilla dearest," he asked, "where is our little son?"

She shook herself together.

"I know not," she replied, "They would not let me know, for fear that the usurper—may he rest beyond the waves—might force the secret from me. But our country is more important than our child. While we tarry here the battle rages. Quick, to the upper levels, and let us take control."

"We cannot do so without a message from their king," her husband asserted. "Let us therefore bring them one."

Stooping down, he picked up the dead body of Prince Yuri and flung it across his shoulder.

"Lead on!" he said.

As they emerged up a flight of stairs into the main hall of the palace they saw a frantic throng of palace guards piling tables, chairs, and other furniture into a barricade across one of the doorways. Evidently the troops of Emsul and Hah Babbuh had penetrated the palace and had driven the defenders back to this point.

The golden-curled Lilla, standing straight and slim in her black gown, stopped all this work of fortification with an imperious gesture.

"Desist!" she cried. "I, your princess, command it. The war is over. Yuri, the usurper, is dead."

"Prove it," snarled back the guards like a pack at bay, recoiling from her regal presence.

"Here is your proof!" Myles Cabot shouted, stepping forward and casting Yuri's body down before them. "Your king is dead."

"'Tis true," one replied. "The king is dead."

"Yuri is dead," another echoed. "Long live King Kew!"

"Long live King Kew!" shouted all the palace thugs, just as the besiegers stormed over the barricade with leveled rifles.

But at the shouts within, and at the sight of their princess and their intrepid earth-man leader, they grounded their arms and, holding their left hands aloft, gave the Porovian greetings:

"Yahoo, Myles Cabot! Our regent has returned from Minos to rule over us!"

Then one guardsman had an idea. "Come," he said, "let us mount to the upper terraces, haul down the yellow pennant of King Yuri, and restore the red banner of the Kew dynasty."

From one of the balconies above came a boyish voice: "It has already been done, Myles Cabot."

Every one looked up, and there stood Yuri's younger brother, the loyal Prince Toron, wearing the insignia of admiral of the Cupian Air Navy.

"I hope you don't mind, Myles," he said as he descended. "I made myself admiral on my own hook. You see, while all the bees were here at Kuana bombing your men, I captured the air base at Wautoosa with a crowd of ex-aviators whom I had assembled for that purpose.

"We had been hiding in the woods for several sangths, with spies at Wautoosa to inform us when there was an opening. When the time came we walked right in, killed a few old bees who were on guard, reconditioned the planes which have lain in storage ever since my brother seized the throne, painted them with silver paint, flew up here to Kuana, and put the bees out of business.

"The silver paint was my own idea, and I must say it seemed to work. The bees couldn't see us at all against the silver sky. The plaza and the fields beyond are strewn with dead and dying Hymernians, and my men are tracking down the survivors."

And he would have chattered on in his boyish excitement, had not one of the soldiers brutally interrupted with:

"Thy brother lies dead, O Toron."

The young prince followed the pointing finger of the guard until his eyes rested on the crumpled body in its blood-stained yellow toga. Then he flung his arm across his face to blot out the sight. For a few moments he stood thus, while all respectfully kept silent. At last he uncovered his eyes and addressed the earth-man.

"May he rest beyond the waves!" he said. "I crave the corpse so that I can give my brother a decent funeral."

"He shall be buried with full royal honors," Myles Cabot replied, "for he was a brave and regal Cupian who would have served his country well if his inordinate ambition had not blinded his judgment."

"My cousin shall have royal burial," echoed the Princess Lilla. "It would be due you, Toron, for your share in the victory, if for no other reason."

"I appreciate this courtesy more than words can express," Toron replied.

The news of the capitulation had rapidly spread, and the huge hall was filling with Cupians from without. Among them came Emsul, Nan-nan, Hah Babbuh, Oya Buh, and even Poblath the Philosopher. Warm were the greetings between the friends.

"But where is our king?" Myles asked, as soon as he could free himself from all the congratulation.

"Now it can be told," Poblath replied. "He is safe in the care of my wife Bthuh, in our villa at Lai."

"The darling! I shall go to him at once," Lilla announced.

"And I too," Myles added.

"But no," Hah Babbuh interposed, "for the populace are already gathering in the stadium and are demanding a speech from the great liberator."

"So be it," Myles said with a shrug of resignation. "Affairs of state cannot wait even the presence of the king, it seems."

"But shall these black-togaed guards be permitted to retain their arms?" Emsul asked.

"Why not?" the earth-man replied. "Their only crime is that they fought loyally for their leader. Besides, this is a free country. One of our grievances against the usurper was that he deprived us of our rifles."

Then, to the palace soldiery: "Care tenderly for the body of Prince Yuri, and lay it out in state pending our return. Oh, and I almost forgot—there is a crazy woman bound in one of the cellar rooms. Turn her over to the mango of Kuana for incarceration in the mangool, and under peril of your lives do not permit her to escape."

"All hail our regent! And our most beautiful and beloved princess!" shouted the guards, as Myles and Lilla left the palace.

A kerkool awaited them at the gate. Getting into this, they proceeded at a slow rate through the city and across the plaza toward the stadium through lanes of cheering Cupians. Prince Toron, Emsul, Hah Babbuh, Oya Buh, and others of their retinue followed them.

The plaza and the fields beyond were strewn with bodies—mostly in fragments—of the once great race of the Hymernians. One of these bees, as they passed it, gave sign of still possessing some life. A faint whistling noise assailed the antennae of the passing procession.

Cabot gave one look in the direction of the sound, then signed the kerkools to stop, dismounted, and approached the dying creature.

Adjusting his control to the wave length of bee speech, he sadly said, "Portheris, once my friend, whom I made king of the bees, it grieves me to see you lying thus, struck down in a war against my people."

Raising himself feebly, the dying Portheris replied, "I bear you no malice, Myles Cabot, and I pray that you will bear me none. Although I opposed the war, yet when it came to a fight of race against race I was loyal to my own, as any honorable individual would have been under like circumstances. Perhaps it is just as well; for do you not remember that when you were driving the ant-men off the face of Cupia, you said: 'There is no room on any given planet for more than one race of intelligent beings?' Now the last Formian is gone, and the last of my own people is gone. May Cupia be at peace. It is the sincere wish of your old friend."

The huge bee fell back, quivered a moment, and lay still. Thus died Portheris, the last of the Hymernians.

"May you rest beyond the waves, dear friend," the earth-man murmured as he returned sadly to his car.

They found the stadium packed with cheering throngs in gala attire. Everywhere fluttered flags of the Kew dynasty.

After Lilla had been comfortably seated and Marshal Hah and the others had arrived, Myles stepped to the transmitter and was about to broadcast some appropriate remarks to the assembled multitude, when an airplane arrived overhead and settled softly into the arena.

From the plane there stepped Poblath the Philosopher, followed by Bthuh, his dark and beautiful wife. Both were smiling, and Bthuh held in her arms a baby Cupian.

Then Cabot spoke into the microphone: "Behold your king!"

It was the shortest speech he had ever made—and the best.

Thus came Kew XIII into his own.

There is not much more to tell.

Prince Toron retained his self-given title of Admiral of the Air Navy. Hah Babbuh was restored to his professorship at the Royal

University. Oya Buh was promoted to full professorship. Poblath the Philosopher again became mangool of Kuana, and his wife was made governess of the infant king. Emsul, the veterinary, was given the title of court physician.

Owva, the Holy Leader, died shortly after this, and Nan-nan was selected by the Great White Lodge as the fit person to reestablish the lost religion publicly throughout Cupia.

Myles and Lilla, leaving their friends to reconstruct the capital, departed for a vacation at Luno Castle.

Thus end the story of the adventure of Myles Cabot, the radio man, on his return to the silver planet Venus, as received by the Harvard scientists and myself over the long distance radio-set at my farm on Chappaquiddick Island, Massachusetts.

Made in the USA
Las Vegas, NV
01 July 2022